The air in the tunnel was thick and dank,
and as black as a shadow's shadow. Our single flashlight was woefully inadequate. Darkness encased my brother and me while its offspring prowled the concrete corridors searching for us. I'd been fighting for survival my whole life, but never before had I so thoroughly felt it.

The Darkest Sum

by

Micki Miller

The Darkest Sum

Cover Art by *Rae Monet, Inc. Design*

The Wild Rose Press, Inc.
PO Box 708
Adams Basin, NY 14410-0708
Visit us at www.thewildrosepress.com

Publishing History
First Mainstream Fantasy Edition, 2017
Print ISBN 978-1-5092-1576-8
Digital ISBN 978-1-5092-1577-5

Published in the United States of America

Dedication

To my dear Vegas friends.
You keep the monsters away.

Chapter 1

I wondered, not for the first time, if the thing had eyes.

Did they shimmer within its unformed shape and blend with the traces of it I could see, or were they, like the rest of it, still undeveloped? If it did have eyes somewhere in that faint mass of shadow against shade, I may well have been staring into them. The thought was disconcerting, yet I did not look away.

In the unlikely event some lost soul who'd wandered this far down the east end of the Las Vegas Strip should see me standing there, I would certainly have looked the fool, roasting in the blistering sun, staring into that dark-as-deep-space opening to the storm drain. But even though I could not enter, I couldn't leave.

Blessed shade, a commodity of jackpot proportions waited only a few feet before me in what to anyone else would appear as nothing. Still, I stayed where I was, burning beneath a sky so bright and so hot it blanched the blue. I stayed where I was because I knew a portion of that shade was alive, and hungry in ways I was too terrified to analyze.

Before me were two six by six openings bisected in equal parts by a vertical cement divider. Both tunnels led to the storm drains, though to different parts. The three hundred or so miles of subterranean tunnels housed approximately two hundred people beneath the glittering city.

For almost a year now my brother Jacob, three years younger than my twenty-two years, and I have called this place home. I need to get back. He was sick, awaiting the return of his big sister, and though he would never admit it, he was afraid.

Using my hand to shade my eyes, I glanced up toward the street where cars passed by in a steady stream. Far off to the left, palm trees front the ever-golden Mandalay Bay. Beyond that was the massive, black pyramid of the Luxor. Its Egyptian theme appeared a transplant from one desert to another, except for the reflective shine and the valet parking.

No one was walking in my direction. I turned my head the other way and mostly I saw desert.

Fifty or so yards to the right in the middle of the street sat the legendary 'Welcome to Fabulous Las Vegas' sign. It's often busy there with tourists waiting in line to get their picture with the famous landmark. Sometimes movie crews are set up there half the day to get a five second shot. On a day like today, when the afternoon sun was aggressive and the temperature was well into the triple digits, I didn't see a single car parked in the small lot.

Looking back toward the tunnel entrance, I saw the thing was still there and wished for the millionth time we had an actual home where we could go and live in blissful ignorance of its existence, like everybody else who doesn't live underneath the city. We can't, though, not yet.

Another difference between the open world above ground and those of us who lived down here, was more than the obvious cash flow and often ill-gotten clout. In fairness, it wasn't all the people up there, in my estimation at least, causing this trouble before me. It was a segment. However, they were a powerful segment.

I lay this trouble at the feet of people who talk a good game of scruples, but didn't nuisance themselves with the rules. They affected those of us living down here in ways their smug minds could not imagine.

You see, all the wickedness they sloughed off with their loofahs of sanctimonious bluster found its way down here. Much like Frankenstein's monster, the evil genius of happenstance stitched the dead parts together without benefit of a normal brain, and in the many shadows of our domain, created a new and very frightening kind of life form.

There was a convention in town. Some ultra-conservative political group, according to the newspaper I'd skimmed while waiting in line at the drugstore. I didn't spend even one moment reading the backs of any books, though I very much wanted to. Their covers drew me with pictures and titles that left my brain pining.

I loved to read. I missed it. At our camp, I had one battered old book, and I'd read it many times. I planned to read it a few more. Not being able to buy a book, or get to one of the libraries to check one out, was a loss that often kicked me. I learned not to let a new book tease me with an invitation to a good story I can't afford to buy. So, I stuck to skimming the newspaper and the monotonous nonsense of politics.

Having so much of my life consumed with survival, I'd never had the time or inclination to explore beneath the shallows of how our government worked. All I could claim for actual experience was that Uncle Sam pocketed a fair amount of the measly paychecks I used to earn, and used a good chunk to pay elected officials way too much money.

Some of these people, the extreme moralistic types especially, fed the thing that blocked my way. They're the kind of people who would blame the very evil they enhance on some segment of citizens who don't measure up to their particular brand of moral standards, or rather, double standards.

Politicians and religious leaders always generated the most sin here in Sin City. I knew this because that was when the evil in the darkness underwent its most notable growth spurts. When the porn convention was in town, or a gay pride event, a march for animal rights, or even a legalize marijuana demonstration, the evil diminished a bit, as if oppressed by the candor.

It swelled whenever a politician screamed family values as his eyes roamed in search of his next extramarital affair. It flourished when a religious zealot preached his puritanical, anti-homosexual rhetoric, so often committing treason against the people of his own true self. At those times, the evil grew fervent, thriving on all that boisterous duplicity.

I think the hypocrisy nourishes the thing. It's one of the more potent evils. That's probably because it required so little effort and yet could gain so much. All a person had to do was shed their conscience, perfect a sincere smile, and learn to speak in virtuous tones. Money and supporters would not be far behind.

Of course, those were just my opinions and were worth less than the journal I'd write them in if I could afford such a splurge as a journal. Long hours with little to no light, depending on our candle and battery situation, were fertile ground for a mind sober enough to insist on thought. While I was not so drunk on sobriety (pun intended) as to believe all my thoughts were indisputable, on this I truly believed I was right. For I had witnessed cause and effect.

The high and mighty perched upon their holey holy vows, their right hands raised in pledge to God and country while with their left hands they pilfered and profited. They had no idea how, in fact, they fed the evil against which they so heartily declared themselves.

Padded by the fat of their yields and blockaded from true grace by their fortified, squeaky-clean facades, they did not understand the malevolence they nourished; did not notice a bite or two missing from their rot.

As things were, that very malevolence suckling on the foulness of lies upon their collective breaths stood between my wretched home and me.

The two entrances before me led to a complex system of storm drains running beneath Las Vegas. To the left of the concrete divider was simply a shadowed square. Our camp was through the entrance on the right.

I wondered, as I had in the past, whether the thing could pass through cement. I didn't think it could circle the front of the divider. Doing so would take it into the sunlight. It lived strictly in the shadows.

I wished I had given a more thorough exploration to the left entrance. Maybe there was a roundabout way to get to our camp, a side door of sorts. It wasn't the time, though. The tunnel on the left could take me miles from where I needed to be. So, I stood in the blistering sun while the monster coated the shade, and waited.

Through that dense and terrifying portal and about three quarters of a mile in, my baby brother was sniffling from yet another cold. Jacob was only nineteen years old. His immune system, however, had suffered six years of serious alcohol abuse, as well as a fair amount of whatever drug his eager hands could grab.

In my hand, I held a plastic grocery bag containing generic cold medicine. The nearest drugstore was a mile and a half walk, one way. Beneath the desert sun burning over Las Vegas in late July, I swore I could feel the seeds of melanoma burrowing into my pores. I imagined it waiting until I got our lives up and running before dumping another tragedy on the last two remaining members of the Linden family.

I spent the bulk of our precious dollars on cold medicine for Jacob. I didn't buy the box of feminine products. This month, again, I would do as our foremothers did and use rags. Sunscreen was also a luxury we could not afford.

As I stood there on the downward slope, sun-roasted concrete beneath my tattered sneakers and eight feet up on either side of me, I felt more than saw the evil.

It showed itself with a subtle sheen in the darkness, a sporadic, spastic shimmer. An occasional splash of wetness, as if the monstrous part of that darkness salivated in anticipation. Mostly, though, I felt its presence on my nerve endings, where no one was sure of its existence but me.

I'd never seen more of it than vague traces, a movement where there should be none; a momentary sheen I wished I could blame on tired eyes and a goaded imagination. Nobody else had seen even that much. In fact, its very existence at all was a periodic point of debate within our underground community.

Some of the few people we knew in the tunnels disagreed with me. They thought I was too free with my imagination. Of course, many of them were either riding some kind of a high or falling from one. Not all of us, though. Hard times can generate despair, and then unite with it, to strike down even those of us who made the best efforts.

No matter how vehement the opposing arguments, they had never been able to convince me what I saw was a manifestation of my many fears. I wanted to believe that was true. I so wished I could. But as I said, I felt its existence, and my feelings were rarely wrong.

My most shameful fault lay in my unexplainable resistance to follow the good instincts nature had given me. If that thing, that entity, had a positive, it was instilling a lesson my parents should have taught me— Listen to my instincts.

I'd been trying very hard to not rebel against what few positives I possessed. I did that sometimes. I used to do it a lot. Again, I didn't know why. Maybe I was afraid there was some sort of trick involved. Sometimes I felt like if I showed such arrogance as to believe in myself, I'd be punked by life yet again.

I had gotten much better at making use of my instincts. Which was what I was doing, as I stood beside the shallow stream of water. It rolled in a slow flow down the center of the storm drain and into the mouth of the tunnel.

Benny had hinted at belief. Chester, Silvia, and

several of the others in the tunnels who we'd become friends with over this past year would say I was being ridiculous. They'd shake their heads at me standing out here and frying to crusty embers. I continued to wait it out, though. I truly believed it was there.

If it was as mindful as I thought, it thought of me. I heard the conceit there, but I felt it to be true. On several occasions, our minds had grazed each other. That is how I knew it was dangerous. I also knew it was vulnerable, though I didn't know in what way. And I had to wonder how much it knew about me, and if and how familiar it was with my weak links.

Though it had never harmed me, at times I felt it wanted to. Whether it was practicing restraint when it came near or whether it for some reason was reluctant to touch me, I am unsure. Whenever possible, I kept my distance from it. It had been a very, very long time since I'd had a good night's sleep.

The base of my skull was stiff and at times, felt electric. When I felt the tingle, I knew if I looked around, I would see a dark layer of living shadow. When the tingle became a buzz, I could see its dampness. For me, its existence was not in doubt.

If the manifestation in question had eyes, it was staring at me. I was equally sure if it had a mouth, it was grinning at my predicament. I sensed a certain giddy humor in it, like a Bond villain on the verge of world domination.

Having left our jug and a half of water in the tunnel with Jacob, after my long trek in the dry and brutal summer heat, I was in a bad state of dehydration. Whatever perspiration my body had been able to produce had long evaporated into the desert furnace.

I swallowed, thinking the act would produce some saliva. It only made my tongue stick to the back of my throat. It was as if some kid had painted my tongue in lumpy paste. For a few seconds, I feared choking on my own thirst.

Jacob must have been getting pretty worried. He knew his big sister would never desert him. If I didn't get back soon, he'd be sure something bad happened, and he would panic. For Jacob, panic would be a more than worthy excuse to backslide.

Poor as we all were down in the storm drains, somehow alcohol and drugs were not hard to find. It both saddened and angered me, but an excuse to drink was a scenario Jacob might welcome.

Ten feet in front of me, the damp-patched monster in the dark, of the dark, waited. Maybe it was curious to see what I would do. All I *could* do was squint at its varying depths.

I couldn't pass through the thing. True, I never tried. Maybe nothing would happen. Maybe it was all shiny intimidation and its power wasn't more than psychological, but I didn't think so.

We'd all heard screams in the tunnels; had known someone who one day just vanished. It was far from unusual for people to pick up and leave the tunnels. Still, I had to wonder if the others believe the short-lived screams of terror we sometimes heard meant little. That they were no more than vocal expressions of frustration by someone who could not believe what their life had come to. I always thought that was something the people down here told themselves so they could go to sleep. I envied their delusions.

Far above me, a foolish, arrogant cloud had the gall

to mosey beneath the sun that burned most clouds away without mercy or regret. For a brief moment, I relished the reprieve as the temperature dropped to, oh, I'd say a frosty one hundred and four degrees.

I squinted at the sky, hoping for more clouds. There weren't any. When the lone cloud passed and the sun made its victorious return, I looked back to the tunnel entrance. By sight, it was almost the same. But the evil that lurked there a moment before was gone. The darkness was once again flat, harmless, and its implied coolness inviting. My nerve endings no longer sizzle.

I crossed the threshold.

Chapter 2

My steps were cautious so as not to splash the widened stream of runoff water from the city and get my socks wet. A few yards in, I retrieved the flashlight from my old patchwork purse. With the continuing downward slope and after the first corner, twilight squashed almost all the sunlight coming through the entrance.

Before rounding the turn, I glanced back. Pale gray concrete made a square telescope out to the desert. Traffic muffled to almost nothing. There wasn't a chance of anyone out there seeing me now. To man and beast, I had once again become a nonentity.

Though the batteries in my flashlight were new, after the turn, the beam would shine no farther than a few yards. It's as if the darkness was compressed, packed as thick as the surrounding concrete. It was night tenfold.

I couldn't tell you how many times I came upon a stranger, my light shining in his face with a suddenness that can frighten a person right into a heart attack. Sometimes I got an abrupt grumble or a cursing out. I tried to ignore strangers, and after their initial reaction, they usually did the same. Nobody was here to socialize.

Every now and then, I passed someone else walking with a flashlight and got a brief but friendly hello. That's nice, a brethren of the downtrodden. Other times, my light found a tooth-rotted leer over a smoldering crack pipe. Those are almost as scary as the monster.

Eventually, I came to the part of the tunnel where the cement floor starts angling upward a bit. This is so during the infrequent rains we get, the rush of water coming through will slow.

Although real downpours were rare, they did happen. It didn't take a tremendous amount of rain to send water gushing through the storm drains. The desert ground was hard and doesn't absorb water well. Even a light rain can transform the stream to a raging river in the time it takes to see your life flash before your eyes.

Some have died trying to ride out a storm down here, or when they were too far gone in a drug-induced haze to realize what was happening.

A few months ago, in one of the more dangerous tunnels, a middle-aged man named Luke who had never climbed out of the depression of a divorce he'd not wanted, was carried off by the fast-moving waters. Two days later, someone found his body in the Las Vegas wash. The papers called it an accidental death. I call it suicide by nature.

Black widows enjoyed the damp climate down here enough to invite their friends and family to come and stay. Other spiders and bugs made their home in this concrete maze, too. They crawled about the filth and debris and the innumerable mounds of hopelessness. In some areas, there were crawfish. They gave me the creeps with their pinchers and blood red shells. Some people in the storm drains eat them. I had a great fear of becoming that desperate.

Occasionally, there was a freak out that could turn dangerous. Drugs and disparity can be a volatile mix. Along with of all of that, there are particular fears for a woman that men cannot truly understand.

Often I was utterly alone in a place where no one would hear me scream. And even if by chance someone did, I would have to beg hope for the unlikely combination of sobriety, compassion, and heroics.

Those are some of the many cons of our life in the storm drains. There were, however, a few pros.

The police tended to leave us alone. Those down here who do drugs, which are many, could do so with far less anxiety than what plagues them and often spoils their highs when above ground.

We were not an eyesore for business owners and their patrons who looked at us the way I looked at the crawfish. We had walls, a roof, and the blessed coolness (a twenty-degree drop), was great incentive for those of us with few if any options.

Some, like Jacob and me, have been able to create a threadbare semblance of a home with odds and ends others have discarded. Chester, a sweet man with a terrible gambling problem who lived two tunnels over, had a single burner stove. When he won a little, he bought some propane and did a bit of simple cooking. If it was a good win, he shared.

Benny, a heroin addict who lived in the vicinity, though I didn't know exactly where, had a radio he let us use when he knew he'd be gone for a while. Having a radio was a real treat for us. Down in the tunnels, we viewed our blessings through a magnifying glass.

After a couple more minutes of walking at a steady pace, I came to a wall with two holes approximately four feet in diameter. These were equalizers, slowing the water and keeping it going exactly where the planners had intended. I climbed through the hole on the right.

Except for a bare trickle of a stream running down the middle, the floor was mostly dry here. For a short while, I left damp footprints that would evaporate before anybody saw them.

I kept the light moving so I could see as much of what I was walking into as possible. As the beam swept the walls on either side of me, I could see large, spray-painted vulgarities both in words and in explicit drawings that weren't fading fast enough.

I was almost home.

To my left sat a gold and yellow couch cushion with a raised paisley print, sliced open and gutted by a vandal with no respect for usable trash. I knew what was coming next.

Though I hadn't stopped to look at it in some time, I always slowed at this point. I didn't want to. The picture bothered me. It frightened me. Sometimes it drew me, and that scared me most of all.

Ahead, a striped light ten feet long and almost as broad as the storm drain came into view. The grating in the ceiling of the tunnel allowed plenty of sunshine so I could turn off my flashlight for a minute or so and conserve batteries. Several yards before I was to turn left and centered on the wall beneath the grating, the mural of Jesus appeared.

The artist painted His hands raised about hip high, palms up. A white robe hung on His body in a soft, draping flow. His eyes, bluer than the sky the iron bars of the grate split into lines, watched me. His head tilted to the right, conveying pity through His well-crafted expression.

Usually I passed it with little more than a glance. The mural called to me, so I stopped.

Our parents were not religious people. The only time we ever heard the word "God" in our home was when it preceded the word damn. Dad never went to church. Mom would go on Christmas Eve. She never took Jacob or me. I suppose she didn't want to rub her sins in God's face.

Whoever painted the mural did so with love and a heartfelt pursuance of perfection. Only a person who believed in God as strongly as I believe in the monster could have painted it.

Others in the tunnels believed in God. Sometimes they came to this spot, trudging through spider webs and garbage, past addicts with fickle sanity, on stomachs empty of everything except guilt and regret, so they could worship. Keeping faith in such abysmal conditions as these bewildered me. How could they still believe there was a God?

What kind of *loving* God would allow His children to live like this? And what kept His followers from losing their faith through the pain of their hunger and the degradation of their circumstance? How did they still feel His love, still gain comfort and consolation in the presence of a mere painting? *How,* I wondered, as my fingers curled into my palms.

I spun away from the mural and walked at a brisk pace toward our camp, envy swirling in my wake.

At the intersection, I turned right. The floor was dry. It hadn't rained in more than two months, and that was light. The walls were a hopeless shade of gray, but this far in, at least they were free of crudeness and illusory propaganda. Being so close to home calmed me. That should have bothered me far more than it did, considering what our 'home' was.

At the same time I lost the water, I also lost the light of the grating. Without my flashlight, the darkness would have swallowed me whole.

Shortly before I got to it, I smelled the alcove coming up on my right. I kept it as clean as I could, but it was still an unventilated cement cubby. Whatever was the purpose of the small room, we'd never been able to guess. Jacob and I each kept a metal bucket in there. It was our bathroom.

On I walked.

"Lizzie?" Jacob called.

His voice was weak from his illness, and lined with apprehension. Every now and then teenagers came through, mostly boys revved up on testosterone and boredom. If they traipsed through now and were in the mood for violence, Jacob was in no condition to put up any kind of defense.

"It's me," I said as I entered our concrete camp. Even those two small words were hard to form with a mouth as dry as the desert floor.

"About time," Jacob grumbled. He lumbered to a sitting position on the scavenged mattress that was our bed. Even in the light of a single candle, he looked grouchy.

After turning off my flashlight, I set it on the overturned, blue plastic crate that served as one of our tables. I tossed the bag from the drugstore to my brother, resisting the urge to hurl it at his ungrateful head. I then lifted a jug of water from the table and drank in big gulps. It was liquid heaven.

When I needed a breath, I lowered the jug and with as much sincerity as I could muster, said, "You're welcome." Then I drank some more.

With a great weariness I had earned, I carried the jug toward the foot of the bed to the lawn chair we salvaged from a trash dumpster a couple of months ago. I sat down like a frail old woman. I would have liked to just fall back, but it wasn't sturdy enough for such heedlessness and even a small injury could cause major problems for both of us. We had to stay vigilant of so many things.

After a few more healthy gulps of water, I set the jug in my lap, replaced the cap, and surveyed our camp. With just the light of a single candle, it was quite dark. My eyes soon adjusted, however, and I knew the place well. *Too well.*

There were times when I felt somewhat connected to other creatures living underground. In an odd way, I gained comfort from that. It was good to know I was able to adapt. On the other hand, the fact that I had adjusted so well to this place was unsettling.

My acclimation to living in the storm drains running under the city was gradual. I could not name any turning point where I could say 'yes, that's when it happened'. I wondered if it would be the same when someday we got out of here, or if I would fall back into normalcy, if I would be able to at all.

Chester once told us he used to have a brother who spent more time in prison than out. Upon his release after one especially long incarceration, he found he was unable to adapt to the outside world. Six weeks after gaining his freedom Chester's brother hung himself from the monkey bars at Lorenzi Park in the middle of the night.

That story never left my mind. I tried not to let a day go by without picturing the day we'd leave this place for good, so I would be prepared in every way. I pictured it, even as I looked upon these familiar dismal surroundings.

Our lucky find of a mattress sat on a great many cinderblocks Jacob and I carried down here one heavy block at a time. So far, our bed has stayed dry through the one light rainfall that visited Las Vegas since we lugged it down here. We had some decent bedding we got at a yard sale. We took it to the laundromat when we took our clothes to keep it nice.

Sharing a bed with my brother is far from ideal, but I reminded myself we were very lucky to have a bed. A couple others down here do, but most sleep on old blankets and/or cardboard pallets.

Other than our bed and four plastic crates for tables, our furnishings included three rescued lawn chairs. Two are white plastic, as clean as I could get them. The one I sat on was the most comfortable; red, white, and blue striped fabric stretched across aluminum poles. Only two of our duct tape patches spot the colors.

We have an old, baby blue chest with three drawers. Jacob had the third drawer down. The middle was mine. In the top drawer we kept some canned goods, and a few other precious items. It once had four drawers, but the one on the bottom was missing when we found it. The chest, with a fair amount of chips and scratches, sat on cinderblocks, too, to keep it safe.

An oak end table, bearing the scars of an abusive

past, held a burning, fat white candle on a sea green, chipped salad plate we retrieved from a dumpster. The table also held a somewhat pretty, plastic daisy in a clear plastic vase I found in the same dumpster.

The table had a long crack in one of the legs when we found it, tossed off in the desert, but Jacob fixed it with some duct tape. He was a talent with that stuff. Patches of it were on almost all our furniture.

Getting these things in here was always a long ordeal. Much of it wouldn't fit through the equalizers. We had to haul it the long way around through one of the other entrances we'd explored.

It was a bother and sometimes, like when we were struggling to carry the mattress, I wondered if it was worth it. It was. This section of the tunnels was more difficult to get to from the outside, which could be a real pain for us, but it also kept us safer than we would have been in some of the other places in the storm drains.

The east opening, closest to our camp, faced the Las Vegas strip. Sometimes a curious adventurer came through, but not often. Tourists didn't come to town to explore the dark and fearsome storm drains. If someone stumbled by us, it was usually another resident. Every now and then, a stranger wandered through. So far, we'd been lucky and they just wandered out again.

The west opening was not easy to see from the street. It took some maneuvering over a rocky hill to get to the big hole in the fence we disguised by plugging with numerous tumbleweeds. That was often enough of a deterrent for those who would make trouble for us. Even though it was longer, I used that route today so no one would see me coming or going. Since it was daytime, discretion was wise.

Another big plus was it didn't flood here as bad as it did in some of the other tunnels, so I thought it was worth the extra hassle. Jacob and I had made a reasonably comfortable home for ourselves down here. Lately, I worried we had become a little too settled.

I looked up from the jug in my lap. Jacob was tilting the bottle of cold medicine as if he was chugging a beer. "Hey, take it easy with that stuff," I told him. "You have to make it last."

"How much money do we have left?" Jacob asked me before taking another big swig.

A line of expensive red syrup slid down the stubble on his chin, staining the pale blond color that matched the hair on both of our heads. He wiped the wasted medicine off with the palm of his hand and then wiped his hand on his faded purple shirt. Even after all these years it amazed me how little effort my brother had to expend to annoy me. I held my tongue, though. It was too thick and heavy to argue anyway.

"We have about four dollars."

"That's all?" he said with a mix of surprise and fear he tried but failed to hide from me. He screwed the cap back on the bottle of medicine. "I think by tonight I'll feel good enough to do some credit hustling."

Credit hustling was our only source of income. We would wait until two or three o'clock in the morning and wander the casinos along the Las Vegas Strip trying not to look destitute. Tourists who drank far beyond their limit because they were on vacation often left credits on their machines. We could usually count on coming home with fifteen, maybe twenty dollars. Sometimes it was more.

Once, about eight months ago, Jacob and I found almost three hundred dollars on a machine. We treated ourselves to a cheap motel room where we could have real showers instead of the sponge baths we take here. Watching television all night with a real toilet and sink nearby was a grand treat we savored until our eyelids fell shut.

The next day we took the bus to buy a few articles of clothing at the Goodwill store and spent the rest on food. Well, I told Jacob that's how we spent the rest.

I'd managed to squirrel away a nice chunk to put in my special hiding place. It was comforting to know it was there for emergencies. I hoped we didn't have any, though, so I could save enough to one day get an apartment for us, which meant an address to put on a job application. An emergency would have to be dire before I would even consider touching that money. I had almost five hundred dollars in a long wallet I had duct taped to the underside of my dresser drawer.

"We'll go out tomorrow night," I told Jacob after he finished a short bout of coughing. "It's too hot to cool down much out there and you're pretty weak."

"Yeah, maybe," Jacob said. He set the cough syrup on the crate next to his side of the bed and flopped back against his pillow. "What do we have to eat? I'm hungry."

"We still have some bread and peanut butter."

He scrunched his face and said, "I'm sick of bread and peanut butter."

Before answering Jacob, I blinked my eyes in a slow motion I hoped would be cleansing. It wasn't. My eyes were dry. The heavy lids scraped against my eyeballs and I didn't want to raise them again.

"There's a can of green beans and I think a can of corn," I told him.

"I'll take the corn," he said, as if I were his waitress.

Though fixing Jacob his meal consisted of nothing but taking the can out of the top dresser drawer that served as our pantry, opening it, sticking a spoon in the can and handing it to him, I was too exhausted. Even going to the bed for a nap was going to take effort.

"In a few minutes," I told my brother. "I need to rest first."

My head was fuzzy and light. My skin radiated heat. The desert sun had roasted me clear to my core. Even my ponytail was expelling heat, as if my walk in the brutal afternoon sun left my hair fevered. When I was able to work up enough energy, I would dampen a cloth in our washbowl and wipe myself down.

"Fine," Jacob said. The word ground with irritation. "I'll lie here and starve while you relax."

"Jacob, then open the damn can yourself," I told him. Since drinking the water my mouth was lubricated enough to make my annoyance clear.

"I'm sick."

"You were ready to go credit hustling a few minutes ago," I pointed out.

"God, Lizzie, sometimes you're a totally unreasonable bitch."

He was right. Sometimes I could be an unreasonable bitch. This, however, was not one of those times. My bitch had withered in the sun halfway home from the drugstore. All I had left was tired aggravation.

"I just walked miles in the blistering sun for you," I reminded my dear, ingrate of a brother.

He laughed at me. "Yeah, your skin looks like one of those crawfish."

Sometimes I hate my brother.

"Fine," he said after a moment on a sad, put-upon sigh that often gets to me. "I'll get it myself."

Moving with far more energy than I had, Jacob got off the bed and stepped over to the dresser where he opened his own can of corn. He sat on the edge of the mattress in his T-shirt and underwear, facing me while he ate. After a quiet minute or so, my stomach rumbled and I remembered it had been quite a while since I'd eaten.

"Let me have half of that," I said. It was not a request.

"Eat the green beans."

"I don't want green beans. I want corn." Actually, I love green beans and they would have been fine, but that wasn't the point. I couldn't say what the point was, just what it wasn't.

"Fine, you spoiled brat," he responded with a half-grin I knew was trouble.

Jacob shoveled two heaping spoons of corn into his wide-open mouth before leaning off the bed to hand me the can. I took it, tilted it toward the candle light, and looked inside. A few kernels were floating around in the liquid at the bottom of the can. I ate them, and then drank the liquid.

"So what's going on out there in the great big world?" Jacob asked as he scooted back on the bed and propped himself up on our two pillows.

"Heat," I answered. "Lots of it." After a moment I said, "There's a convention in town. A political group."

Jacob rolled his eyes and then gave me his

disgusted look. "Don't start that crap again."

One night, after a discussion about the monster I believed lived in the dark, I told Jacob about my theory on it. That was a mistake. When he's feeling cocky, which is more times than not, he teases me. He can be relentless when he gets going. If I remember to, I remind myself that is how he handles his fears.

When Jacob was scared, he blamed me for whatever popped into his mind. It was usually something ridiculous, like I'm stingy with our money, or I ate the apple he was just thinking about eating. That's when my bitch came out.

I threw at him angry accusations that, while true, were still cruel. In a voice lacking all empathy, I would remind him we lived the way we did because of his drug and alcohol abuse. I would remind him how I kept a job at a pizza parlor until his legal expenses and rushing off to the emergency room or to the county jail cost us our rent money and me that job. I would remind him of all the job applications I put in after, and that I had some real possibilities. Two places called me back for a second interview. One of them paid even more than the pizza place had.

Then Jacob totaled our old but dependable car on which I carried only liability insurance. Even though I had no problem riding the bus, employers always asked if I had a car. It mattered more to them than it did to me, which in turn made it matter to me.

Maybe they saw it as a sign of prudence and responsibility. It didn't help when they called my previous employer they found out how sometimes I ran out in the middle of my shift after a call from, or on behalf of, my brother. Suddenly I'd become un-hirable.

That's the point in the argument when my brother gets weepy and apologizes to me until I felt guilty enough to award him winner of the fight by letting him be the victim. This was our routine.

After I'd told Jacob my theory about the monster, he told me I was turning crazy like Silvia. She was an addict/prostitute who sometimes lived in the tunnels (and I think Jacob had a little bit of a crush on her)

He laughed at me and asked if I'd taken Silvia up on her offer to share her pipe. I should have known not to tell him such personal thoughts. It never ended well for me. But he was my brother, my only family, the closest thing I had to a friend, and sometimes a woman needed to talk things out.

"Jacob," I said, thinking to change the subject before he could start in on me. But my mind was too tired to think faster than his rested one.

"There ain't no monster down here."

"Isn't."

"Yeah," he said, all snotty because of my correction. "That's what I said. There *isn't* a monster. God, what are you six?"

"I know what I know, Jacob."

"Yeah, yeah, evil flows down here like the water." Jacob rolled his eyes before continuing. "Why come here? Seriously, Liz, why here? Wouldn't it be more profitable for Satan to take from those who have so much more to lose than we do?"

"It's not Satan. There's no such thing. But there's good and there's evil. And evil thrives here. Besides, I told you, I don't think it can live in the light."

"So instead of living in the basement of some fancy resort it chooses to live in the storm drains?" he said, followed by a sarcastic snort of laughter and a cough.

It was a valid point. I hated when he made valid points. "Maybe it's a bottom feeder and it's that we're easy prey."

"Goddamn it Liz, stop it you…freak! Sometimes you're so creepy."

His words were angry and mean, but they were a cover. Fear ran beneath, and I could hear the flow. Jacob believed at least in the possibility of the thing. To acknowledge it, however, was to open himself to more fears.

"I'm sorry, Jacob. I guess I'm just too tired to think straight. There's no such thing as monsters."

"Of course there ain't, isn't. I don't believe in monsters."

A grin tugged at my lips, but I didn't let it show. In that sentence, my little brother sounded like the cowardly lion proclaiming a disbelief in ghosts.

"You look tired," Jacob said. His tone changed to one of brotherly concern. It's the part of him that keeps me whole. "Why don't you come here and lie down for a while?"

Jacob fluffed my pillow for me and put it back on my side. I stood up. My legs were shaky and weak, and I felt much older than I should. I took off my shoes and lay down on our bed.

"Turn over. I'll rub your back for you."

This was Jacob's way of saying he was sorry. I graciously accepted his apology and let him.

Chapter 3

"Come on, lazy bones. Wake up."

"I'm tired, Jacob. Let me sleep a little while."

He continued to shake me. If I weren't so beat, I'd have punched him.

"Come on, Lizzie. We have four dollars to our names and we're running out of food. We need to go out."

He was right. Money was low, food was low, the only thing we had in abundance was need.

"All right, all right," I said, and I pried open my eyes. They were hot and gritty. I wished I had some eye drops. "Just give me a minute."

The mattress gave a wobble as Jacob hopped off the bed. I closed my eyes again. The heat had drained me of my energy, and water and a nap had only given me a partial refuel.

Jacob made some sounds, shedding his clothing and then sloshing water in the bowl as he washed. I rolled over so my back was to him to give him some privacy. This courtesy had evolved between us without discussion.

He'd lit the candle on his side of the bed. It flickered a bit with my movement. Without looking, I knew the light made a few quick swirls against the cement walls of our home, giving off a cozy illusion.

"Don't forget to shave," I told him through a yawn.

"Maybe I'll grow a beard."

"No. Your beard is too scraggly. It's better if we look clean." He grumbled. Then I listened to the sound of him getting out his razor. He understood the value of inconspicuousness. "Do you want me to wash your hair for you?" I asked.

"Yeah, after I shave."

Jacob coughed a couple of times, mostly a dry cough. He sounded much better than he had the last few days and that helped to settle my nerves. And he was motivated. That was something I always tried to encourage in him.

As my brother dressed, I rolled onto my stomach and stretched, coaxing myself into waking. We really did need to go out. Jacob had been sick for the better part of the past week and I'd been loath to go credit hustling without him. A woman wandering alone late at night was foolish enough. Leaving my brother unsupervised for such a long stretch of time was also a concern.

Jacob's dresser drawer scraped open. As he was putting on his clothes, I sat up and rubbed my eyes. The action made the skin on my face burn. The burning sizzled across my arms and legs as well. It covered all my skin that had been exposed to the sun on my walk to the drugstore. It was as if I'd spent the afternoon rotating over a hearty campfire.

"Jacob, hand me that bottle of lotion."

Jacob took the bottle from the top of our dresser and handed it to me. His thorough glance lingered in a way that failed to suppress the full measure of his alarm, and I knew my sunburn must look as bad as it felt.

"After you wash my hair, I'll go get some fresh water for you," he said to me.

My brother was being nice, thoughtful, and his voice was kind. I must have looked awful.

"Okay," I told him, knowing I'd better take advantage of this ration of good will while it was here. "What time is it?"

Jacob picked up his watch from the top of the dresser and carried it over to the candle, turning it toward the soft light. "Almost two o'clock in the morning. Stupid drunks must have left us something by now."

In the interest of starting the night without an argument or harsh feelings, I resisted the temptation to point out to my alcoholic brother that phrases like 'stupid drunks' were unkind. Especially considering those people were in fact supporting us. Not to mention while in the throes of drunkenness, he had done far more stupid things than leave a few dollars on a gaming machine.

Even after totaling my car, Jacob continued his substance abuse. Eventually, stress led me to complain to my brother. I'm only human. Not that complaining did any good. In fact, it had the opposite effect.

Suddenly, Jacob could justify his drinking because his bitch of a sister was on his back all the time. Instead of listening to my instincts and shutting my mouth, my complaints increased in volume and ire. My bitch grew, Jacob drank more, and our troubles reproduced like Gremlins in a pond.

My boss fired me, with good reason. I cursed him out anyway. Making matters worse, I did so in front of customers and other employees. He was angry and embarrassed, and I knew he would have loved to slap me. But my young boss was better than that, so, he did what he could do, which was to send me packing with a hard promise to warn off any prospective employers who might call in the future for information about me.

With no real skills, no car, and a terrible reference from my previous boss, even the crappiest jobs wouldn't have me. Two months later, we were living here.

It's been almost ten months since Jacob has had a drink. I tried to remember that and not dwell on the night all those months ago when we split up in the Mandalay Bay Casino. That night left a nasty bruise, and it was stubborn to heal.

The intensity of my anger had frightened me. It frightens me still. My build-up of misery-infused fury broke loose and ran through my veins like the vilest of toxins. That day at the casino, the bitch in me could have killed my brother.

Jacob found eight dollars in credits on a poker machine. Instead of cashing out, he played them back, one at a time at a slow pace, scoring several free drinks for himself.

At the time, we'd been living in the storm drain for almost three weeks and I didn't think things could get any worse. Jacob, I was so sure, could see what his drinking had done to us and he had learned. We could only go up from there, both figuratively and literally.

I'd found him sitting at the gaming machine, playing back the money we so desperately needed. He was flirting with the cocktail waitress and laughing his loud, drunken laugh as he slipped one of our precious dollar bills onto her tray. At the site of it, sharp blades of outrage plunged into the depths of my despair and unearthed a blinding rage.

My in-his-face stance was nothing less than shrewish. I screamed at him, names so foul they'd never before passed my lips. If it hadn't been for a security guard telling us to tone it down or leave, I believe I would have become violent.

At least I'd held onto enough sense to stifle myself, even apologize to the guard so he wouldn't kick us out. We needed that place. It was close enough so we could walk there in a reasonable amount of time. We had to split our visits among as many casinos as we could to avoid repetitive recognition.

For a while after that, Jacob said nothing about my keeping him under a microscope. He did what I told him to do, period. He had never seen me so angry, and I think it scared him almost as much as it did me. Good. Our living conditions hadn't put the fear he needed into him. But I did.

If I could look back on that day from a couch in our living room with electricity, a stocked refrigerator, and a real bathroom with running water, I could chuckle at the scene I'd made. I might laugh outright at my brother cowering from me as if I was bigger and stronger. Until that night, I'd been the docile one in the family, the good little mouse whose pliable spine bent with the circumstance.

Sometimes I thought of that night as I lay on the old mattress somebody dumped in the desert. Some days it played back in my head when I woke up in the daytime to pitch dark because there were no windows in the storm drains.

And sometimes, I thought of that night when Jacob

was sleeping, and I counted my secret savings, and realized how very far I still had to go before I could get us out of here. If on occasion I had to be a bitch to do it, then that's what I would be.

Though I wouldn't savor a recurrence of consuming rage, in a way it was somewhat empowering. After that night, at least for this good stretch of time, the dynamics of our relationship changed.

Jacob grumbled sometimes when I told him what to do, but I was the one making the decisions, giving the instructions. I held the upper hand and, oddly, since that night when I lost control of my temper, I'd been more in control of my own life than ever before. I didn't know how much longer it was going to last. The fact was, lately, the structure of this commander/underling relationship had worn thin in patches.

For Jacob, the incident at Mandalay Bay had faded far more into history than it had for me. In recent weeks, my brother's irritation at my mistrust had grown, and he was less and less inclined to stifle his grievances. No matter how I phrased it, I couldn't convince him of my justification. He saw himself as the victim of adverse circumstances and he refused to accept he caused his own troubles. This frustrates me to no end.

"Okay, I'm ready now," Jacob said. He dipped his head into the washbowl sitting atop a blue, overturned plastic crate. Beside the washbowl, we keep a bar of soap on a pretty, little floral-patterned plate with only one small chip on the edge. I insist on cleanliness and on that Jacob abides me with little fuss.

When we lived with our parents, we lived in filth. Our parents existed too immersed in their individual infidelities and adventures in sobriety-avoidance to care whether their children, or the home they lived in, was clean.

There was a broom leaning against our dresser and it was in reasonably good condition even though we found it in a dumpster. I kept the floor of our concrete camp swept. While rummaging through the castoffs of others, I kept an eye out for a usable rug. A rug would make a nice addition.

I made my way to the dresser and picked up our bottle of generic shampoo and conditioner in one. Using only as much as I needed, I rubbed suds into Jacob's hair as he leaned over the washbowl. I gave his scalp a good scrubbing before pouring some water from one of our jugs over his head to rinse.

As he dried his hair with a towel, Jacob whistled a tune. I stretched and winced as a blaze flashed along the surface of my skin.

"Be right back," Jacob said.

He poured the water from our washbowl into the metal bucket we kept right there for dirty water. He wiped and then refilled the bowl with the last of the clean water from the jug. He then walked toward the south opening managing to carry a flashlight, the bucket of dirty water, and both of our now empty jugs. He made a right and his light soon disappeared from my sight.

A few yards from the tunnel exit, near the end of the Las Vegas Strip where our part of the storm drain opened up, was a working spigot. Surrounded by nothing but desert, its reason for being there was inexplicable.

There must have been a plan for it. Probably some sort of construction coming in the future, or maybe it was a remnant of a previous plan never brought to fruition. Like the alcove we use as a bathroom, I didn't know why the spigot was there, but I was ever grateful for the water source.

While Jacob was gone, I made the bed using stiff motions. A silly bit of tidiness, really, but I worry about losing touch with the simple habits. Surrendering the minutia of life was the first step in surrendering.

In an effort to wake myself, I stretched again. The tightness of my searing skin made me cringe. Trying to ignore the pain, I went to my dresser drawer and took out some fresh shorts and a clean T-shirt.

In between laundry trips, I washed my underwear by hand and laid them out to dry so I always had a clean pair. Tomorrow, though, we'd have to go to the laundromat. We'd go early before the heat got too bad, or late, after the sun has set. The way my skin felt, I voted for late.

"Here you go, all fresh and clean," Jacob said upon his return.

He carried the flashlight in his armpit, freeing his hands to carry two full jugs of water and the handle to our empty dirty-water bucket tucked into the curl of his fingers. He set everything down, and then poured some fresh water into the bowl for me to use. While I undressed, he sat with his back to me and played with the Rubik's cube we found on the side of the road a few weeks ago.

My skin eased at the water's soothing touch. I should have done this before I lay down, but I'd depleted even my reserves too much to seek relief.

After drying, applying more lotion, and getting dressed, Jacob helped me wash my hair. He even helped me towel dry it. While I combed out my hair, I sat in one of our lawn chairs. Being clean did much to revive me. I was feeling human again.

"I think we should start at the Desert Star tonight," I told my brother.

The Desert Star was a very small casino at the end of the Strip. It's across the street, but still nearest to us. We usually only stopped there on the way home.

Jacob gave the cube another twist and glanced over at me. "Start there? Why? Our chances of finding much there aren't great."

"I told you, there's a convention in town. All of the casinos will be busy this weekend, even there."

And the Desert Star is close, so if Jacob isn't feeling well, it won't be so far to get back. "Besides," I said, "They have better deals on food and we're pretty tight."

"Okay," he said in an amiable tone. He was so happy to be getting out he'd agree to almost anything. Jacob cleared his throat and brightened further with a thought. "Hey, maybe they'll be handing out some of those two-for-the-price-of-one coupons for the buffet."

"Those coupons aren't good on the weekends." I hated the disappointment on his face. I was sure it was on mine, too. We could stuff ourselves at a buffet and keep our bellies full for a good long stretch.

His mood lifted again and he said, "Well, I'll see if I can find one of those coupons anyway. People are always dropping them on the floor. We can go back during the week." Jacob was smiling again.

"Good idea," I told him, because it was.

"Are you ready yet?" he asked.

Jacob was pacing, his hands fidgeting. He was anxious to get going. I couldn't blame him. For days now, all he'd had to occupy his mind while his body was healing was his Rubik's cube and a few pages of a ratty old sports car magazine. He'd read it at least half a dozen times already.

"Let my hair dry a little more."

I wished I could use a blow dryer and give my hair some style so I would fit in with the tourists better. But I'd learned brushing it in a certain way until it was dry, or close to, helped.

In the meantime, I carried the burning candle from the crate to the dresser, adjusted the round mirror on a stand atop it with a crack running along only the far right side, and I applied a bit of pale peach lip-gloss. The tube was the last of my make-up and down to a thin stub. A few more uses and it too would be gone.

Jacob stopped in his pacing and faced me. He was working up the nerve to ask for something. I already felt like a tyrant.

"Hey, if we get real lucky, do you think we could hit a matinee this week? I saw a poster on the wall near the movie theater in the Luxor last time we were there. There's a new Avengers movie out. I'd *really* love to see it."

"If we get real lucky," I said, trying to put some hope in the sentence.

I faced the mirror and Jacob's reflection, a little to my right. He lowered his head and nodded in the slow way of disappointment. After so many blows, my hopeful inflection was crippled. Besides, it really didn't matter if I sounded convincing. We both knew the odds of us getting so lucky were not great. It happens, though.

Several times, we found seventy or eighty dollars on a single machine and I allowed a treat like an afternoon movie. For my brother's sake, I wished for that tonight. He needed rewards more than I did.

"Okay," I said, turning to my brother. "How do I look?"

I already knew the answer. I looked burned. My appearance didn't worry me too much. After a hot, sunny day like today, there would be plenty of tourists walking around with sunburns, too. If anything, it would help me look the part. Locals knew better than to be outside for so long without sunscreen.

The look I was going for was casual effort, as usual. That's how the bulk of the people out there would appear and the better we blended in, the better we would fare. Security guards kept a lookout for our kind.

Jacob scrutinized me and pretended not to notice the redness of my skin. "You look like a hot babe," he said with a grin and a nod.

Well, the hot part was right, just not in the way he meant it. I was on fire. And even if my skin wasn't the color of an irritated rash, I'm realistic enough to know I was not good looking. I wasn't hideous or anything, well, not usually. At my best, I was a mediocre-looking girl with a personality too wrapped up in our survival to present much of anything to anyone else. And today I was not at my best.

"Thanks," I said, appreciating his effort. "You ready?"

"You bet. Let's go."

I grabbed my purse while Jacob picked up a flashlight. We headed toward the east exit that would deposit us a few yards away from the Las Vegas Strip.

****

The nighttime temperature had dropped into the nineties. It was still hot, but tolerable without the sun pounding on us. I tipped my face toward the sky for the sake of having all that space over my head, not out of expectation of seeing any stars. Their tiny lights twinkled elsewhere, lacking the strength to outshine the strip.

We crossed the short expanse of desert and stepped onto the sidewalk near the glowing 'Welcome to Fabulous Las Vegas' sign. As front yard ornaments go, it wasn't bad. A sign like that might scream 'dated' or even 'gaudy', if it lived some place else. Here, though, it had substantial beauty, a nostalgic tether in a place of perpetual change.

The sign shone proud as tourists, even at this late hour, stood beneath it with cameras and smiles. How many people have taken pictures in that spot? It must be millions. I'm sure none of them knew that only a short distance away was a storm drain where many of the homeless in Las Vegas live.

It was about a ten-minute walk down the Strip to the Desert Star. Even though it was only another three or four hours until sunrise, tourists still wandered below the sporadic motion of colorful neon.

Most looked tired with their bleary eyes guiding their slow yet eternal pace. Some were more energized, high on free drinks and a lucky streak. Others had that 'in Vegas only' ability to look both electrified *and* exhausted. Somberness overtook the worn out highs of a few, a sure sign they lost more in the casinos than they'd planned.

The Desert Star was very old, hiding out at the end of the strip where no one ever thought to tear it down, or remodel. The ceilings were low and painted black with tiny flecks of white. At one time, it was probably supercool, maybe even groovy.

What must surely be a rickety filtration system cleaned the cigarette smoke at a pace too slow to keep up with the need. As a result, the faux night sky was always foggy and its stars a bit jaundiced. Many of the gaming machines were an era behind and the carpet was a patchwork of remnants, leftovers from the big resorts. The ladies room still has the old Pepto-Bismol pink sinks. Jacob told me it was sea green in the men's room. The kitsch was what drew people.

Stepping into the Desert Star gave us a finely chilled blast from heaven. The cool air whooshed along my burnt skin like a refrigerated salve. The burly security guard at the door gave us little more than a glance. Even though Jacob wouldn't be twenty-one for two more years, the drugs and alcohol had aged him. I knew stress had aged me. Neither one of us had ever been carded.

The sounds of the casino were as lively as ever, as I had suspected with the convention in town. The frenetic tones of the machines, the fake sound of real money printing out on tickets, cocktail waitresses taking orders and making deliveries to patrons still out for a party, all sounded promising to me.

"Do you want to split up, cover more ground faster?" Jacob asked me.

While covering more ground increased our chances of finding some credits, it also increased the chance of Jacob scoring a free drink or two, or more, while out of my sight.

We were several notches below our regular state of desperation. The last thing we needed was a rerun of my fit in Mandalay Bay. My brother must have read my thoughts on the scorched surface of my face.

After a breathy huff, Jacob said, "I'm fine, Liz. Look, it's a little place. I won't be out of your sight for more than a few minutes."

He was in the bud of agitation because I didn't give him my full trust. He had a lot of nerve. I had good reason not to trust him, and he knew it. But his point was valid.

Apart we could cover the place faster. And since the Desert Star was so small, I figured he wouldn't try to sneak a drink where it would be so easy for me to catch him. I spun it to his favor, though, letting him think I was giving him my trust. It might make it easier in the next place where I would not.

"Okay," I told him. "I'll meet you right back here in twenty minutes."

He looked so pleased with himself I was glad for the bit of freedom I was allowing him. I hoped he wouldn't turn my joy into disappointment, as he has so very many times before. We didn't have the luxury of time to have a fight or to call it an early night. We needed money and we needed it soon. With the sad tally of our present finances, we didn't even have enough to do our laundry tomorrow.

I wandered at a slow pace down an aisle, machines at the hands of their players blinked and beeped on both sides of me. I did my best to look as if I was in the depths of analytic thoughts, sizing up the machines, deciding which one to play, emulating one of two basic styles of players. This was something I learned watching others, and I think I was good at it.

The gamblers who were out for no more than little fun would plop down at any machine with a game they liked, or maybe something trendy to the populace, a TV show, a movie, a celebrity, etc. They wanted a side of fun with their win.

Then you had the more serious players. They would travel the rows of slot and poker machines at a slow cruise believing they would get some sort of psychic feel for one about to hit. No matter how many times this theory failed them, they couldn't let it go.

Chester, our friend in the tunnels who lost everything he ever owned, and some things he did not, to the casino games, still got a rush of excitement when he *felt lucky*.

Across the aisle, in the next row, something looked promising. The man was in his early thirties. His clothes, a collared, dark blue shirt so new it had not yet faded, and khaki shorts ready to check into the clothes hamper. The bottle of beer in his left hand angled at a precarious tip while his right hand dragged back and forth across the buttons of his machine.

The man's shoulders were slumped and he was listing in the opposite direction of his beer bottle. His body was buff and his skin looked healthy. This state of drunkenness was not the norm for him. The next time he woke up he probably wouldn't even remember this moment of his life.

With a covertness I'd perfected, I kept a watch on

him.

His head swiveled as he cast an awkward, visual sweep of the casino. It nearly cost him his balance. The man appeared unaware of the dips his body was making. He kept searching for someone. His head stopped and bobbed a little from side to side. He was looking in the general direction of the restrooms. He wasn't looking for a person, but a place.

The man shifted his wobbling head back to squint at his machine. The slight action threw him into a sway. He caught himself before he fell, but not before a good splash escaped his bottle of beer. His shorts gained an obvious wet spot near the top of his thigh. He didn't notice.

In a move quite sudden for someone so intoxicated, the man popped up from his machine and lurched straight to the men's room. I wandered over and stood behind his vacated seat.

I shot a quick glance to his game. The man had been playing video poker, Deuces Wild. He'd left a little over twelve dollars on the machine, twelve beautiful dollars. After a few minutes, he staggered out of the men's room, made a sharp right, and lurched toward the elevators. A moment later, the man stumbled inside and hit a button. The elevator doors closed, I hoped taking him to the right floor.

Sliding into his seat at the machine, I hit the cash out button. The ticket printed to the music of coins clinking in a metal tray and I snatched it out before I stood up and spun around, anxious to share the good news with Jacob.

"Hi," said a giant of a man.

He had to be at least six three, broad shouldered,

and he stood no more than two feet before me. I could smell the musky scent of his aftershave. At five four, I had to tilt my head to look up at him.

Although he leaned on one leg in a casual stance, it was like standing before an armed guard at the ready. The guy had to have played football in high school, which looked to me to have been about ten years ago.

He wore a dark suit with an appropriate, somber tie that blunted his attempt at a regular-guy smile. The neat cut of his midnight hair gleamed clean beneath the artificial light. His strong-jawed face had a fresh shave. In the sharp, azure of his eyes lay a great deal more awareness than his casual pose implied.

I was immediately on alert.

I did my best to gather my cool and ignore his largeness, and the fact that he looked like an F.B.I. agent. I took a quick study of his face. He was handsome, but not in a plastic way. This worried me. He probably wasn't narcissistic enough to disregard me. His friendly expression worried me, too, for he had no good reason to shine his attentions my way.

Between his brows were two slight, vertical indentations that would eventually deepen. At the same time, I could see laugh brackets had formed around his mouth, less pronounced than the frown lines. Though the man was serious, he did at least grin on occasion.

I had to wonder if in this man's mind having a good time meant making trouble for someone like me. Some people were like that. Some people played cruelty like a sport.

Because of the poker machine right behind me, I could take no more than one small step back. Standing in between the two empty seats, he was too big for me to scoot around, and anyway, by the official look of him I thought that would be a bad idea.

Clear, penetrating eyes bore into me with a casino-bred knowledge that put me on edge. A small gold tag pinned to the breast pocket of his jacket read 'Joe'. He worked for the casino; a position of some importance was my guess.

He smiled at me, waiting for a response. His teeth were straight and sparkling clean. The lift at the corner of his lips indented a dimple on the right side of his face. His place on the handsome meter ticked upward.

There was a sudden dampness in my armpits that had nothing to do with my burning skin or even the myriad of problems I might be facing. For the first time in a very long time, I found myself wishing I looked pretty.

"Hi," I returned.

"You got lucky pretty quick. Wasn't someone else just sitting there?"

His voice was deep, the kind that could be seductive, or intimidating, depending on the man's preference and the given situation. He looked muscular from shoulder to toe, big enough and strong enough to be a bouncer at a biker bar. I took a nervous glance around. If Jacob were to walk by, he might not have even seen me on the other side of this guy. If my brother did see me, I hoped he would know better than to approach.

I looked the man in the eye, knowing to do otherwise would be a sure sign of guilt. Though what I did wasn't illegal, it was unsavory. Casinos frowned on unsavory. Maybe that's how he got the creases between his brows.

His gaze was intense, though not overly critical. When he spoke to me, he made it sound like he was making relaxed conversation, but we both knew better. I was under investigation.

A trickle of perspiration made its way from the base of my neck down my spine.

"Was there someone sitting there right before me?" I asked, trying to paint my nerves with a good coat of casual. I tagged my words with a pleasant expression. "Yeah, I got lucky fast. All I put in was a couple of bucks." Video from one of the many casino security cameras would tell him different. I crossed my mental fingers and hoped it wouldn't come to a review.

"Hit a little jackpot right away." I smiled a little wider. "Gotta cash out when you're ahead."

"Well, the smart ones do." he said, giving me a broad, beautiful grin. I wondered if it was as false as mine. The thought made me a little sad.

I maintained eye contact and hoped my lips didn't show the tremble. Getting eighty-sixed from a place wasn't such a big deal to most people. Las Vegas offers a million other places to go. We had to walk the long distances between them, though. And we didn't go there for fun.

"Well, I'd better go find my brother. He'll be getting worried about me."

And if Jacob saw my plight, he might act the hero and do something utterly foolish. I shuffled a small sidestep, as if to go around the big guy. He didn't budge, so I stepped back until the button ledge of the poker machine pressed into my back. I tipped my face up to his. His gaze softened and that confused me. What was his game?

"I've seen you in here before." He tipped his head slightly as if trying to place me.

I had the feeling the effort was a façade. I hoped it was my imagination and he didn't recognize me from the other times we'd been in there. For the time being, Jacob and I needed to maintain flight beneath the radar of pretty much everyone.

"We're locals."

"You and your brother live around here?"

"Not too far."

His response was a placid, two-tip nod. He glanced away for a moment, and then turned back. His mouth opened a bit, as if he wanted to say something to me, but didn't know how. It's how I'd always imagined it was for beautiful, kempt women when men approached them. *What was his game?*

Finally, the big man stepped back and said, "Well, enjoy your night."

Just like that, he was letting me go. I passed him and was a quick three feet away when he said, "Wait."

My dark thoughts had been right. He was playing with me, a cruel hunter, toying with his prey. My heart pounded harder.

This man could make loads of trouble for us. If he called in the police, I would have no address to give them, no place of employment. Even my driver's license was expired. Although the law rarely bothers those of us who live in the tunnels, living there is illegal so I couldn't tell them the truth of my situation. To do that would be to rat out everyone down there.

During this past dreadful year, I'd had to do some lying, but I'm not comfortable enough with it to be good at it. After no more than a few questions, professional interrogators would regard everything I said as suspicious.

I didn't think I could be arrested for credit hustling. At the very least, though, I was sure they could come up with some reason to haul me away. And then what would happen to Jacob if I were gone for a day or two? I knew the answer. I just didn't want to think about it.

The man's hand slid inside his jacket. I expected a cell phone to emerge and prepared myself to make a run for it. Jacob and I had discussed the possibility of such a situation, and he would know to meet me back at our camp. However, it had been a while since we'd had that talk and I worried he might not remember.

The sorting of my panicked thoughts halted when the man slid a long ticket out of his pocket and held it out to me. After I looked at it for a few seconds, I closed my thumb and forefinger over it, but he held on until I looked up at him.

"In case you didn't read my nametag, I'm Joe. I work here. This ticket is good for two for one at the buffet. You can use it Monday through Thursday. You and your brother come back during the week to eat." With that, he let go of the ticket.

I know I should have been grateful. I was grateful. But the obviousness of my unfortunate situation filled me with humiliation that burned worse than my skin

In a moment of senseless pride, I almost tore the ticket in half and threw it in his handsome face. I wanted to scream 'we don't need your charity'. However, the fact was, we did. We needed it very much. I swallowed yet another chunk of my battered pride, and took the ticket.

Not able to look him directly in the eye, I tipped

my head until my gaze rested on my poor old sneakers. The pose was too pathetic, so I lifted my head and looked away, as if searching for my brother, blinking back tears. I didn't say thank you. I was afraid if I did, the tears would show and flaunt my humiliation. Was my state of affairs really so obvious?

I knew I was skinny, but so what, lots of people were. My few articles of clothing were old, and all were well worn, but they were clean, and so was I. Maybe I didn't clean up as well as I thought. I suddenly felt obvious, an object of a fine man's pity.

Though I couldn't see past the big guy in front of me, I was sure all eyes in the vicinity were watching me. More sympathy I didn't want, attention I didn't need. It riled my temper, but I managed to rein it in. This was my lot in life and if Jacob and I were going to survive it then I had to be tolerant. Sometimes, though, it killed me.

Joe said nothing more, so I turned and walked away. The temptation to kick him before I left was close to overwhelming. My face heated, degradation giving my sunburn a booster.

"What did he say?" Jacob asked me. He was waiting for me at the end of the row and turned to walk with me. Since he was a little taller than I am and his legs are a little longer, he had no trouble keeping up with my brisk pace.

"He gave me a two-for-one ticket for the buffet," I told my brother, angrier than I had a right to be.

"Why'd he do that?"

"Because I look pathetic, that's why."

Jacob beamed. "Cool," he said, skirting a bulbous man in a Hawaiian shirt.

I stopped and scowled at my brother as if he was a parasite. "It's not cool, Jacob. It's humiliating."

"Fine. You be humiliated. I'll be full."

"We can't even use it till Monday." It was a lousy comeback, but it was all I could pluck from my flustered mind.

"Something to look forward to," he said through his big, stupid grin. I didn't think it was possible, but his smile grew even wider.

My brother's good attitude was a row of sharp tines raking over my wounded dignity. We had nothing. We were hungry and broke, and lived in a storm drain with drug addicts, alcoholics, and prostitutes who invite strange men into our secret place. We fear the rain and the dark, the criminals and the police. We didn't have a lock on our door. We didn't even have a damn door.

I felt my bitch rising, but my stomach was rumbling so I managed to stop her before she stopped us. I let my short fingernails dig half-moons into my palms as I channeled my frustration into a cyclone within me until it wore itself down to a manageable size. It settled in my stomach, where there was plenty of room.

"Let's go to Mandalay Bay," I said. Weariness bore down on me again. My sunburn ached and my pride was in tatters. I wished I could go home, lie down on our mattress, and then sleep for a week.

"Cash that out first." Jacob pointed to the ticket in my other hand. "How much is it for?"

I'd forgotten all about our twelve dollars and change. Without speaking, I showed him the ticket nestled against the buffet coupon.

"Cool," he said.

We walked to the closest cash out machine where I slid it in.

"We can share something at the café first," Jacob said. He was staring at the money as it slid out of the slot and into the tray, gazing at it as if the machine had already converted it into food.

"No, I want to leave. We'll eat at the next place." I put the money and the buffet ticket in my purse.

"Come on, Liz. I'm starving. Besides, everything at Mandalay Bay is too expensive."

I was hungry, too, very hungry. And he was right. Mandalay Bay wasn't the kind of place a person goes to for a cheap bite to eat. But I wanted to get away from Joe and his pity. I wanted out of the Desert Star. The place was staring me down and I was ready to look away.

"We can go to the food court at the Luxor," I told Jacob.

"Hey, why don't we do this?" Jacob said brightening the way he does when he gets an idea. "We'll go straight to the Excalibur, go downstairs to their food court for something to eat, and then scout for credits there. After that, we can hit the Luxor and Mandalay Bay on our way back. Make full use of the night."

That meant a long walk past two huge resorts. I didn't care enough to care, though. I just wanted to go. "Sure, that sounds good," I told Jacob.

Maybe I would feel better after I ate. Being hungry always made me cranky. So does being humiliated. I'm going to have to work a little harder to get through this perfect storm.

Chapter 4

With our bellies full and forty-seven dollars in my purse, I did indeed feel better. In the cavernous food court at the of the Excalibur, Jacob was able to scarf down a submarine sandwich and an order of fries like it was little more than a snack. He didn't slow down until the thin white bag with grease spots showing through held only about five or six French fries. At that point, he ate at a leisurely pace. It was more an act of extending the meal than finishing it.

I savored my sandwich in small bites, taking my time chewing. We shared a cup of water. Afterward, I treated us each to a donut. I chose a jelly-filled while Jacob, child he so often is, picked one with white frosting and colorful sprinkles on top.

After we'd both eaten the last of our meal, we sat there for a while. Although our stomachs were full, we still enjoyed the sights and smells of food. Even the French fry grease was wonderfully aromatic. When people carried orange plastic trays holding their food past our table, we always peeked to see what they had. For a while, we played a game born in this very place I called, 'next time I'm getting that'.

We did a little people watching. That never got old. People wander through these resorts in everything from raggedy cut-offs to formal wear. Sometimes a wedding party passes through. Every now and then, we spot

Elvis. Mostly, though, we just liked being some place other than 'home'.

Since we had paid good money for the food we'd eaten, my brother and I had a right to be there, the same as everybody else. What set us apart were the things for which we were grateful.

We enjoyed sitting in the plastic chairs that were not previously somebody else's garbage. Being inside somewhere safe where inconspicuousness took little effort. Relaxing in a room where the air was cool and clean. Sitting some place where hot food and clean bathrooms were close by. Electric lights. We had a great appreciation for things most people took for granted.

Sometimes I wondered if, when times were better for us, that appreciation would fade away. I didn't think so. If I should feel that happening I would, with utter clarity, summon up these days.

After a brief conversation, Jacob and I changed our plans. We crossed the strip and cruised through the casino at the Tropicana. We hadn't been there in more than a week. If anyone had seen us then our common, unremarkable appearances would have faded from their minds by now. Jacob and I had become apt at ordinary.

The Tropicana is a classic, one of the few old time resorts that survived the implosion epidemic that purged the town of most of the originals. It had been there since the fifties, but, unlike the Desert Star, its caretakers had preserved the resort.

I liked the classic feel of it. I enjoyed imagining the old days with the guys of the Rat Pack and other big names of the time all dressed up in their best clothes, as people did back then, having the time of their lives. It must have really been something. It still is. Chester once told us they have a pool at the Tropicana with a swim up gambling table. I didn't know if that was true, but I liked the way the scene looked in my head.

We did well tonight. Even with all we ate, we went home at dawn with enough money to do our laundry the next day, and enough to eat again. Feeding ourselves was always at the forefront of our thoughts and efforts. As soon as one meal was finished, we started worrying about the next.

Later, after Jacob fell asleep I would put five dollars of our score in my secret hidden wallet. All in all, it was a good night. I should have been happy. But that Joe guy kept popping into my head and spoiling my good thoughts. And the whys of it were not as clear as they should have been.

Joe was good to me when he could have been rotten. Plenty of others would have been; in fact, had been. We were undesirables; burned out light bulbs, smudges on an otherwise clean pane of glass. But Joe didn't look at me with disdain. He looked at me with pity, the only way he would ever look at me. For a reason I can't explain, that bothered me much more than it ever had before.

Jacob and I passed the great shining pyramid of the Luxor with its giant beam of brighter than bright light shooting straight up into space, literally into space. I hardly noticed. I was thinking about other girls my age.

We saw them all the time. They went by us like radiant butterflies bypassing dead flowers. They fluttered through the casinos in pairs or in groups, dressed in short skirts and high heels, pealing laughter as they made their way to the next club or party.

They acted like they owned the world. In a way, I guess they sort of did. By way of their enchanting veneers, they cast a spell and usually got what they wanted. Even hardened men of power became malleable in the heat of their radiance. Maybe I was jealous.

Normally I didn't let my mind put me in their pretty shoes. It was too depressing when I blinked and saw I was still standing in my own. On that night, though, with Joe lodged into the layers of the more important matters constantly plaguing my mind, I couldn't stop myself. I kept wondering how he would look at me if I had the sheen of one of those girls.

He had the appearance of a man who would have a girlfriend like that. She was probably some beauty queen who had a standing appointment at the salon and bought new clothes all the time, even if they weren't on sale. She was happy and giggled a lot, except when she chipped a nail or didn't get her way.

Due to her surrounding abundance, she fretted over gaining weight, not keeping it. She probably wore perfume every day. Because men gave it to her, she must have a lot.

A woman like that was up on the latest fashion and was diligent in her birth control because men wanted her and she wanted them back. Sex was a fun pastime. Maybe it was romantic, too, with candles lit for mood and not a light source. I wouldn't know. At twenty-two-years-old, I was still a virgin. Aside from a quick peck on the cheek from Eddie Hale in the tenth grade, no guy has even kissed me. I had been looking after my brother for as long as I could remember. It had been a life-consuming job.

In high school, I didn't date or play sports or join any clubs. I worked. I studied whenever I could, especially if it involved reading a work of fiction. There wasn't enough free time to establish any solid friendships.

When I was seventeen, nine weeks before graduation, Dad had a heart attack and died.

I had to quit school and turn my part time job at the pizza parlor into a full time job or we wouldn't have had next month's rent. Six months later, Mom overdosed on an odd mix of drugs she'd collected and stashed away.

Nobody ever knew for sure if her death was deliberate or not. When I'm feeling fanciful, I tell myself it was. She missed my father so much she couldn't bear to live without him. When my honest streak shined a callous light where I didn't want it to, I knew that's wasn't true.

Our parents often fought as if they hated one another and cheated on each other with regularity. They only stayed together because they were too lazy and too broke to get a divorce.

During my teen years and beyond, between school, doing for Jacob, and working, there'd been little time for me to do any primping and none for dating. Even when our parents were around I mostly took care of myself as well as my little brother. Often, I took care of our parents, too.

Seeing how everybody turned out, I guess I wasn't very good at it. I was trying to do better, though. I was trying very hard.

And during all this trying and mostly failing, while my parents were drinking themselves to death and my brother was following in their footsteps, the experiences of youth circumvented me, scared off by the drag from which I was inseparable.

I didn't like to think about dying a virgin, but I always knew I wouldn't be the kind to take up with any guy that came along either. That's what our mother did. And then she got pregnant with me and married our duplicitous father. She once told me he'd convinced her he had far more than he did, and then she was stuck for the rest of her life in a miserable marriage. I vowed long ago, that would not be me.

Not that my standards mattered at all anyway, nobody was asking. Even if someone like Joe did ask me out what would I do, give him directions to our camp in the storm drains? Tell him to call out before he walked in so I didn't freak out and accidently stab him with the kitchen knife I kept next to the mattress for protection?

Shaking my head, I had to give myself another scolding. There I went again, spoiling the good points of the night with my dark thoughts. Things were bound to get better eventually. I had a plan and I was saving for it. What I should have done is remind myself of the positives more often. There weren't a lot of them, but the ones we had were big.

Jacob hadn't had a drink in months. I should dance for that blessing. We were both reasonably healthy. My secret savings were gaining bulk. Someday we really would be out of the tunnels, in our own apartment with furniture and dishes and running water and a door with a lock. That's not a fantasy. It will happen. It *will* happen, I told myself.

Jacob's coughing fit jerked me from my thoughts.

It was the first one he'd had this evening, or had I been too lost in my own self-pity to notice?

"Hey, Jacob," I said, clapping him on the back several times. I could hear the rumble in his chest when he sucked in a deep breath only to cough it out again. It wasn't nearly as bad as it had been, but he wasn't all the way back from his illness.

"I'm all right."

"You know," I said, as his coughing subsided. "We have enough money for right now. Why don't we call it a night?"

Jacob must really be feeling bad because he nodded without hesitation. Usually I had several false starts before I could coax him back home. I understood. He was a young man and the only excitement he got out of life is when we went credit hustling.

"You should have told me you weren't feeling well."

"I felt pretty good until about half an hour ago, but I didn't want to go back yet. It was too good to be out. But I'm ready if you are."

I nodded. "I'm ready."

And I was. My skin hurt and I was tired. I was tired in new ways. Fortunately, I was too weary to explore them. Maybe if I get lucky, by morning our daily rituals of survival, of plodding through our present and heading into the future, would once again be so consuming I wouldn't be able to give the lacking in my life much thought.

We'd already made it to the front of the Tropicana. It was near dawn and there weren't many people around. I turned my head for a quick sweep of our dazzling surroundings.

They had not gotten old. Maybe it was because of the dramatic contrast of the Las Vegas Strip compared to the grim solitude of our home in the tunnels. Our two worlds could not differ more, but I think the blatant contrast was only a contributing factor. I couldn't imagine any town outshining this one.

On the other side of Tropicana Avenue sat the M.G.M. It was a gargantuan resort with a magnificent golden lion posed in a proud stance right on the corner of the property. Across the Strip from the M.G.M. was New York, New York. The Statue of Liberty stood with the same tall dignity she did in the real New York. Red roller coaster tracks ran past her and through a city's worth of buildings.

Farther down Las Vegas Boulevard were dancing waters, a volcano that erupts on schedule, the Eifel Tower, a grand palace and much, much more. It was a beautiful town, with creative architecture, the sum of which exists nowhere else in the world. Every time we emerged from the gloom and darkness of the tunnels, this greeted us all the way down to the Lucky Dragon.

Jacob was right. It was good to be out.

We turned around, rode the outside escalator back up to the overhead pedestrian bridge, and crossed Las Vegas Boulevard. From there we rode the escalator down on the other side where it deposited us right in front of the Excalibur, a medieval castle with colorful turrets and a stationary drawbridge. Jacob still appreciated the magnificence of it all, too. His head swiveled as he gazed at sights he'd seen many times before. From the Excalibur we headed south. We were about to begin our pass before the Mandalay Bay when Jacob perked up.

"Hey, Silvia!" my brother called out. He was looking behind us, as he often does. His chest heaved out one big cough, but I didn't think he even noticed.

I turned around. Silvia strutted down the boulevard in her eye-catching uniform, red three-inch heels and a bright purple dress as short as it was snug. She looked magical with the giant, glowing sphinx in front of the Luxor over her right shoulder. I always thought there was something kind of magical about her anyway.

Silvia was so full of love and life it broke my heart knowing what her life was like, believing, as I did. she could be so much more. I wished I could help her, but my own struggles have my hands filled to overflowing. Besides, Silvia didn't want to change her life. She told me so herself one afternoon.

A bad night had left her battered and bruised and I asked her why she didn't quit the prostitution business. She told me she had no desire to stop her 'partying' or to get off the streets. The business part of it, she said, she didn't mind at all, but I didn't believe it for a second. I think Silvia only said that to ease my worry and salvage her pride.

I knew she drank hard and enjoyed her drugs. Sometimes she was strangely happy. Other times, though, she got so very depressed I worried she'd commit suicide. I hoped she'd quit the drugs. I hoped she'd quit before it was too late for her to keep what she had left of herself. Maybe when we get our apartment she'll come and stay with us.

Silvia was still young, maybe a little older than me, and pretty, too. But at the rate she was going, she was going to hit the wall long before her time. I'd seen it before.

Every once in a while, longtime druggies come right through our camp trying to find the one they'd set up somewhere and lost. Sores patched their faces, a mark of their drugs. Often they were missing teeth. And always they were aging at a rapid pace.

So much waste of human life, at times it made me angry how they threw it away. Sometimes though, like when I get to know a person like Silvia, it was more depressing than I could bear.

I didn't know Silvia's last name. I had a feeling Silvia wasn't even her real first name. Most of the money she made selling her well-endowed body she spent on drugs. I knew she smoked a lot of pot. Often she reeked of it. Sometimes the smoke made its way from her part of the tunnel into ours.

She liked meth and every now and then heroin when she could get it. Ecstasy was her favorite. If she couldn't find drugs, she could manage for a while with alcohol. Sometimes she mixed them. She paid no heed to the dangers of this. I didn't know her past or what led her to this life, but I knew she was better than what she'd become. For all her problems, Silvia had a heart as big as the world and I worried about her because she deserved my concern.

Sometimes Silvia got a motel room or she crashed with someone for a while. She knew a lot of people. Often, though, she lived in the storm drains not far from us. Our first night there she let us stay in her camp. She was the reason we found our shelter.

We first met Silvia when she was 'taking care of business' in the desert across the street from a German restaurant. Several of us without homes had set up a camp of plywood, cardboard, blankets and tarps. Jacob and I were sitting on a dusty blanket surrounded by our few belongings stuffed into plastic grocery bags. When we left our apartment, we were only able to keep what we could carry.

The heat was retched and the windstorms were at times dangerous to us. Our fragile shelter could be picked up by the powerful desert gusts and easily injure one of us on its way to who knew where. Also, out in the open we were easy targets and often harassed by someone.

We heard from others that charity people sometimes visited and brought offerings. The only kind of people Jacob and I ever encountered in that place, other than those who shared our pitiful circumstance, were troublemakers who thought we were there for our laziness and their sport.

Jacob and I were eating a pizza and listening to Silvia conduct business on the other side of our cardboard wall. After her customer had gone, she'd peeked around the corner with the biggest, friendliest smile I'd ever seen and sniffed in the direction of our pizza. As dismal as our situation was, we couldn't help but grin back at her.

She apologized for bothering us with her business, and said it was just an occasional office. We shared our pizza with her and in turn, she told us about the storm drains. We packed up that day and moved. Silvia also taught us how to credit hustle for which I will be forever grateful. After paying for that pizza, we were down to our last thirty dollars. I don't know what would have happened to us had we not met her.

"Hey kids! What's up?"

Her words slurred a little, but she wasn't too far-gone. Silvia gave us each a hug. We hugged her back even though she reeked of beer and cigarette smoke. Jacob minded less than I did because she nuzzled her large breasts against him.

I didn't know how old Silvia was. Her skin was the color of dark chocolate and showed only a hint of tiny wrinkles around her sparkling eyes. But her lifestyle was rapidly sucking the light from her glow. She'd become more forgetful. Sometimes she forgot right in the middle of a sentence.

Cigarettes added some gravel to her voice and her teeth were yellowed from neglect and smoke. Somehow, though, Silvia still managed to shine.

She was wearing her blonde wig. It was big, brassy and bold, sprayed stiff in fancy curls. Underneath, I knew Silvia's hair was very short against her head. Sometimes she wore a red wig. The hair on that one was stick straight and cut even at her shoulders.

"We were out doing a little credit hustling," Jacob told her. As usual, he was having trouble keeping his eyes on her face. I couldn't blame him. Silvia had the goods and knew how to display them. If her neckline plunged any lower, her nipples would pop out.

"Oh yeah, baby? You guys have any luck tonight?"

I wanted to nudge Jacob, but there was no way to do it without her seeing. I would share our last bite of food with Silvia, but to share with her our money so she could buy drugs was not something I was willing to do.

"A few dollars," Jacob said. "We spent it all on dinner."

Good boy, Jacob.

"Well, I had me a big ole meal so I guess we're all good for the night." She treated us to her happy hoot then. I'll say this for Silvia; sometimes she was the happiest homeless person I've ever met. However, when she was low, she was the epitome of desolation.

"You guys heading back to the tunnels?" Silvia asked, adjusting her tight dress. She swayed a little on her high heels and Jacob placed his hands on her waist to stabilize her. She rewarded him with a flirtatious grin and a ruffling of his hair. It was cute to see him blush.

"Yeah, we're calling it a night," I said. "You, too?"

"Yeah. We'll walk together. Safety in numbers you know. Oh, lord, girl," Silvia said with sympathy upon closer inspection of my face. "You were out in the sun way too long."

"Oh, yeah. I got a little toasted."

"Poor baby."

"How was your night?" Jacob asked as we walked. He had a little crush on Silvia, I think since we first met her.

"Had me a good night. With that convention in town, the whole weekend's been good. Tomorrow is Sunday, right? Yeah they'll all be leaving tomorrow. Too bad. Met me a real nice guy tonight. He fed me before he bed me."

She hooted again at her joke. We laughed, too. When she was in a good mood, Silvia had a jovial affect that made everything sound funny. Over the previous weeks, though, her lows had been working to overtake her highs. The drugs were gaining ground. I wondered if she could see it.

When we got to the tunnel entrance, I removed the flashlight from of my purse and gave it to Jacob so he could lead the way. I did that because of Silvia, so Jacob could play the brave and chivalrous role. It's a small way to keep his self-worth boosted, but I figured enough small ways could add up to much. The three of us rounded one sharp corner. At the next, we would part ways.

"Silvia, did you bring a flashlight with you?" I asked.

"Oh yeah," she said, patting her glittering, silver bag of a purse. "I'm like a boy scout, always prepared. Don't worry about me."

I did worry about her, though. Her line of work was dangerous. She'd staggered back to the tunnels after nights that left her robbed, beaten, raped, or so disturbed by someone's perversions she couldn't even talk about it. And even when the transaction went well, most of the money she made was spent on drugs.

It was heartbreaking because I knew she could be so much more. Silvia struck me as someone who could do something with her life if she only saw things clear enough to get herself straight.

As we neared the corner in our concrete hallway where we would turn left and Silvia would keep going straight, my nerve endings sprung into a quiver. The feeling was as strong as it was sudden. It was as if my body was a guitar string, plucked hard and unexpectedly in a room packed with silence.

For a mere flash of a second, my mind darkened as black as the space behind me. Then a sharp draft that shouldn't be this far in the tunnel parted the back of my hair. Something grazed my neck with a chilled, moist tongue.

"Jacob!" I shouted.

"What?" he said as he spun around. The light sliced like a pale light saber before he focused it on my chest.

"Shine the light back there," I cried out, motioning behind me. He did. Nothing was there. But it *was* there, and not far off, maybe ready to make another pass. The patch it left on my neck was still cold and damp. It was as if it had tasted me.

"What's the matter?" he asked. Annoyance snagged his tone on the way to fear.

All I could do was stare into the darkness at nothing, yet something.

When I didn't answer, Silvia said in a pitch higher than normal, "Did we walk through a spider web?" She started brushing at her bare arms in frantic swipes. "Damn it, damn it, damn it! I *hate* spiders!"

Jacob shined the light over to help her look for creepy crawlies, leaving me completely in the dark. I stepped closer to Silvia.

"No, it's not a spider web," I said. I twisted to stare back again, to see what didn't show but for some reason, wanted me to know it was there.

When I didn't elaborate, Jacob turned an angled head toward me before letting loose a sudden grunt of disgust and saying, "Oh geez, Liz. Are you seeing monsters again? Grow up and get over it."

His voice was condescending, but he shined the light all around the tunnel, all around us. No matter what he said, Jacob was not convinced the monster was all in my head.

Silvia laughed and waved me off. "Girl, you believe that crazy story? You musta been listenin' to Benny again. He's back on the needle, you know." She patted my shoulder and then gave it a gentle squeeze. "Honey, there ain't no such thing as fairy tale monsters, just the human kind."

Her words were a kindhearted conveyance for comfort. Jacob's snort of laughter, however, was deliberately belittling. He knew I believed whole-heartedly, knew I was frightened, yet my brother wanted so much to look cool and tough and manly for Silvia, he was willing to humiliate me to do it.

Jacob shone the light straight into my sunburned face, forcing me to hold up my equally sunburned hand and close my eyes.

"I think you watched too many monster movies when you were a kid," he said with an unmistakable sneer in his voice.

And then he laughed again and shoved my shoulder harder than simple playfulness should allow. He wanted me to shut up before I embarrassed him in front of Silvia. I wanted to put a fist in his face.

"Oh, don't be too hard on your sister now. These tunnels can be creepy," Silvia said in a scolding tone to Jacob.

Her chastisement struck better than my fist could have. Had I not been so frightened I would have been tempted to gloat over my brother's fallen expression.

It only took Jacob an instant to recover. He puffed up his chest. "Don't you girls worry. I'm here to protect you."

With his macho words, Jacob put his arm around Silvia and walked away with the light. I had to hurry to catch up. A quick, yet satisfying fantasy played through my head where I gave my brother a good martial arts kick to his skinny, hairless chest and deflated it.

"Hold on a minute," Silvia said after a moment, then paused and leaned against Jacob so she could unbuckle her high-heeled shoe and slip it from her foot. She sighed as she wiggled her toes. While she unbuckled her other shoe, I couldn't help but look back over my shoulder, as my nerve endings had not yet settled.

It was there.

It lingered in the fringe of our light no more than ten feet behind us. The formless concentration of shadow appeared to be striving for solidity.

In varying places of its being, it became denser, more visible. Then it faded again. With each attempt, it shimmied with its efforts, like a weightlifter testing his limits. Two, blunt-ended extensions like arms stretched from the center of its pliable mass before retracting, as if an outer layer was too thick for them to penetrate. It reminded me of a commercial touting the strength of a garbage bag.

The thing was abstract, both form and shadow, clinging to the dark. An obvious sheen of dampness covered it and for a reason I can't explain made me think it was perspiring. The black lake effect of it appeared and disappeared, and then appeared again, shimmering in and out of view. It was part darkness, part its own entity, though I was certain it wanted to be all its own.

The outer, undefined edges of it melted into the shadows, blending in until its border was indiscernible. But in a sizeable section in its center, its ever-shifting darkness was less shaded than its surroundings. Not lit, exactly, but not quite as dark where it bulged in a paler mound.

I stared in fascinated horror as the mound in its center shifted. It quivered. Then for a moment, it held still before quivering again, this time with more violence. Its center swelled, emerging through its damp shell. It was as though the darkness was trying to give birth.

It flattened out again, heaved a couple of times, and then settled. The thing looked to be, exhausted. But after the span of a breath or two, it recovered. It shifted, and then it quivered again before calming into tranquil motions.

The thing developed two spots of light near the top where, if it had a head, its head would be. Like the formation of its appendages, the lights struggled for life. Within those two silver-dollar sized circles, however, it flashed dim, white/gold pupils that sparkled effervescent. The two lights receded, and then returned to flash bright before receding again. They returned once more, holding steady this time.

And then, to my sickened dismay, to my heightened horror, with focused eyes the thing shifted, and stared at me.

"There it is!" I shouted.

I lunged toward Jacob, grabbed the flashlight from his hand, and turned the beam toward it. Nothing was there. I shifted the light, slow at first, then growing more frantic. Wherever the beam landed, though, it shed light on nothing but drab, gray concrete.

In flashes, I could see it just outside the beam. Its eyes must have closed, or receded, or whatever they did when I could not see them, for I could only see its shadow on shadow mass, dry now, as it evaded my light.

It was impossibly fast, scurrying without a sound up and down the wall and across the ceiling or floor whenever I got the light close to it. Maybe it was afraid of the light. Or maybe, it was playing with me.

"Enough, Liz! Shit!" Jacob yelled as I slashed the beam of light through the darkness.

"Don't you see it?" I shouted, hearing the hysteria in my own voice, wanting them to see what I could see. "Look, it's barely outside the light!"

Jacob stepped toward me. "Nothing is there!"

"You're just tired," Silvia said in a soothing voice. She put an arm around me and to Jacob said, "You need to put your sister to bed. She's all burnt up and tired."

I continued to look for the thing. Though I could no longer see any of it, and though the intensity of my sense for it weakened, its presence still tingled on my skin.

After a moment, Jacob's arm replaced Silvia's arm. With gentle hands, he took the flashlight from my hand, murmuring words to soothe me. I hated myself for doubting his sincerity, for thinking he was putting on an act for Silvia. My brother had a good heart. I knew it. Maybe he couldn't help it if sometimes he was a jackass.

In a voice quelled with unmistakable surprise, Jacob said, "You're trembling."

Until he said it, I hadn't known. My brother's hand that had been merely resting on my shoulder then gripped me with love and comfort. Sometimes I felt it was *always* my brother in need of *my* support. Not only was that egotistical, it was untrue.

Jacob kept me goal-focused. Maybe not on purpose, but his very existence kept me from crumbling to a sobbing ball of tears when I was feeling besieged by adversity. Having someone need me was much more inspirational than needing. Later, when my nerves settled, I would remember this moment and be sure to tell my brother how much I need him.

"Come on, Lizzie, let's go home," Jacob said to me in a voice so kind I nearly wept.

I looked back again, but the thing was gone. I didn't know where it slithered off. Maybe it just disappeared. I only knew it was gone. Because, unlike my racing heart and struggling lungs, my nerve endings were calm. Weary, but calm.

Silvia took her flashlight out of her purse and we said our good-byes. When she was out of sight, Jacob kept his arm around me so I knew it wasn't for show. He even drew me close for a moment to put a kiss on the side of my head. It was the best part of the whole night. Even if he was often a jackass, my brother loved me. He cared.

We rounded the corner that put us in our home and Jacob lit the candle next to his side of the bed before turning off the flashlight. I brushed my teeth first while Jacob turned down the bed and took off his shoes. While he brushed his teeth, I put on my nightgown. When we were both in bed, Jacob leaned over to blow out the candle.

"No, Jacob, leave it on for a while, please."

This must have disturbed him. I was very conservative with our candles. We had to make everything last as long as possible. He didn't say anything, though. He just lay down next to me.

"Do you want to read for a while?" he asked before muffling a cough into the crook of his elbow.

I glanced over at the red, overturned plastic crate on my side of the bed that served me well as a nightstand. Next to the unlit candle was my copy of 'Paper Moon' by Joe David Brown. Between its tattered blue cover the book was fat with oft-turned pages. I found it in a dumpster and, since it was clean and had all of its pages, considered it a real treasure. I'd read it a couple of times already and I was about halfway through reading it again. It was my only book. It was a good thing I loved the story.

"No," I said, knowing my eyes would close after reading a page, two at best. As Silvia said, I was all burned up and tired. But I wanted to stay awake for a while. I wanted to stay awake until I couldn't.

"You sure? I'll come over and light your candle for you."

"Thanks, Jacob, that's sweet. But I don't feel like reading right now."

"Do you want to talk?"

I kind of did. Not about anything important, just chat for a while. As things stood, though, Jacob and I were about to close this day on a good note and I didn't want to risk spoiling it.

"No, you need to sleep so you don't get sick again."

"Okay. Well," Jacob said on a yawn. "Good night, Lizzie."

"Good night."

Jacob curled up on his side, his face toward me and away from the burning candle. I stayed on my back. Every few seconds my head shifted from left to right. There was nothing to see, nothing to feel, well, almost nothing. The monster in the dark may not have been close by anymore, but fear of it sat heavy upon my chest.

Why couldn't anybody else see it? Jacob and Silvia had been right beside me and hadn't seen a thing. Even among the others in the tunnels who believed in it, none of them had ever *seen* it.

They spoke of it with the elaboration of a campfire tale. It was a story, the bogeyman, a good reason to get wasted. No one, *no one* else had ever gotten a visual.

Why me? Why me?

Chapter 5

"Come on, Liz, today."

It was Wednesday and I'd been putting Jacob off since Monday. The way time moved in our world, with previous, now, and next all attached without the junctions of normalcy, that was not a long time, except when it came to food. He was anxious to use the buffet ticket Joe had given me. I would rather go hungry.

For the last couple of days, I had us credit hustling all the way down at Bally's. By the time we made our way that far, we were starving hungry. We'd been such a distance from the Desert Star it was easy to talk him into eating some place else.

I knew it was irrational. A buy-one-get-one-free at a buffet is a real treasure to us. But the thought of seeing Joe again had kept me away. I didn't want to feel humiliated in front of him. What I hated even more was that I cared. I was in no position to care what a man thought of me. I didn't even know him. To let my pride stand in the way of a full belly was pure foolishness.

"Okay," I told Jacob as I tied my shoelaces with due regard for the fray, and gathered some indifference. "We'll go to the buffet today."

It had to happen this week anyway before the ticket expired. Maybe Joe wouldn't be working today. I hoped not, and then scolded myself for caring.

"Yes!" Jacob cheered, shrugging into his shirt as he

did a ridiculous hula dance. I had to laugh at my little brother. Sometimes he was so cute.

Since my sunburn was almost gone, except for a little peeling on my nose, and the night before I had slept well, my mood had improved. I haven't felt or seen the monster in the dark since that early morning we were with Silvia. Maybe it left with the political conventioneers.

Or maybe it was dormant, awaiting the next round of counterfeit do-gooders and sly over-dogs. Though it hadn't been around to taunt or frighten me, it had not left my thoughts.

Realizing it sounded paranoid, I still couldn't help but feel it had targeted me, though I couldn't begin to guess for what. It hadn't tried to kill me. It often had the opportunity, like when I went to the bathroom, as I was always by myself.

Maybe I was paranoid after all. I wondered about this during the frequent breaks in my sleep. Sometimes I thought it just liked to scare me.

While it got close to me that night, even going so far as to touch me, it did not actually harm me. Then again, I was in the company of others. Maybe it had an aversion to witnesses. My head sometimes spun with thoughts and guesses, with frustrations and fears I was not free to express. Sometimes I thought I'd go crazy from it. If that was its goal, it was succeeding.

"Come on, come on," Jacob said as I tied my other shoe. "I hear the dessert bar calling my name. Oh god, I hope they have cherry pie today."

"Food first, Jacob," I told him in my motherly tone, though I was smiling when I said it. We both had a sweet tooth we do not often get to indulge.

"Dessert is food." At my frown he laughed and said, "Of course, food first."

****

When we entered the Desert Star, I tried hard to look like I didn't care who else was there. I had an ugly suspicion that by doing so I had the opposite effect.

My incompetence in this arena was embarrassing. The venues in which I excelled were a pitiful few, but in this, I was usually a star. I was an expert at inconspicuous strolling. Or so I thought until I caught my eyes scanning the casino like a neurotic stooge on the verge of attempting an Ocean's Eleven heist. But I couldn't help myself. I scolded my eyes and continued to pretend I wasn't looking for Joe.

The small casino was busy with play. All around us, slot machines clanked and beeped, some of them spoke excited invitations in computer-generated voices.

Above some of the slots were brightly striped wheels, like colored-in spokes of a bicycle. They spun while eyes anxious, sometimes desperate for a big win, gazed in hopeful anticipation. Some people tapped their knuckles in a lucky rhythm on the numbers of their keno machines. The poker machines and their players were the quietest, imparting a solemn maturity to the game.

In the row to my right, a young man's escalating encouragements erupted into a cheer and the voices of his companions chimed in. A couple of people stood up to peek over the tops of their machines to see what kind of jackpot he hit. One skinny, middle-aged woman with red, rebellious hair flopped back down on her cushioned seat and glared at her own gaming machine as if it had betrayed her.

There were too many people, most of them sober, or close to, for us to do any credit hustling this early. I was glad for it. The last thing I wanted to do is hang out at the Desert Star.

I felt awkward, as if I was on the brink of a stumble and I couldn't get it together. At any other time, as I said, I was very good at presenting a cool façade. It's funny since I'd never been even near to cool. I was just good at the pretense.

Feigning aloofness was a survival skill I honed since childhood. In a place like the casino, it helped me to blend in. When I was a kid, it helped calm the tensions of my parents.

If I fought my mom and dad, they fought back bigger, more so when they were drinking. If they couldn't rattle me, I was no fun. If I was lucky, they found my cool so boring I became virtually, and blissfully, invisible to them. Unless, that is, they needed me for something. Then I was 'hon', or 'sweetie'.

In the Desert Star, my old pal cool had abandoned me. If Joe spotted me, he would think me a nervous flutter-bug.

My hands joined in front of me. My fingers intertwined in order to tone down the fidgeting, and on I went, trying and failing to stop looking for his fine physique. I was a fool, brainlessly dancing about a paradox, as I wanted to see him while hoping I didn't. Reining in my stooge would be good.

Demanding the return of what few abilities I called my own, I looked around as if I was observing, much like when we were credit hustling. Toned down, I didn't think I looked like I was looking for him, even though I was.

It was a compromise. One I thought would satisfy my stooge and tempt the return of my cool. It was a good thing Joe was such a large man. With his height and breadth, he would be easy to pick out without too much scrutiny.

Without knowing when the thought started, I was wishing I could have used a curling iron before we left. I had to leave that luxury item back at the apartment, where the landlord shoveled it into the dumpster with the rest of our belongings. It didn't matter anyway. Our new home had no outlets.

My hair was clean and combed but hung in limp locks past my shoulders without the benefit of a style. It never bothered me much before, but suddenly I was fretting over it. I ran fingers back over my scalp, trying to give my hair some lift. There I went again, caring. To quote Silvia at the thought of the unwanted: damn it, damn it, damn it.

"Aw, man."

"What's wrong?" I asked Jacob. I followed the line of his sight as I spoke.

"Look at that."

The long line of hungry people waiting for the buffet wrapped around three brass posts upon which were latched red velvet ropes dividing the lines into order. We'd be waiting for the better part of an hour.

"Why don't we come back later," I said. "Or tomorrow."

"No," Jacob said with defiance.

He hadn't spoken to me with such opposition since before he totaled my car. After that night, he pretty much turned control of our lives over to me and rarely disputed my decisions. Anticipation of a great feast had revved up his testosterone.

I didn't want to argue with my brother a little more than I didn't want to be there. "Come on," I said. "Let's get in line."

The wait was long, the line slow moving. The whole time, we could smell all that wonderful food and it made me glad I let my brother convince me to stay. Jacob kept raising himself up on his toes so he could get a better look through the window that was the top half of the wall. I too kept my back to the casino, but for a different reason.

No matter the effort, though, every now and then I couldn't help but shoot a quick glance behind me into the casino. I didn't see Joe. Good. For a reason I didn't want to credit, though, I was disappointed. It made no sense. I didn't want to see him. He was so far out of my league we might as well have been from different planets.

I hoped I wasn't turning into one of those pathetic types who would suffer any kind of humiliation for the sake of some particularly fine man's attention. I had enough problems.

"Last corner," Jacob said with a burgeoning grin as we rounded the final brass post.

The aromas sang to us louder than ever. Plates clacked and silverware pinged in a musical promo, with the low murmur of conversation as back up. And they summoned us to join in.

My brother breathed in the wonderful food smells deep through his nose. His stomach made a loud rumble and guilt had its way with me.

"Hey Jacob," I said. "How about after we eat we go to the arcade and play a few games?"

"Really?"

I didn't want to stay there one minute more than was necessary, but guilt trumped my ridiculous feelings and the Desert Star had classic arcade games for which they charged less than the other places.

"Sure. We can afford to spend a little bit. We've done well the last couple of nights and our food drawer is pretty well stocked."

We actually hadn't done as well as I would have liked, but we rarely do. And our food drawer was far from packed. Every so often, though, we had to treat ourselves and do something that makes us feel more human than mole.

Jacob's reaction was worth every precious penny I was about to spend. He beamed with the smile of a severely deprived nineteen-year-old boy who had before him an evening of buffet eating and game playing.

As we got to the front of the line, I glanced at the two women who stood in front of us. One of them held a two for one coupon, too. When I handed ours to the cashier, along with the money, I was the same as everybody else. Finally, during that moment, I shared Jacob's joy.

We followed the hostess through the large room packed with people and tables until she stopped at one of the very few empty ones. We didn't bother to sit for our drink order before winding our way to the source of all those wonderful smells. Las Vegas has, without a doubt, the best buffets in the world. Of course, I've never had one in another town. I've never been anywhere else. But that's what the people in line always say, and they're from everywhere else.

We surveyed the long and ample row of American, Italian, Mexican, and Chinese food, displayed with the colorful flair of an artist. In the center of the restaurant was a huge soup and salad bar. A crisp rainbow of nature's best, ending with big silver pots tagged with signs telling what awaited us inside. Next to that, a dessert bar almost as big as the salad bar. It's beyond imagination what else they *could* offer.

We started with the salad bar. My brother wasn't thrilled about that, but he was too happy to complain. Even as Jacob filled his plate with pasta from the Italian section, his favorite food in the world, I reminded him to eat plenty of vegetables, too. That's about the only health care we can get, so I take it seriously. Jacob grumbled about vegetables taking up room on his plate. I shut him up with a reminder of his recent bout with illness.

To Jacob's delight, and mine too, they did indeed have cherry pie on the dessert bar. We ate until our bellies were near to bursting.

Once again, Jacob suggested I stuff some food into my purse for later. Once again, I declined. I didn't have to give him the lecture on honor and theft. He'd heard it from me enough times to have it memorized. If I was going to teach my little brother about doing the right thing, I had to set an example.

I realized credit hustling dipped a toe into a murky pool. The money didn't really belong to us. However, the people it did belong to were usually long gone. And on the rare occasions when I saw someone walk away from their credits, like the drunk man the other night, I needed only to remind myself how dealing with drunks was a waste of time. They're difficult and at times even dangerous.

I believed this, but in all honesty, I had to admit it was, at least in part, justification. I wasn't perfect, but I was trying. I was doing my best.

We spent eight dollars on games. If I thought too hard about wasting a chunk of money like that, I'd make myself sick. Of course, looking at the joy on my brother's face, maybe it was not wasted money, but rather a cheap form of therapy. Yes, I liked that view. It made the pinch in my wallet a little less painful.

"It's still too early for credit hustling," Jacob said as we lumbered out of the arcade still as blissfully stuffed as two teddy bears fresh off the conveyer. He looked around, I think hoping he'd been mistaken and it wasn't too early. He wasn't. It was. Jacob then said, "But I don't want to go back yet."

"Me neither," I said as we made our way toward the door. Our stomachs were so full we would have been miserable if not for the huge dissimilarity from our norm. Stuffed was uncomfortable. Hungry was painful and distressing.

"We could walk down the Strip; see if anybody's dropped a wallet or something."

"Wallets have ID. We'd have to return it." At his silence I said, "Hey, let's walk down to the Bellagio and look at the summer flowers."

At the Bellagio, they had an atrium with a plant and flower display that must take a sizable and diligent crew to maintain. The arrangements change on a regular basis and are always fantastic, with colors and decorations to suit the season. There was no charge for strolling through.

"Sure, that sounds good," he said. Not so long ago

he would have cringed at the suggestion we go look at flowers. Both of our perspectives have changed in ways I hoped we never, ever forgot. "Hold on a minute."

I waited as Jacob knelt to tie his shoe. Suddenly, my head sprung above the lethargy that comes in the aftermath of a large meal. Some kind of strangeness flowed through my spine. It was a gentle, warm surge, yet no less a thrill than finding a jackpot of credits. Its meaning, however, was beyond my understanding.

For a moment I panicked, thinking the monster from the storm drain had followed us. But, although I was alert, even wary, I did not feel so much as an inkling of fear.

It must have been the night of food and fun, I thought, wanting to laugh at my foolishness. That evening we had lived like royalty, at least by our snake-belly standards. My mind and body were not used to such indulgences and it must have been throwing me off.

My head swiveled in a slow sweep of our surroundings. It was almost like a hand was tugging on my chin, so strong was the draw. As if clicking into place, my head stopped and in the sudden halt, my feelings tumbled like the little white ball falling into a cubby on the roulette wheel. Joe was about ten feet away from where I stood.

He was gazing at me in a piercing way no man ever had and some foreign, sublime part of me floated into his eyes. Warmth blossomed in my core and it had nothing to do with the desert heat. Joe was there, and swirling my thoughts into deeper mystification, he was smiling, at me.

The tempo of my heart grew rapid. A joy I

shouldn't feel rushed me, a desire to which I had no right. Still, I drank it in. I couldn't stop it if I wanted to, and with shame, I had to admit, I didn't want to.

He looked so handsome in his charcoal gray suit, white-as-new dress shirt, pressed tie and shiny dress shoes. His large, muscled frame, combined with the kindness in his eyes gave the impression of uncontaminated authority. He was strong and safe. I could feel it.

When I didn't turn away from him, his eyes sparked a gleam, as though I'd made a decision in his favor. I can't say how long we stood there looking at each other. I certainly couldn't explain why he looked so happy to see me. It was obvious, however, why I couldn't take my eyes off him.

Without a doubt, Joe was the most attractive man I'd ever seen in my life. Strong body, strong features tempered with benevolence that radiated from him. His smile was dazzling. His hair was the color of a raven's feather and neatly cut, but long enough to show it wanted to wave. Clear, focused eyes held me in place.

The tan of his skin was from being outside, working, exercising, who knows, but not lounging in the sun. He was not a lounger, but a doer. I sensed that too. If I were being logical about it, I would say I was infusing too much daydream into my perception. It felt so real, though, I had to concede.

The survivalist in me told me to run, even though I sensed no danger. But I couldn't afford to trust anyone. In my head, my brain worked toward directing me to the door. My bitch, selfish to the highest order, told her to shut up.

"Hey, that's the guy who gave you the buffet

ticket," Jacob said. Joe was walking toward us. His eyes stayed on me and I'm not sure if I didn't look away because I didn't want to or because I couldn't.

I should have responded to my brother, but my brain was blinking and I couldn't steady my knees. I hated feeling like this, yet at the same time I wanted more. Maybe living in such close proximity to insanity had rubbed off on me.

"Hi," Joe said, glancing at Jacob to include him, though he made it obvious who he'd come over to see. When he dragged his eyes from me to look at Jacob, it was pure civility. After enough seconds had passed to satisfy proper etiquette, his gaze popped right back to me.

I didn't know how to take it. All I could think of was I must have food on my face. "This is my brother," I said, motioning toward Jacob. When Joe turned back to my brother, I made a quick swipe with my fingers across my face.

"I'm Jacob,"

"Joe."

"Thanks for the buffet ticket," Jacob said with bubbling enthusiasm. "It was great, really. I wish I could eat like that every day. Seriously."

I wanted to kick Jacob. His overabundance of appreciation was making us out to be desperate and impoverished. It doesn't matter that we were. I still hated sounding like it to anyone, especially to Joe.

"Nice to meet you, Jacob," Joe said, looking him in the eye.

He put out his hand to shake and Jacob took it. My brother lifted his chin, proud to be treated so. I liked Joe a little bit more.

"I'll have to round up another ticket for you two for next week, since I know you'll use them."

"Oh yeah, we'll use them!"

Shut up Jacob. Just shut up.

Jacob glanced at me in that sly way he sometimes did, and then to Joe before looking back to me. He was up to something. The dread of it fell heavy on the knot of my full stomach, but I was helpless to do anything since I didn't know what idea was rallying his thoughts to action.

"I'm going to the bathroom. I'll be back in a few," Jacob said. And then the little brat abandoned me.

Panic blossomed in my chest. I didn't know what to say, what to do. My limited social skills lived under the strict guidance of my survival skills. On their own, I knew they were feeble and inadequate from disuse. Thankfully, Joe spoke before I had to think of something to say.

"I'm glad to see you here."

His voice was deep, velvety without the menace such virile men often convey. At the low timbre, his voice had the power to soothe. I had a feeling, though, it could rise to unquestionable dominance if need be.

The few words he'd spoken to me sounded so sincere. A part of me hoped he meant what he'd said, that he was glad to see me. The rest of me, though, had sense enough to know better, but not enough to stop daydreaming.

"Are you going to be around for a while?" he asked me.

He tipped his head a little to the right and my eyes stayed with his irises, deep, indigo blue, I could see that being so close to him. They made me think of a spring sky, darkened from holding back a portentous storm.

"I get off in ten minutes. Maybe we could get some coffee or something."

Tell him no. Tell him you're leaving now and won't ever be back, my brain shouted.

After a slight pause I said, "I was about to take my brother to the arcade to play some games. We'll be there for a while."

Apparently, I was not only a part time bitch, but also a part time idiot. Joe probably knew we'd already spent time in the arcade.

"Great. I'll meet you over there."

He didn't ask if he could join us. But I had the feeling I could refuse without a hassle. "Okay," I told him.

The moment Joe walked away Jacob returned to my side grinning like a fool. "Bathroom my foot," I said.

"Boy, he's hot for you."

"Shut up."

Jacob laughed. "So you're taking me to play some video games, huh?"

"You shouldn't listen to other people's conversation. It's rude."

"So is lying."

He was right, so I ignored him. When we re-entered the arcade I gave Jacob two dollars from my purse. That made ten dollars spent on fun in one night. My head ached at the thought of it.

"Make it last," I told him.

He looked at me at me as if he'd caught me at something he could at some point hold over my head. I ignored him again for the same reason as before.

Chapter 6

It was the first time in my life I'd ever had a cup of coffee. I always associated it with my parents' hangovers and never had the desire to try it. Sitting in the cozy little coffee shop decorated in the hunter green and burgundy colors of another environment, listening to cerebral music for grown-ups, I gained a feeling of growth. I followed Joe's lead and added a packet of sugar to my cup. After one sip, I added another one.

We sat opposite each other in cozy, fluff-stuffed chairs nice enough to be in somebody's living room. The sound of an acoustic guitar being strummed by deft fingers drifted from the speakers and the small crowd within spoke in quiet tones, as if all had agreed beforehand to keep the atmosphere serene. I took another sip of my coffee. Self-conscious pride helped me to resist the urge to add yet more sugar.

Joe was watching me. He looked like he was about to ask a question and since I had no good answers to any I asked one first.

"How long have you worked here?"

"About a year. I transferred over from Caesar's Palace."

"That's quite a downgrade," I said. Half a second later, I wanted to cut out my tactless tongue. "I'm sorry. I didn't mean…"

"It's okay." He said with a grin. "It *is* a downgrade.

I wanted to be here, where I could be…more useful."

He'd left Caesar's deliberately? I thought the arrow of my *faux pas* struck at his getting fired. I couldn't understand why someone would leave the grand Caesar's Palace to work at a little nothing of a place like the Desert Star. He must have taken quite a drop in pay. I didn't say anything, though. Whatever he earned, it was way more than I did.

"What is it you do here, if you don't mind me asking?"

"You can ask me anything."

He said it with a nod and no expressed humor, as if trying to impart great earnestness in his reply. That was some invitation considering he hardly knew me.

"I'm in customer relations," Joe said. "Casino promotion, that sort of thing."

"In other words, you smile at people and give them things like buffet tickets."

His easy grin gave way to a laugh.

"Well, yes. But I don't smile at everyone and I don't give buffet tickets to everyone, and I've never invited a customer for coffee before."

I wrapped my hands around the porcelain mug. I liked the warmth against my palms. In the back of my mind I thought, when Jacob and I have a home of our own, I'm going to have a mug like this and drink coffee.

"Why me?" I asked.

"I wanted to."

"Just that, you wanted to?"

My voice carried suspicion and I was glad. He should know I would not fall over silly because he was so attractive or because he gave us a half off buffet ticket and bought a cup of coffee for me.

"I have great intuition," he said simply, as if that was any kind of explanation. For a moment, he said nothing. He was either waiting, or maybe expecting, me to say something. I didn't. At my silence, he continued. "My good intuition is why I can work about any place I want to."

"But you want to work some place like this instead of Caesars Palace? What's the attraction?" I was well aware my tone had become confrontational. I didn't care anymore if he was insulted. There was something going on here.

"Why, Joe? Why would you work here when you could work at Caesars?"

Without pausing for thought he said, "I rarely saw *you* when I worked at Caesars."

I was speechless. He didn't seem to be flirting. Of course, no one had ever flirted with me before, so maybe it's not as obvious as I had thought.

Anger bubbled up from a crack in my core. He was playing with me. Of course, he was playing with me. Nothing else made sense. I was furious at myself for letting this happen. This man was not attracted to me. Impossible.

My clothes were well worn and far from stylish. What little make-up was in my purse when we left our apartment was almost all gone now. Chester gave me my last haircut, by candlelight, with dull scissors. I was no beauty to begin with. Like this, my desirability was as low as our home.

He'd probably lost a bet with a coworker, stood to make a pile of cash if he could get the pathetic little nothing into one of the beds upstairs in the hotel.

Maybe they even had cameras. I'd heard of such things happening.

"That doesn't make any sense," I spat. My bitch was back and she was angry. He'd left Caesars by choice. He'd done so to see me. Yeah, right.

"Listen, Lizzie…"

My spine stiffened. I put my hands on the table, ready to bolt as I said, "I never told you my name. You never asked and I never said it. How do you know my name?"

"Calm down. It's not what you're thinking."

"Now you're a mind reader?" I stood up.

"Not exactly. Please, sit down. I only want to talk."

I glanced to my left. The coffee shop was open on one side and I could see Jacob across the way. The video game had his full attention, an evil grin on his face as he slew some make believe dragon.

"Please, Liz. All I want is to talk to you. That's it. I promise."

I swung back to Joe. He hadn't risen from his chair as if he would stop me should I run. He was leaning forward though. We were both well aware he had the strength and authority to stop me if he wanted to. And he wanted to. Even though he was calm, I felt his anxiety. I *felt* it.

I glared down at him, hoping my dominant position would give me the appearance of an advantage. "Why do you want to talk to me?"

"Because you're…special."

"Special. I'm special." Then I knew he is playing with me. I was the least special person who ever existed. I made wallflowers appear vibrant.

"Thanks for the coffee," I said, though there was

no gratitude in my voice.

Joe sat back, as if resigned to what I was about to do, as if he was helpless to stop me. He said nothing more, but his eyes stayed on me. I could almost believe him imploring, apologetic. No, I wasn't buying it.

When I marched to the arcade to collect my brother, Joe did not follow me. While I didn't look to see if he was watching, I was certain he was. When we walked out of the arcade, I glanced back once and made a quick scan. There was no sign of Joe.

Chapter 7

"I thought you'd like that."

"Thanks, Benny," Jacob said in all sincerity as he sat on the edge of our bed. His eager fingers turned the dial on Benny's old battered and beloved radio. He found his favorite rap station. Angry puffs of urban poetry pulsed from the small speaker and put a lift to Jacob's face. I'm a rock girl myself. Later we'll take turns.

"Sit down," I said to Benny.

He settled into one of the plastic chairs. I sat in the chair strung with red, white, and blue fabric and duct tape. Between us was our table with one plain white candle burning. It flickered from our movements, making our shadows dance against the concrete wall before burning vertical again.

I wished I could offer Benny a cold drink, set out a bowl of chips, maybe some nuts. He understood, though, since he lived down there too. That I could offer him a chair, by storm drain standards, was living well.

"So where are you off to this time?" I asked.

The way the question was phrased it sounded like he had a great many choices, as if he was a traveler of sorts. The truth was Benny's choices were only a little better than ours were.

He had a brother named Bobby he stayed with

every now and then. They didn't get along, though, and Benny always came back to the tunnels.

Every time he left the storm drains, Benny thought it was for good so he gave us his prized possession, his old radio. He never asked us to return it. He would show up one day, within a week or two of his leaving, and say it didn't work out with his brother. We always acted as if it was a loan and not a gift, giving him back the radio, and thanking him for letting us use it while he was away visiting. It was a precious item down here and we appreciated getting to have it for a while.

"Got myself into a rehab program," Benny said, removing his worn out Detroit Tiger's baseball cap. On the left edge of the bill was a mustard stain shaped like an upside down teardrop.

There was a line at his temples where his fair skin stayed light because of the hat's protection. He smoothed back his very salted brown hair he had tied in a fresh ponytail. Chester, who used to be a barber, must have cut his hair, as his ponytail now hung a little above his shoulder blades instead of all the way to his waist. Making an effort to clean up for his fresh start, I suppose. That was new. And I thought a very good sign.

Like the rest of us who lived down here, Benny was lean, and not from the latest fad diet. I think at one time, he must have had a muscular build. Maybe he played sports or worked out at a gym. Even after all the years of living down in the tunnels his calves still had a noticeable bulge and his shoulders had not completely succumbed to his life's plunder.

Benny put the baseball cap back on his head. He looked from my brother to me. His broad smile showcased a space between his stained teeth where he was missing a top tooth right in front. The expression also boasted his pride and emphasized the multitude of wrinkles carved deep beneath the stubble on his face.

Benny's eyes were clear. He was trying to kick his habit. While my mind was callous with doubt, in my heart I held hope. Even at my most optimistic, though, I could not deny sitting on the other side of our burning candle were the depleted remains of what was once a community asset.

"Yeah," Benny continued, his damaged smile beaming. "I'm gonna get myself all cleaned up."

We'd heard this story before but always without exception, his expectations were fresh. And always Jacob and I hoped for his future. Benny could be ill tempered when his withdrawals got bad. Sometimes, he even got a little crazy with nonsensical rants, but I believed he had much good in him. It often shined through and when it did, it was warming.

He checked in on us, sometimes gave advice that helped us to better survive down in the storm drains, often acting as a father figure, which touched me deeply. He was generous even though he had so little to give. Sometimes he showed up with two cans of peaches for us, a grand gesture in this life.

Benny was prone to bouts of depression that sometimes expressed itself in anger. Chester, who lived in the tunnels about a half a mile away from us, told us it was because he used to have so much, and then he gave it all to heroin.

He warned us to be wary of Benny. Though Benny had never been violent toward us, he attacked Chester one night over some silly disagreement and left Chester with a black eye. They made up the next day. Benny and Chester have been friends for the better part of a decade. I imagine they cling to the human contact; pretty much all any of us down here had to offer.

Benny sometimes had facial tics and his hands often twitched. He always seemed on the verge of something good, something bad, or something secret only he knew. Often he forgot things, or worse, remembered them wrong.

I didn't know how much of a recovery he could make. The drugs had eaten into him, and much of what he once was had already been digested.

"I feel real good about this program," Benny continued. He smiled at me and nodded. His tongue poked through the empty space between his discolored teeth.

"I'm glad to hear that, Benny." I said. While I did believe it was not too late for Benny to have a better life than what he had down here, I think the one he used to have, the one he pined for and thought was but one more effort from his grasp, was forever gone.

At one time, Benny had a wife named Maria. I'd seen her picture. He carried it in his thin and tattered wallet like a talisman. She was lovely. Her hair was the color of cream-less coffee, smooth, straight, shiny with youth and health. Her brown skin was flawless. Her dark eyes sparkled with life. In the picture, she was looking at the camera, which Benny told us he was holding, smiling like a woman in love.

I didn't know how long ago he took the picture. Sometimes Benny said two years ago, other times as much as eighteen years. He so often gets confused and forgetful. Maybe that's just as well.

Before heroin had introduced itself to Benny, he worked for the Nevada Power Company, and so did Maria. He told us that's where they met. They lived in a nice house with a pool in the back yard and often had friends over for parties on the weekends.

When speaking of the good ole days, Benny always followed up with something like "I can't wait to get back there again. Probably the lawn needs mowing and I'll have to fertilize. Yeah," he always said, nodding with confidence and anticipated joy. "I'll be a good husband this time."

I never tried to inject realism into this dream; it was only the hope of it that kept him reaching upward.

Benny says he's thirty-eight years old. He's probably at least a decade older. It could be, unbeknownst to him, the drugs have devoured those ten years, along with the house, and the pool and the beautiful wife.

As he sat beside me in his nicest T-shirt, the faded green one without any rips, stains or a logo, I wanted to believe this time Benny would find his way.

"So the radio is all yours now, kids. Enjoy it."

"I'll think of you every time I listen to it," Jacob said, letting his gratitude show.

Like me, he gave the impression he believed Benny was leaving for good. Though we've never discussed it I didn't think Jacob believed it, but I gave him credit for a worthy facade.

After a brief conversation about the endless summer heat, Benny said he'd better get going. We stood up and he gave us each a hug. The pungency of a long-unwashed body forced me to hold my breath while I savored the affection. He got teary-eyed and told us we were like his own. He invited us to his house for a party next Fourth of July. We told him we couldn't wait.

Benny walked toward the exit. Jacob lay down on the bed with the radio next to his ear, bobbing his head and grinning in a way that made him look so very young. When I saw him like that, I realized how often I forgot my brother was not as old as he had to be.

Benny flipped on his flashlight and stepped out of the designated space of our home, and then he turned back. He made sure Jacob wasn't watching before he shifted widened eyes to me. The action was secretive, and might have been comical had it not been for the dire expression he cast my way. He motioned for me to come over.

I passed my brother on the way. With his eyes closed, his feet were tapping a rhythm to rap.

"Lizzie," Benny said in a hushed tone. He peeked at Jacob again, who was oblivious. Then he rotated his head to look over his shoulder into the darkness.

Moving the flashlight in a thorough, methodical sweep across the gray concrete walls, ceiling and floor, he seemed in search of something, but nothing was there. He shifted the light, left to right in a zigzag, then up and down. As soon as the beam of light veered , utter darkness closed in behind it like water behind a swimmer.

He then turned back to me, pointing the ray of light low enough not to bother our eyes, yet high enough for us to see each other's faces in the eerie glow.

He suddenly looked nervous. His cheek twitched and the fingers of his free hand convulsed into a weak fist. Before he spoke, Benny twice shoved his tongue through the space in front of his mouth where he used to have a tooth. I feared his confidence was waning and I didn't want him to lose his belief that this time he could beat the drugs. It *was* possible. In my head, I scrambled to prepare a pep talk.

"You be careful now, Lizzie," Benny said in a low and ominous voice. He glanced over his shoulder once more, swished the light around again, though faster this time. When he turned back to me, his gaze was clear and direct, and frighteningly sober.

"It's getting stronger," he whispered.

My breath caught and my stomach tied itself in a knot. This wasn't at all what I was expecting him to say, and I almost stumbled at the ill-omened turn.

"What is?" I whispered back after a moment, afraid, because I already knew.

"That thing. You know, you know, that *thing*."

"You've seen it?"

Benny nodded. "Heard it, too. It used to buzz, but not really like a sound. I think it's kind of electric, you know?"

"Yes. Yes, that's it. I know," I said, both relieved and sickened at the confirmation. "I've felt it, Benny. My skin tingles. It's like I'm too close to raw electricity."

And then I thought about something I learned back in school when my home life didn't have me too distracted and I could actually learn something.

A teacher in my science class was talking to us about neurons. She talked about how electrical impulses carry messages from the brain to different parts of the body. I remembered picturing tiny businessmen with tiny briefcases holding very important messages, running through my body.

I wondered about the thing in the dark, about it having electronic messengers. It *feels* electric. Then I thought, if it had neurons, they are more like construction workers than like messengers. But I also thought their business suits and briefcases awaited them.

"It's dangerous, but you might be able to hurt it, maybe even kill it. It's afraid of you, Lizzie."

"Afraid of me?"

Benny gave me no explanation, just a fierce nod.

"What is it, Benny?"

"It's evil. Pure evil. That much I know. I think it's been around a long, long time. At least down here. I've heard the stories for years, but, you know, I always figured it was crazy talk."

Benny paused for a moment before continuing. "I started seeing that thing myself a few months back. It's kind of like a shadow, only thick, and it's darker…and *alive*. I don't think too many other people have actually seen it, at least not anyone who's still around."

Not anyone who's still around. I was tempted to ask what he meant by that. Had some people been so frightened they left the tunnels, or had something far more sinister happened to them? I didn't ask because I really didn't want to know.

After another nervous glance over his shoulder Benny said, "It's gotten stronger lately. When I first got here, it wasn't any more than a little spot, you know, a shadow on the wall that shouldn't be there. I'd see it every now and then, wonder about it. Sometimes it would make these rippling movements, like a puddle after someone throws a rock in it. After it got to be about the size of a big dog, that's when I could hear it."

Benny paused and shot a quick peek back. "A tiny buzz back then is all it was. There's some power to it now. It can stretch away from the wall a little. I think it wants to get out. It's already strong enough to hurt people. Oh, Lizzie, it hates you. It wants to hurt you most of all. I'm sure of it."

I didn't want to think about that thing wanting to hurt me. I was already afraid enough. "What do you mean, get out?" I asked Benny.

"Out of the tunnels."

I found myself glancing off into the darkness and wishing Benny would shine the light there again. Lowering my voice, I asked, "How do you know all this?"

Benny pushed his tongue through the space between his teeth two more times. He looked downward and frowned, as if ashamed. His cheek twitched again. "Sometimes, it talks to me. It kind of talks in whispers, but real loud. It knows no one will believe me."

"I believe you, Benny."

Benny lifted his head and looked me straight in the eye. Even in the peripheral glow of the flashlight beam, his teary gratitude for my faith was unmistakable, but I spoke the truth. I believed him.

Benny's fear was raw. Maybe that's what lit a fire under him to try rehab again. Ironically, maybe this monster had scared him enough so he'll stick with it this time. Maybe knowledge of that *thing* living down here will keep him straight. Take that, you evil son of a bitch. You've done some good.

"I don't know why it hasn't killed me," Benny

said, looking sad and bewildered. "I know it can. It could suck me up into the wall, into *it*. It likes the taste of sin." He paused there, I think reflecting on the flavorful sin of his self-destructive past.

"Yesterday," Benny continued. "When I was asleep in my camp, it was there. I don't know how long that damned thing was with me. I woke up and I could hear it, like an electrical current running through my place. So I turned on my flashlight. Sure enough, there it was. At first, I wasn't too sure because it was flat, like a big splash of black paint on the wall the size of a kitchen table. That's what I hoped it was. Sometimes kids come through with paint, you know?"

I nodded, and understood his hopefulness all too well.

"But then I saw it bulge out from the wall the way a 3D movie does. It looked like a giant slab of wet, black clay. It was thick, at least a foot thick, but it's hard to say because its shape kept changing. Sometimes it was the size and kind of the shape of a dog. It grew, right in front of me, got to be as big as an extra-large football player is. And then it got a little bigger. It stayed attached to the wall. But like I said, it bulged out, and it was moving a lot. Changing its shape seemed to take a lot of effort, but it could. One minute it was a squirming blob, then a big bat, then a giant spider with glowing white eyes. I think it was putting on a show for me. When it finished changing shapes, it turned back into a blob. The thing looked all damp, like, I don't know, all sweaty or something."

Benny's eyes turned wild and he loosed a mad chuckle in two quick breaths. I said nothing.

"I don't know what gave me the nerve, maybe it

was because I hadn't been able to score and I was, you know, moody, but I just got so pissed off it was down here. This shithole is all we have. Well, I stood up and yelled at it and told it to go shrivel up and die."

Benny's fingers convulsed. The beam of light shook. The defiance fell from his face and he poked his tongue through the gap in his teeth two, three, four times before he spoke again. Benny looked like he wanted to weep.

"It turned itself into a circle and grew these fat, spiky things around the edges, like a little kid's drawing of the sun. Only it was a black sun, like a sun in Hell. Then the spikes curled out from the wall and they all pointed at me, started shaking at me all wild and violent. I was scared. I've never been so scared in my whole life."

Benny took two stunted breaths before continuing. His eyes were wet. He was trying not to cry.

"One of the spikes punched me, punched me hard in the chest, knocked me over like I was nothing but a cardboard cutout and then the other spikes stretched out from the wall and pinned me down, then spread out on top of me. I couldn't move. I tried, but I couldn't. It was so powerful."

Benny chugged in a gulp of air. "Then it stretched across my face and around my neck. It was all wet, and slimy and strong. It was so *strong*. And it smelled rotten, like kitchen garbage left out in the sun. It started squashing me. I couldn't breathe. I couldn't get it off me. I couldn't even move a little bit. It stayed like that, choking me until I almost passed out. I thought I was going to die, Liz. I really thought I was going to die. Then, easy as can be, it slid off me."

Benny's hand rose to massage his throat. He didn't have any bruises there, but I didn't need proof to believe him. His wild story was true.

"While I was lying there trying to catch my breath it rolled itself up on the wall like a joint and said, 'Don't I look good to you now? It started laughing in this rough, whispery voice, and then flattened itself out again and skidded real fast along the wall and into the dark until I couldn't see it anymore."

I was horror-stricken. It had more powers than I had seen, or maybe it was growing faster now. And it could speak. I wanted to say something to help Benny, but the only words I could say were, "Oh, Benny," because I was also trying not to cry.

"I'm okay, honey," Benny said. He squared his shoulders, making a show of the bravery he strove for, but he continued to push his tongue through the gap in his teeth. "Don't you worry about me. Besides, I'm leaving this place. Maybe you and Jacob should leave, too."

It was my want of all wants. But there was no place for us to go. The shelters were often full, or so I've heard. We never actually sought one out. I worried about putting Jacob so close to people haunted by the same demons as he is. It would not be a good place for a young man too easily tempted by those appetites. I didn't know how many more emergency room visits my brother had in him, ending with him still alive.

I looked back to Benny. "You said I might be able to kill it. How?"

"I don't know, Lizzie. It's not afraid of anybody or anything, except you. I figure there's gotta be a good reason."

"That doesn't make any sense. I'm nothing. Why would it be afraid of me?"

"I can't explain it. But it said something to me about alcoholics and pretty girls. It said it liked pretty girls, like my little blonde friend with the brother. I knew it was talking about you and so I got real mad and yelled at it, 'You stay away from Liz!' Just like that. When I said your name, it flinched, like I hurt it, or pissed it off real bad. Then it yelled in that rough, voice. No words, all I heard was 'Ahhhhh!' After that, a little hole opened up in the middle of it and it spit at me, spit, like human saliva, warm and everything, and then it slithered away."

Benny shook his head before looking at me, an idea lifting his brows. "Why don't you and Jacob come with me when I get out of rehab? Bobby and his wife, oh, I can't remember her name, but they would love to have you. We could all be a family."

Even Benny didn't sound like he really believed that, much as I knew he wanted to. His brother, Bobby, with his hands full with his own wife and kids, must have a difficult time opening up his home to give his problem-riddled brother yet another chance. I can only imagine Benny's brother's reaction were he to show up with us.

"Thanks, Benny, but Jacob and I have our own plans. Someday soon we'll be getting out of here too."

Benny nodded. From him I sensed the same desperate hope we had *for* him. I wondered if he had the same unspoken doubts in regards to our prospective progress.

He stabbed his tongue through the space in his mouth three times fast. He was thinking hard, his mind working against the damage done to his brain, trying to dredge up solutions from a well too few ladles away from dry.

"Besides," I continued. "You said it's afraid of me."

"That's true. But being afraid of you makes it hate you even more. Maybe it'll find a way to hurt you. Maybe when it gets stronger…"

I said nothing. The maybes were all too possible and a savior but a fantasy. Like Benny, my mind was thinking hard too, thinking and terrified, and sick to death of being stuck in a miserable situation.

"Hey I know," Benny said, bright with a solution. "I'll be going to rehab for a few weeks, but after that, instead of going back to my brother's for a while before I go home, I'll go straight to my own house with Maria. She's a good woman, that one. We have plenty of room there for you and Jacob. She'll welcome you guys, I know she will. Please, Lizzie, say you'll come and stay with us."

This he whole-heartedly believed. If only all of that were true. Tears filled my eyes and blurred my vision and I found myself envying his delusions.

"That sounds great, Benny. We'd love to come and stay with you and your wife."

Benny nodded with renewed enthusiasm. He hugged me again, darted his flashlight around the tunnel to make sure it was safe, and left without another word. I stared until the darkness closed in behind him, separating me from my friend.

I stepped back into our camp and stood there for a moment while my brain decided it was a good time for a headache. Jacob had gone to sit in one of the chairs and was playing around with different music stations. He didn't notice me. He was staring at the radio as if it was a television, probably imagining the video. I wish I could picture the same.

My mind was churning out pictures of little electronic construction workers building a monster.

Nervous energy infused me. I picked up our broom that was just sparse enough to be garbage. As I swept the cement floor, Benny's story kept running through my head. His were the ramblings of an abused brain. I repeated the mantra several times before letting it die a respectable death. Benny was telling the truth. I was as sure of that as I was my own name.

After some more thought, it made sense, at least the part about that thing talking to Benny. No one but me, or maybe another drug addict, would believe anything he said, something sounding so crazy. Surely not anyone with any kind of authority would believe it. The monster retained its anonymity while it was growing. Being afraid of me, though, that was hard to swallow.

My only weapon was a kitchen knife. My only protector was my skinny little brother who I still had to remind to eat his vegetables and brush his teeth.

I wasn't brave or especially clever. I had no talents whatsoever. But if I was to believe the other things Benny said to me, I'd have been a fool not to believe that part. I still couldn't understand it, though. Worse still, I didn't know what to do with it.

Jacob continued playing with the radio stations and I continued to sweep. He didn't seem to notice he'd had to lift his feet three times for my broom. All his attention was on the radio.

I listened to the music over the soft sound of broom bristles scraping the cement floor. He'd switched from rap to rock. I must have been rubbing off on him. I recognized the tail end of a Green Day song, then the beginning of one of my favorites by The Foo Fighters. Before the end of that song, he played with the dial again, pausing on various stations.

Jacob was as a starving man dropped for a limited time near a table full of food; grabbing everything, everything he could, while he could, to fill the emptiness that would return all too soon.

Eventually, Jacob stopped at a news station and listened to a weather report. The heat was going to continue. No surprise there. It was summer in the desert. *I* could report the summer weather with almost the same degree of accuracy; hot, hot, and more of the same.

A chance of rain next week, the newsman said with hope in his voice. Rain was a blessing in this desert town, except for those of us who lived in the storm drains. We all had to watch the sky with great vigilance, and be ready to run for our lives.

The reporter hopped on to upcoming events. Some big boxing match was upcoming, a car race too, tickets on sale now. The Reverend William P. Merriweather would be in town this Saturday. A rally would take place.

My broom stilled.

Reverend Merriweather was an activist who fought hard against gay rights under the guise of preserving family values. Most people had sense enough to ignore him and his nonsensical rants, but he had a following. They were a small group, but vocal and with minds' the width of a cocktail straw.

His present mission was to put a stop to gay marriage. He was furious with the Supreme Court. He had it in his head that homosexual marriages would somehow damage heterosexual marriages. The argument shunned logic just as its spokesperson shunned compassion. Then again, bigotry has never been on speaking terms with logic *or* compassion.

His was fear mongering and frankly, I thought, plain cruel. Live and let live, tolerance, the golden rule about treating others as we would want to be treated; the good lessens we're taught as children, if not by parents then by teachers, were concepts to which the Reverend Merriweather preached but did not practice.

And the good reverend hadn't a clue about the monster his malevolence helped to spawn.

Two years ago, following one of his rabble-rousing speeches he spat throughout the Bible belt, two young men attacked and brutally beat a twenty-two year old gay man. The thugs felt justified because they believed the rhetoric.

By way of a connective string I could never understand, they were of the belief they were doing God's work, ridding the world of sinners. They left the young gay man in a barren field on a cold November night where in the early morning hours he died, broken and alone.

Reverend Merriweather accepted no culpability whatsoever. He said it was not his intention to incite violence and took no responsibility because those boys had 'misunderstood'. He said that on the six o'clock news as the right amount of tears veiled his eyes.

For a couple of days the video reran on every news

station. He left me with the distinct impression that after the news conference, the Reverend Merriweather strutted back to his hotel room and carved another notch into his crucifix.

While Reverend Merriweather's occasional presence in my town used to merely aggravate me, I became terrified. For I knew about the evil his self-righteous sermons produced, the building materials he supplied for those little electronic construction workers. He was a truckload.

His anti-gay rants were nourishment for the monster. That thing grew stronger with every visit from Merriweather, and all the heartless fools like him. I thought of Benny's encounter. I thought of the arms trying to form and how they couldn't quite stick. Would they develop after Saturday's speech? How strong could the thing get? I wondered, and how powerful?

I continued to sweep our floor. I swept and thought, and swept and thought. Our floor was as clean as one in any well-tended house, and still I had no answers.

Chapter 8

For the next couple of days life was normal, well, it was normal for us. Jacob and I did some credit hustling, we ate, I squirreled away a few more dollars in my hidden wallet. Benny had not come back. I thought about him often. In my mind, he was doing well enough to grieve the loss of his wife and he was learning a new life. Maybe this time he would, for this time he was inspired by a new emotion, fear.

I woke up very early to Saturday; the day the Reverend Merriweather was due to hold his rally. According to news reports we listened to on Benny's radio, he had already held sessions in a couple of chosen churches. Most churches, to their credit, refused his request to speak.

What trouble had he already caused, I wondered, and what was yet to come? While I did not know the answers to these questions, I was sure they were terrible. My nerves had been working themselves into a slow build. Nausea had made a home in my stomach and my head ached all the time. What little sleep I had the night before had been fitful.

At some point in the early morning hours as I laid in our bed, my brother breathing softly beside me, my thoughts turned toward the mural of Jesus.

There was no real reason for this. I was not a religious person, nor had I ever been. My parents, in their frequent, screaming battles, often used the word 'hell', but never in a biblical context. To me, religion had always been a fringe anecdote. Churches were buildings with parking lots where kids who were lucky enough to have bikes could ride them every day except Sunday and days when they hosted a wedding or a funeral.

It was probably desperation injecting new thoughts into my head. Of late, I found I believed in things I once thought nonexistent; like monsters that live in the dark.

Before drifting off to sleep again, I made the decision to visit the mural once more. I didn't know what I expected to discover. My prospects lacked hope and my hope was evasive. I just didn't know what else to do.

For lunch, Jacob and I shared a can of green beans and one slice of bread with peanut butter for me, two slices for Jacob. After cleaning up, Jacob settled into a chair with Benny's radio. He'd been good about resisting the temptation to run it too much so he could make the batteries last. His good sense and self-discipline made me proud. He was growing.

After cleaning up from our meal, I told him I was going for a walk. My taking a solitary walk wasn't unusual so he thought nothing of it. I picked up the flashlight and left through the north side of our camp.

I didn't turn off my flashlight until ahead of me stripes of sunlight from the grating above lit my way. Dust motes floated thick in the shafts of bright sunshine. Particles of dirt drifted down from the desert floor above on even the mildest of breezes, and there was almost always at least that.

A moment later, I was standing beneath the grating and staring at the mural of Jesus. I didn't know what I thought might happen, what might be different. Only that maybe since I was going with a more open approach I might experience an epiphany of some kind. And with that, in a pious presence, I would get some answers. Maybe even the voice of God telling me what to do.

I stood, I stared, and I waited. Nothing. Empty minutes elapsed. Enrichments did not come to my mind, my spirit remained low-slung, and my silent pleas remained unanswered.

I considered speaking, but that was too much like prayer and, given my history of skepticism, it would be hypocritical. Besides, if there were such a thing as God, He would already know my thoughts as well as my desperation. And if He were a loving Father, surely He would help me.

I was not asking for jewels or for stardom, or a winning touchdown. Never have I wished for excess, never expected anything I wasn't willing to earn. Could it be I was simply unworthy? Maybe I was just a fool, staring at a picture on the wall of a storm drain, trying to see a sacred wonder in paint and concrete.

For a time I stared at the eyes of the picture, created blue and lively by manmade paint and human brushstrokes. How long I stood there gazing at the mural, I could not say, but I was reluctant to go. It wasn't because belief was taking hold, but because from there I didn't know where to turn.

After a while, I stepped back to lean against the wall opposite the mural. When my legs tired, I slid down to sit on the hard concrete, setting the darkened flashlight beside me.

Sometime later, much later, apparently, because enough time passed so the sun shifted and put the mural in shadow. I could still see it, though. Nothing had changed, and nothing had come to me. I heard no voice, saw no vision, received no divine insight, or even hope this route would save us. Salvation was not merely evasive, but nonexistent.

Aggravated with everything and ashamed of my despairing grapple with religion, I stood up from the floor that had gotten too hard for sitting and brushed off the seat of my shorts.

I was wasting my time. But as I had nothing else to do with my time, I didn't beat myself up too much over it. As many in desperate situations before me have done, I was grasping at straws. The fact that my hands came back empty was old news to which I should have become long accustomed, yet the disappointed still gouged.

I didn't have to be anywhere in particular. I could walk to the exit for some fresh air. The idea fled an instant after it arrived. I was tired. More emotionally so than physically, but it was just as wearing so I decided to be satisfied with the air drifting down from the grate.

The easy downdraft was hot like an oven set to bake, but fresh compared to what I got in our camp. Although, I could swear it was heavier than usual. That was probably my emotional tone weighing down everything in my world.

With my head resting back against the cement wall I closed my eyes and breathed in deep through my nose the sun-roasted air, dust motes and all. Knowing I could stand before this mural till the end of time, and it would never be anything more than paint on concrete, made me feel foolish for my fairy tale hope. I was glad I hadn't spoken my mind to Jacob.

The child I never was, beckoned. I wanted to burrow in the arms of an old-fashioned TV-like dad and I wanted him to make it all better. It's stupid, I know, and certainly fruitless, but the feeling was strong. As I'd never sought or received comfort from my own father, it was not a memory, but a fantasy; one in which a woman who must be ever resilient should not indulge.

As if on a rusted hinge, my head dropped forward, chin to breastbone. My breath hitched and there was a distinct ache in my chest. A broken heart; not from the loss of a lover, but for the want of a decent, normal life that at the very best times had only grazed my fingertips.

For a moment, petulance seized me. I wanted to stomp my feet and shout, actually considered it. However, the appeal of a good fit withered in the sweltering might of my helplessness.

So I just stood there, with my back against the wall.

Suddenly, tears poured from my eyes. It was a strange thing. Astonishing, given my circumstances, it would be strange at all. But it was.

I'd held on to my fortitude out of necessity. I had to, for Jacob more than any other reason. If I fell apart, he would have no reason to stay sober. He would see it as the end of days. And if I lost my brother, I would have no reason to go on.

Jacob wasn't here now. I was alone with a mural that mocked me with its disregard. It had been a long time since I cried. The last time was so far in the past I could not recall. I covered my face with my hands and wept with all the despair I had tried so hard to, and up until now, successfully, ignore.

When my eyes finally opened, they met a mass of drops on the floor of the tunnel. For a moment, I wondered how I could have cried so much. Then the fact spurred my adrenaline. It was not me who spotted the floor, but the sky.

With an audible gasp, my head snapped up to stare through the grating. The dimness was not because the sun had traveled across the sky, but because layers of dark clouds filtered the light.

Drops of falling water sparkled in thin rays of sporadically unobstructed sunlight like shards of broken glass, beautiful, sharp, and deadly. Alarm raised cold goose bumps across my warm skin. It has begun to rain.

They were only sprinkles, but my panic did not diminish. In an instant, sprinkles can turn to a downpour and even a light rain can send water rushing through these tunnels. The desert ground was hard and it would not absorb much. The water would gather on top of the earth, and then it would move.

The city planners spent many millions of dollars to make sure the water ran into the storm drains. And that's exactly what it would do.

It happened once, not long after we moved in. All we had then were our few grocery bags of belongings, which we hurried to gather when Benny ran in to warn us. He'd rushed us out. It was not a minute too soon. By the time we'd sloshed out into the rain, the water in the tunnels had risen almost to our knees.

I bent down to grab my flashlight, my intent to run back to Jacob, rush to gather whatever belongings we could carry and get out.

We would make one sidetrack. We would go to Silvia's camp and warn her. Chester was too far away and his camp situated too far from an exit to make it anything less than foolish for us to try. He was sharp, though. Since he chopped his life low with gambling and not drugs or alcohol, he had not destroyed his brain, and he was vigilant about safety.

I knew there was a grating near his camp. It was the main reason Chester chose that spot. He liked to refer to the grating as his skylight. If Chester was there, he would see the danger and take action.

I spun around, flashlight in hand and ready to run, when my eye caught sight of the mural again. I froze in place.

The painting had changed. An ebony shadow several shades darker than dark covered Jesus from waist to foot. No, not a shadow, I corrected. It was too dense, and it was *alive*. How had I not noticed? I wondered, noting the electrical current emanating from it, causing the entirety of my skin to tighten.

The roundish shadow spread itself wide along the wall, making Jesus look as if He was wearing a black skirt, billowing thick in a wind that wasn't there.

It recessed a bit before bulging out from the wall. In reflex, my foot lifted to step back, but I was already standing against the opposing wall. I should run, but I was transfixed, curious with a need to know. I wondered if, as Benny said, it truly feared me.

As I stared from a very few feet away, two slits opened where its eyes might be. No light emanated. No eyes, like before. Only sockets. Inside, the oblong holes were void of everything except dampness and darkness.

The slits closed and then vanished as if they'd never been there at all.

A moment later a hole the size of a small fist opened about a quarter of the way down from the top. It then expanded, gaping in an exaggerated egg-shaped opening showing nothing but damp blackness before shrinking down to fist size again. It struggled with the effort to pry itself open again, before settling for a cavity about the size of two fists side by side.

Peering into the hole, I could make out something. No, not one thing, many things, separate things. Budding protrusions of varying sizes encircled the inside of the hole. Some of the tops were blunt, others tipped in sharp points. They were thick and porcelain white. Teeth. It was growing teeth.

What I saw next turned me cold.

The eye sockets appeared again, and although they held no eyes, I knew the thing was staring at me. Then the left and right edges of its open mouth lifted upward, forming a distinct grin that was equal parts threat and evil. Saliva dripped in thick globs from several of its newly formed teeth as the outside rim drew back like lips to form a chilling snarl.

The top third of the thing extended a bit farther from the wall, stretching toward me a few inches as it hissed in that loud whispery voice Benny had talked about. I smelled the rot of death on its warm breath. Its hatred of me seethed in a tangible manner, as it never had before. In that instant, the force of my terror crushed my curiosity, because I understood it wanted me to die.

I spun toward our camp and ran.

Behind me, I heard but did not see the thing jump

from the wall. I hadn't a doubt that was what happened. The sound was fat and moist, like an overly wetted suction cup yanked from a window. Then I heard it plop onto the floor.

However, when the thing made its heavy splat, it did not lay dormant. It moved. A wet, sloppy noise reverberated on the concrete walls. The sound was a plop and then a drag, another plop and then another drag. I pictured it in motion, a sodden, obese centipede.

It was coming after me. My whimper echoed off the cement walls.

Terror constricted my chest making it hard to take a breath. However, my legs did not slow. A second before rounding the corner, I stopped, swinging my light back in the direction from which I had come.

The beam trembled as I sliced it through the darkness. Nothing was there. I forced my breath to quiet so I could hear. No sound chased me from the concrete corridor.

I waited.

I shone my light on the walls, on the ceiling and right down the middle in a pattern of fastidious panic. There was nothing to see, nothing but darkness that suffocated my light before it could penetrate very deep.

But then I heard it again.

Not the plop and the drag sound it was making a minute before. There were two plops, smaller, no drag. There was a pause, followed by a huff of breath. And then another plop followed closely by another. It had grown feet. It was taking baby steps. Slow and unequal, as if it was learning to walk, but it was plodding onward, toward me.

I spun around and ran for our camp. In a matter of

seconds, I could no longer hear the thing behind me. Having mastered use of my feet long ago, I was faster. But for how long, I wondered.

Out of breath, I burst into our camp, shouting Jacob's name as I did. For a moment, I held still, panting and panicked. Scanning the small area of our home, I caught my breath, and saw what wasn't there. No matter how hard I looked, how I squinted or shone the light where the glow of the candle did not reach, what I found didn't change.

Jacob was gone.

Chapter 9

A small whimper squeezed through the tightness in my throat as I swung in a rapid succession of rotations to scan our camp. It was pointless, this repetitive search, but in my mind-stifling desperation, it was all I could think of to do.

The single flame of our candle convulsed from the rush of my entrance and the slash of my flashlight. Rather than cutting through the shifting candle-flame, the swinging of my flashlight stirred it into a frenzied work of living, ghoulish art.

Light darted and swirled about our camp in chaotic agitation, giving imagery to the panicked rhythm of my heart, my breath, my very core.

Against the frameless concrete canvas, the rapid fluctuation of lights could have been an impressionist view of a drug-fed rave, cursing me with a moment of vertigo. I shook my head before taking a final look to confirm what I already knew. Jacob was not there.

How could he be gone? Where would he go? Outside, I thought, grasping the viable explanation with both hands. Maybe Jacob went for a walk. Since I hadn't passed him, he must have gone the other way, outside for some fresh air. I sprinted across our camp, my flashlight still on but unfocused as I plunged into the familiar darkness on the other side.

Close on the outskirts of my worry for Jacob, my

attention noted the stream of water on the cement floor, growing right before my eyes. My feet splashed as I ran.

The instant I jolted to a stop outside the exit to the tunnels, a downpour soaked me clean through. Hope slowed my desperate scan near the spigot. Jacob was not out there. Only dimmed desert and rain filled my vision, hard rain, escalating the level of my panic.

In the few minutes since I'd left sight of the mural beneath the grating, the sky had burst open. Water sheeted down on the desert as if to quench a voracious thirst left by the dry, scorching heat of an entire summer. I couldn't even see the 'Welcome to Fabulous Las Vegas' sign posted across the street.

With my chest heaving from panic and exertion, my gaze dropped to the desert floor. The rain was accumulating. Stippled puddles were swelling by the second. Some of them were already bleeding into each other. What had begun as a scattering of mere droplets was becoming a series of small pools.

With this downpour, those pools would grow fast in volume and power. They would join forces to become an unstoppable tide, surging with vigor and violence through the storm drains that served as our home.

A billion little taps on the hard ground united not just in the visual, but also in a ferocious roar that was nothing short of hostile. The storm enfolded me in its wrathful mass, pelted me, and howled in my ears loud enough to echo against the inner walls of my skull.

Worse, and more terrifying, was my understanding that the beating sound of the storm and the growing puddles were but preambles. If this kind of rain kept up for very long our entire underground community would wash away, as if the rain had come to purge the town of our disgrace.

Where the hell was my brother?

Silvia. Either hope or desperation slipped Silvia's name into my head, but once it was there, it made sense. Jacob could have gone to see her. He'd never gone there without me before, but that didn't mean anything. He was still growing, still branching out for new experiences, like a woman who flirted with him every time they crossed paths.

Sinister clouds crawled across the sky above me. Full, and layered thick enough to turn day to dusk, they continued to shed their watery weight in great torrents. Thunder cracked a celestial whip so sudden and loud it made me duck. In this town, thunder was such a rarity it was like a clip from a horror movie, or rather, as if fate had thrown me into one.

Another rumble and boom coupled with the relentless downpour. The voice of a storm proclaiming it would not leave soon, or in peace.

Though all of me was now soaked, my feet were drenched. Looking down at the concrete ditch in which I stood I couldn't see my shoes. Dirty water ran over my ankles. I swung my light back to the tunnel entrance and ran toward Silvia's camp. With every pound of my feet, rushing water splashed up to my knees.

While I ran, too heedless for common sense, it struck me the darkness within the concrete surrounding me had thickened. It was the humidity. It had to be. Still, I couldn't help but feel that somewhere in the storm drains the monster was sucking up all the air, that it would absorb anything life sustaining in order to enhance its own.

I shook aside all thoughts of that thing. At least I made the effort. It was impossible and unwise to pretend it wasn't there, somewhere. But I kept my focus on Jacob. I had to. I had to find my brother and get us out before raging waters that didn't belong in the desert, and a monster that didn't belong in this world, took us from it.

When I splashed into Silvia's camp not even Silvia was there. In her little designated section of the tunnels, the smell of stale beer mingled with the lasting scent of strong perfume. It's what I imagined a bar would smell like in the late swell of a Saturday night. The smell was the most alive thing I found. I swung my flashlight about, the beam slicing through dark air and absorbed by darker water.

Silvia's clothes lay in loose, sopping piles, high-heeled shoes floated here and there. A white crumpled bag from a fast food restaurant was bobbing near the wall beside a couple of brown beer bottles with the labels mostly peeled off.

Her bed was a pile of blankets with one rolled up for a pillow, though I couldn't make it out very well now because her bedding was moving like heavy slush in a flow. All her things were either soaking up water and sinking or floating on the rising tide.

Water dripped from my hair into my eyes. I wiped it away as one of the beer bottles took in its limit and sank into the dark water. A couple of bubbles rose and popped with tiny splatters.

For a moment, I almost gave in to despair. Where else was there for me to look? I couldn't give up, though. Jacob was *somewhere*. The monster slithered through my thoughts again. No, it had been behind me and moving at a slow pace. It couldn't have gotten to Jacob. I forbade my thoughts to go there. I would find my brother. I had to find him.

The only thing I could think to do was to go back to our camp and hope for a miracle. I turned around. The motion took me longer than it should have. I shined the light downward. Water was working its way up my shins. My run back to our camp was half as fast as it should have been and took twice the energy.

When I splashed into our camp, I could have wept with relief. At the same time, I wanted to grab my little brother by the throat and choke him for making me worry. Jacob was there, standing in rising water, grabbing things from his drawer, and stuffing them into a plastic grocery bag. His head twisted toward me the instant I ran in. He'd been watching for me.

"Where the hell did you go?" Jason said, almost in a shout. Anxiety and anger contorted his youthful features. He'd been worried. But so had I.

"I was outside in the pouring rain looking for you. Where the hell were *you*?" I responded, opening my drawer, the one in the middle. I slid it only halfway out so I could get to my things without blocking off access to the bottom drawer where Jacob kept his things.

I grabbed a bag from our surplus and began stuffing it with clothing. At least we both had sense enough to know we had to work while we argued.

"I was in the bathroom." He sounding agitated. "You ran right by me."

The bathroom. He'd been in our little alcove with two buckets and some degree of privacy. The most obvious answer to my question about where he was and

I'd never even thought of it.

"I'm sorry," I said, ashamed at my stupidity. "I should have known. I was worried and went looking for you."

For a moment, he said nothing. My brother was as aggravated with me as I'd been with him. It was our situation, I understood. I think he did too. I knew he let it go when he asked, "Should we take the canned goods or leave them?"

The thought of leaving food behind sickened me. We'd gone shopping the day before and we'd used most of our spendable cash to buy those dented cans of discounted beans and corn and peas, as well as a new package of toilet paper. We had half a loaf of bread and our jar of peanut butter, having just purchased it, was almost full. Practicality had to win out, though.

I didn't waste time with internal debate or grieving the loss. It would eat at me later, when we had nothing to eat. I was going to have to dip into my secret savings, another setback, yet another delay in getting our lives on track.

We would have to leave this place with pretty much what we came with; two plastic grocery bags with some clothes and a few toiletries each, one pillow each and one blanket each that we would carry tucked under our arms. We could not hold more.

"Let's put two cans of food in each of our bags," I told him. "The rest will have to stay. Double bag everything, Jacob. Oh, and grab the can opener." Eight cans of food would not last long, but at least it was something.

I glanced around our camp as if I might be able to take some more of our things. For a moment, I paused for a longing gaze at my copy of 'Paper Moon'.

The book sat upon the overturned crate on my side of the bed with an old receipt sticking out to mark my place. Having read it twice already, I knew I should leave it behind. But it felt like such a great loss. I would make room for it in one of my two grocery bags.

My roving eye then stopped on top of our chest of drawers where sat Benny's radio in quiet anticipation, of being played, of being rescued. This created a dilemma for me. The radio was not ours to leave here for probable destruction. Yet, although it wasn't so big, to take it meant taking up room in one of my small plastic bags and having to leave behind something more useful, like a shirt or some socks, or my book.

Anger flashed through me at being in a position to have to make such a choice. I didn't dream of diamonds or aspire to live in luxury, just ground level basics. Even that was like grabbing for the stars, as if I was materialistic and seeking to place myself above my designated rank, as if longing for an ordinary life colored me an atrocious shade of pomposity.

There wasn't time for me to deal with my recurring anger and frustration, though. I would have to leave something behind to make room for Benny's radio. He entrusted it to us and it was far too precious an item to allow the storm to swallow it. My book would have to stay.

I left it on top of the chest. It was the highest place in our camp. Maybe my book, already worn and tattered enough to make it somebody's garbage, would survive.

Jacob closed his drawer and opened the top one partway so as not to block my access to the drawer that held almost all my worldly goods. I slid mine all the way open. He waved a hand over our canned goods, choosing fast but careful.

Bending low beside my open drawer, I ran my hand along the underside. I acted casual as I removed the long wallet with our savings I had hidden away from Jacob, and anybody else who might wander through here. The sound of the duct tape peeling away drew his attention.

"What's that?" he asked, nodding at the wallet in my hand while shoving a can of green beans in one of his bags.

I stuffed the wallet in my old purse. In a quick and quiet voice, as if to speak of it so would reduce its relevance, I said, "It's our money."

Right away, discovery of my secret wiped from his mind the great urgency under which we were working. Jacob stopped what he was doing when we could not afford to even slow.

If I could have said something to make it right, something to urge him back into action, I would have. I desperately wanted to, and I needed to. But my mind was too overwhelmed to think of anything.

With the quiet intensity of one who has been insulted, Jacob stated as much as he asked, "You hid money from me?"

"It's for our future," I told him, still packing in hopes we could skate over this hindrance to our hasty escape. It wasn't working.

"You don't trust me? What did you think I would do, go blow it on a good time?"

I didn't think that, I feared it. I couldn't say it aloud, though. As it was, my brother was ready to do battle and like most everything else, we couldn't afford it. Still, he stood motionless staring at me with restrained anger as the water rose, creeping toward my knees.

"Jacob, this isn't the time," I said, hoping he would get moving without any more prodding. We had to go. He *had* to see that.

"How much is in there?"

"Jacob."

"How much!" he shouted. The sound seemed very large in our camp that was shrinking by the minute.

"…A little over five hundred dollars."

For a few precious and wasted seconds my brother glared at me while fury ascended through his shock. Water rose and churned around us. The sound echoed against the concrete ceiling and walls, frightening and unnatural in our already unnatural home.

Debris washed in; trash of all sorts, some of it treasures to us down here, all of it garbage to the world outside. Something caught my eye and I glanced over to see water soaking into our mattress. In minutes, the water would ruin it, decreeing it the garbage someone condemned it to be before we adopted it.

"Five hundred dollars! You make me feel guilty for playing a few video games and you're sitting on a fortune!"

"It's not a fortune," I said, even though by our standards it was. But it was a fraction of what we would need to get us started in the real world. I had to make him understand. "And it's not fun money, Jacob. This is to get out of this place and into an apartment. There are deposits, utilities. We have a long way to go before we have enough."

"Still doesn't explain why you didn't tell me about that money."

The room suddenly dimmed and I turned to see the table that held our candle had tilted on a wave, dumping the candle into the water and dousing its flame. All we had left were our two flashlights, both of which lie on top of the chest of drawers, their beams crossing.

Our little wooden table with duct tape wrapped around one leg flipped upside down and floated like a dead cockroach wearing a silver cast.

"Jacob…Fine, yes, I was concerned. How can you blame me? How many times did you dip into mom's purse when she wasn't looking, or mine?"

"That's different! I'm different now than I was then! How long are you going to hold that over my head?"

From his point of view, I was persecuting him for crimes for which he'd already paid. In a way, he was right. He should have earned my trust by now. But there had been too much at stake, too much to venture, too much to lose. To give him full trust was to risk what little financial security we had. However, maybe by not trusting him, I had risked far more.

"Jacob," I started. I stopped at a sound coming from down the tunnel.

It wasn't the water sloshing against the walls, against our furniture, against us. It wasn't the water. It was something *in* the water.

A deliberate splash, followed by another, and then another. The kick of a foot, the splash of a hand, again, again, slow, sloppy, but persistent. It was the sound of someone swimming. No, it wasn't someone. I knew that. It was some*thing*.

I already knew it had grown feet. Did it have hands, arms, misshapen, yet operable appendages? And in gaining such, had it lost its fear of me? Yes, it probably had, if it ever even feared me at all.

"What is that?" Jacob asked, cocking an ear toward the north exit and listening to the sound. He picked up his flashlight and shone the beam toward the sound. It was still too far away to see. Not for long, though.

I turned to my brother, terrified. "Jacob, we have to go, *now.*"

My expression told him more than my words, more than he wanted to know, I'm guessing, for he didn't argue. Jacob grabbed what he could, as did I.

Within seconds we had grocery bags looped around each of our wrists, we both had a blanket under one arm and a pillow under the other. I'd looped the long strap of my purse over my head so it hung crossways, lessening the chances of it slipping off. We each held a flashlight. As fast as we could, we sloshed out of our camp and toward the south exit of the tunnels.

Halfway there we were moving slower than ever as we were walking against a muscular tide. As best we could, we held our bags up to protect our few precious belongings from getting wet. We made the turn. The water deepened.

We were making too much noise ourselves, as was the running water, to hear if anything was swimming up behind us. Sometimes I looked back, though not often. With all matter of debris gliding on the water, things like boards with nails sticking out looking like the treacherous tail of a stegosaurus, we had to have the light in front of us. Besides, I needed my brother to be focused on *getting* out, not *freaking* out.

Every step became a struggle. The water was halfway up my thighs.

Jacob said, "We're not going to be able to get out this way. The water's rising, rushing too fast. We'll never make it. We have to go back. Maybe it'll be easier getting out the north exit. The tunnels run a little higher there."

We had to get out this way. We couldn't go through our camp and to the north exit. That *thing* was there. Bypassing our camp and moving west, going beyond Silvia's camp, was to go to areas unexplored by us. For all I knew it could be miles before we found another exit, or worse. We could come to a dead end and be trapped.

I opened my mouth to tell Jacob we had to get out this way, and a sudden gush of water slammed into me. It knocked me off my feet, and sucked me under the dark water, and into utter chaos.

In an instant, I flipped over twice and lost all sense of direction. I held my breath while my arms flailed trying to find which way was up. The swirling rush spun me, paused but a heartbeat, and then heaved me back into the ferocious current. My ears filled, muffling the riotous sound of water rushing around me. It was as if my body was in the throes of a violent delivery, as if being forced from one world into the next.

My elbow scraped the floor and I flipped around until disorientation made it impossible for me to tell up from down. I slammed into the wall. The hard thud sent pain to my shoulder and to my head. Almost immediately, the current yanked me away again, scraping my left arm and side against rough concrete.

In a natural reaction, I cried out, and lost most of

the air I'd been holding in my lungs. My flailing became desperate. A few more seconds of this and I would drown.

For an instant, my face cleared the surface and I was able to suck in a breath before the current jerked me back under. Water swarmed me, struck me, and dragged me. It played with me the way a bad seed kid plays with a toy.

Through the water filling my ears, I could hear the dampened sound of Jacob's voice calling my name. I needed to answer him, give him some direction so he could help me. I was incapable of doing even that much.

The water held me in a tightfisted, merciless grip. My opponent was mightier. It would not concede. I breathed in a small amount of water and coughed it back out. There was no air to replace it. More water made its way into my lungs. Raw panic warred with despair. Defeat, while not yet touching me, hovered with great optimism.

A moment later, my skull burned when Jacob managed to grab me by my hair. He heaved me up and held me tight against him as we huddled against the wall. Simultaneously coughing up water and gulping air, I found myself engaged in a hard battle against dissolving into complete hysterics.

"Are you hurt?" Jacob asked when my lungs had settled into heavy breathing.

I glanced down at my body, sodden and without a doubt bruised. I was trembling all over. Whether it was fear, trauma, or cold, I couldn't say. Likely, it was a combination of all three. After a quick inspection of my arm, I lifted the side of my torn shirt.

Scrapes ran along my left elbow and upper arm, as well as my side from ribs to hip. Small blood droplets formed in the deeper recesses of the abrasions. There was a bad ache in my shoulder and a milder one in my hip, but none of that was enough for me to complain. I was standing, I was breathing, and I could move all my parts. I was alive. Jacob and I were both alive.

No sooner had the joy at our continuing life touched me than I realized my precious flashlight was gone. And so was one of my plastic grocery bags. Although my other bag was still looped around my wrist, the greedy rush of water had taken my blanket and pillow. At the loss of more than half of my precious few belongings, I couldn't stop myself from weeping.

"It's all right," Jacob said, wrapping his arms around me, rubbing circles on my back. "We'll be all right, Liz."

Through my hiccups and tears I said, "My blanket and my pillow are gone." I sounded like a whiney child. I couldn't muster up the effort to care.

"Mine too," Jacob said on a sigh; commiserating in a good-natured way that belied our dire circumstance.

I looked and sure enough, he had only the two grocery bags looped around his wrists. All our bedding was lost. As I cried in earnest I said through my sobs, "I'm sorry, Jacob."

"It's all right. We'll get by. We always do. At least I still have my flashlight."

He did have that extremely valuable item. Without it, we would be in complete darkness. I trembled harder at the horrible thought. My purse holding all our money was still looped across my body. Those were things to be grateful for, big things.

While I caught my breath and let gratitude bolster me, I looked around. Jacob had hauled me into an alcove, much like the one we used for a bathroom.

The water was rising there too, but it was more placid. I knew from experience we were between our camp and Silvia's. The surge had washed me right past the turnoff that would take us back to our camp.

Jacob leaned out of the alcove and shone his light each way. He turned back to me and said, "The water flowing in from our usual entrance is too strong. I don't think we could even make it back to our camp. We'll have to go the other way."

"Let's try again. I'm better prepared now." I didn't want to go deeper into the tunnels, especially through where we'd never been before. I wanted out.

"Liz, we'll never make it."

"We have to try."

"We'll die trying."

"Jacob…"

"Liz, listen to me," he said, calm and reasonable, with his hands on my shoulders and his eyes holding mine in a look that was kind yet firm. "We can't get out that way. We have to be logical."

Sometime over the last few minutes, we had changed roles. I stood there trembling and crying and making irrational decisions while Jacob stayed cool and used his brain. And he was right.

To try and get out through the south exit would be suicide. The tunnels ran at a slight upward angle closer to Silvia's camp. Benny had told us the storm drains did that in some places to slow the flow of water. I knew it, but I had forgotten that piece of information. That's why the water in Silvia's camp wasn't as high as it was in ours.

"We have to go, Liz. The water here is almost up to our hips."

He was right again. He was right and brave, and calm and I should not have withheld my trust from my brother. "I'm sorry, Jacob." I used my wet hand to wipe warm tears and cold water from my face.

"You couldn't help it. The wave caught you off guard."

"No, not about that. I'm sorry for not trusting you enough to tell you about the money I've been hiding away."

"It's okay. I guess in your shoes I'd have done the same thing," he said. But as he didn't meet my eyes when he said it, I'm not sure he really meant it. "Come on." Jacob took my hand. "Let's go."

Near Silvia's camp, the water was below our knees. Not as high as it had been by our camp and in the alcove, but still rising. After a very brief conversation, we agreed to make a quick check of her place to make sure she hadn't returned. She had not. Most of her belongings had sunk and what hadn't, was ruined. One red high-heeled shoe floated in a circle. I hoped she took some things with her the last time she left.

For a selfish second, our camp flashed in my mind. The flood was even worse there. The waters had surely ruined our precious mattress by now. It had been so much effort to get it there, it and all the rest of our pathetic, valuable things. Everything would be lost or destroyed.

Our home was pitiful and as lowly as a home could be, but it was ours. We'd fixed it up nice, all things considered. Now we were going to have to start all over.

My chest tightened and I gulped a hard breath. Jacob misunderstood.

"I wouldn't worry too much about Silvia. She's probably in a motel or staying with friends somewhere. She knows a lot of people. I'm sure she's fine."

Shame slapped me hard enough to bruise my tenuous self-worth. I wasn't thinking at all about Silvia, but rather drenched in self-pity at our own sorry state. Some friend I was. However, Jacob was right. If our subterranean population voted for someone to be 'most likely to survive', it would be Silvia. Still, thinking was not the same as knowing.

Jacob tugged on my hand. He had been holding on to me since saving me from certain death beneath the cold and filthy water. We left Silvia's camp. For the first time ever, instead of turning right as we exited her home, we turned left, moving through the shrinking concrete tunnel with a single flashlight to cut through the thick darkness and black water.

Jacob and I waded into unknown territory.

Chapter 10

Not long after leaving Silvia's camp, the floor ascended a little before leveling out again. The water dropped to about mid shin and stayed there, making our walk less cumbersome. Still, I was cold and wet. Clothing saturated with filth-laden water suctioned to my shivering body and my warranted fears were trying to thrust me into the welcoming pit of madness.

The air in the tunnel was thick and dank, and as black as a shadow's shadow. Our single flashlight was woefully inadequate. Darkness encased my brother and me while its offspring prowled the concrete corridors searching for us. I'd been fighting for survival my whole life, but never before had I so thoroughly felt it.

Over the next twenty or thirty minutes we made several turns and while I tried to keep my bearings it became more and more difficult. The water rose again.

I had an unreasonable, albeit powerful urge to turn around and run back the way we'd come. It's possible, as Jacob had argued; it would have been suicide, but maybe not. Maybe we would have made it through and been long out of there.

As the cold water buried more of me, creeping upward faster than I was brave enough to acknowledge, that sounded more and more promising.

In all the months we'd lived down in the tunnels, I had never experienced claustrophobia. That was something for which I had neglected to be grateful. However, with us being so far in, with the water threatening to shrink the tunnel to nothing but a concrete box without air and no known way to escape, our home of almost one year might well have been a tomb.

In order to go on and not allow terror to overcome me I did what I always do when I feel close to surrendering to my circumstance. I focused on my brother. Though in all fairness, it was Jacob who'd taken control. He led the way, he held my hand, and although he was afraid too, he kept his fears from me as I had always kept mine from him. I don't know if that made me feel better or worse.

I hadn't a clue as to what was going on outside. Even if the rain had stopped, the water in the tunnels would continue to rise. It was the place where the town shed its' unwanted excess.

Every so often I made a request to Jacob that we stop for a moment to rest. I didn't need to. My legs were strong from all the walking we'd done since becoming homeless and even with the water resistance, I hadn't yet tired. What I needed to do was to listen without the noise of our sloshing through the water.

I didn't hear the sound of something swimming. Maybe, like us, it was walking on actual legs.

A new grade of terror struck me hard. It may still be swimming. Maybe at that very moment it was underneath the water where it could be silent and sly, where I wouldn't know of its approach until it locked onto my legs and was dragging me beneath the surface of the black water.

"Let's go," I said to my brother, and said nothing

more.

Jacob walked in front of me, shining his light ahead. I didn't ask him to shine our only light behind us because I didn't want to put anymore fear into him than what he already had. But I mourned the loss of my flashlight.

With all the moisture, the air was heavy, and it partnered with my drenched clothing and the watery terrain to weigh me down. The surrounding darkness, however, was even thicker than the air, and more the menace. It hovered at my back and at times, though I did not feel the electrical flow I always did when that thing was near, the darkness itself felt alive.

I dared to glance back over my shoulder. It was pointless. The pitch-black night wrapped around us was solid, except for the small porthole made by the forward beam of Jacob's flashlight. The darkness behind us was so complete I couldn't have seen the monster if it was an inch in front of my face, as I knew it well could be every time I looked back.

One of these times, I feared, I may turn my head and still see nothing, but I might smell the rot of its breath when it exhaled against my face. I trembled at the thought, as the possibility was all too real.

Even knowing that risk existed, however, even knowing I would not be able to see, I could not stop myself from turning around to look. Human nature, I supposed; damned human nature.

The thing was changing the last time I'd seen it. It was growing teeth. Would it have a mouth lined with razor-sharp points, maybe even rows of them like a shark? Would it have claws, long and thick, as deadly a threat as its teeth?

Would it have eyes, developed and situated in place, pupils glowing red like the fires of Hell? All I could do was imagine, and wish I had less imagination.

While I was looking back for the millionth time, Jacob tugged on my hand. He had stopped, forcing me to do the same. Before I could ask why, it was clear in the beam of light he shined up and down and back and forth. In front of us, like the barrier to our escape that it was, stood a wall of solid concrete. My nightmare fear of hitting a dead end and becoming trapped had come true.

Two hard beats of my heart later, my terror level threatened to overwhelm me. The slow and steady sloshing of my other, living, evolving terror, as it walked through the water, making its way toward us.

Jacob heard it too. He twisted around with a startled jerk, the beam of light arcing so fast it left a brief trail. There was nothing to see, yet. The sound was still at a distance, echoing in the tunnel, but coming our way. I stared as far as the beam of light would allow. It wasn't far enough, nor was it broad enough. And then the beam of light was gone.

Jacob had turned around. I was about to shout at him to shine it back. As much as I feared the monster, I wanted to see what was coming at me. I didn't want that thing to attack me in the dark. My brother spoke before I could.

"Left or right?" Jacob asked on a quick breath.

"What?" I asked with partial attention. I peered into the dense darkness behind us, ready to grab the light from his hand. Not only did I need it to see what was coming for us, the flashlight was all we had to use for a weapon.

"Left or right?" Jacob repeated. The urgency in his voice was unmistakable.

I turned a questioning glance toward my brother as he shone the beam of light to the right and then to our left. Then, and with immense gratitude to fate, which more often than not has treated us with cruelty, we got lucky. We had not come to the end of the line, but to a crossroad.

While we could no longer go forward, the tunnel was open to the left and to the right. Both ways looked the same in the measly beam of Jacob's flashlight, dark, endless, filling with water.

Feeling both reprieved and rushed, I thought hard. To the left should be north. Our usual north exit was a long walk. Maybe with the distance we'd already covered that way could get us out sooner. It didn't seem likely, but after all that had happened I was having a hard time getting my bearings down here and I just didn't know.

To the right should be the Las Vegas strip. Unless the tunnel had angled away without us realizing it we should be close, by my estimation. But we very well could have angled away. Even if we hadn't it still didn't answer the question as to whether or not there was an exit that way or the other. Of course, eventually there would be, but it might not be for miles. In true Las Vegas style, either choice was a gamble.

"Liz, we have to choose," Jacob said.

Distress tightened his voice as he turned our single beam of light toward the darkness behind us. We could see nothing but a whitish hole in pitch black made with our small tube of light. He swept the beam back and forth, skimmed it across the top of the water, nothing.

We could hear it, though, that thing. It was moving in the water, moving toward us...slosh...slosh...slosh.

Left or right? Either way there was nothing to see. I wished I had more time to think. What I heard told me I didn't. As it got closer, that thing walking in the water no longer sounded awkward or slow. Its gait was as steady as ours had been. And it was gaining on us.

"Right," I said. "Let's go right."

I didn't know if that was the best way or not, and there wasn't time to reason it out further than I already had. We needed to go. That was the only thing I knew for sure. We turned to the right and we walked as fast as we could in the knee-high water toward what I thought to be the Las Vegas Strip.

After about ten minutes, it was obvious. If there was an exit this way, it was not at the same distance as the one we normally used. If it were, we would have already been outside, free from fears and floods and the most terrible of man-made threats.

At the endless horrid scenarios running uninvited through my head, all of which concluded in our ghastly deaths, an escalating panic fought to dig its way into me. It almost succeeded when the floor started sloping downward.

Moments later the water swallowed our knees, and rose in greedy laps to take more. It was too late to go back. All we could do now was go on and hope the tunnel would level out again, or better still, angle upward. Better than both of those choices, of course, would be if these damned tunnels would *let us out.*

Within minutes, the water was climbing up our thighs.

At a glow in the distance, hope sprung. We could

see the tunnel turned ahead, turned to the right. We could see it because there was light. It was dim, but it was there. And where there was light, there was an exit. We sprinted as best we could in the water now licking at our hips.

When we rounded the corner, we could see without our flashlight. Though it was gray, dismal due to clouds piled in dreary, filtering layers, light from the outside world still made its way in. It was not, however, from the exit we'd hoped we would find. The light from above filtered through the cloudy sky, and through a grating in the roof of the tunnel. The grating was a good five feet over our heads.

We could hear traffic nearby. The whir of tires traveling over wet roads was unmistakable. A car horn beeped one long, angry wail before fading into the distance. Along with the sounds of traffic and of the raindrops pattering the earth lying solid over our heads, we could hear the breeze blowing weather-cleansed air across the world above, too lofty to touch the likes of us with its freshness.

Jacob and I stood transfixed, tortured by the taunt. Even if it wasn't the Las Vegas Strip, it was civilization. Through the barred rectangle of the grate, we could see tiers of dusky clouds roving across the sky. The sounds of human life ran close-by: one car driving too fast for wet roads, then a muffler that needed replacing, the rumble growing louder and then fading away.

We could smell the rain-washed scent of the world outside the tunnels. Freedom from this cold, wet hell was right there before us, yet a million miles away.

We stood to the side of the grating, heads tilted

back, staring. A waterfall poured down from one end. Rain sprinkled in through the rest of the grating, though it was coming down much lighter than it had been earlier. The rain, however, was not our immediate thought. We were both trying to conjure up a miraculous way for us to get out through that grating. My brother was far more hopeful than I was.

"You could sit on my shoulders, Liz," Jacob said.

"I still won't be tall enough," I answered, measuring the distance by sight, wishing I were wrong, and knowing I wasn't.

"Let's try. Hurry."

Not moving, I said, "Even if I can make it to the grating and get out, you'd still be stranded down here with no way for me to get you up."

As Jacob's mind searched for nonexistent possibilities, his eyes scanned the bare walls of the tunnel as if a ladder might magically appear. He looked up again. An idea grew in the slight widening of his eyes and lift of his fair brows. Already I knew I would have to crush it. We would not be able to get out through that grating.

"When the water rises, we can reach it," Jacob said. "We'll tread until then."

"We don't know how long that will take or if the water will even get high enough. And if the water does get that high, it'll be running hard. That aside, even if we are able to tread here until then, we don't know if we'll be able to push out the grating. We won't have any leverage at all. Besides, it could be bolted in there, and then we'd be in an even worse situation than we are now."

His mind worked a moment more, as did mine. I'm

sure we both had the same horrible image playing in our heads. The two of us trapped between the grating and the hard-flowing water, holding on for our lives, until we couldn't.

The grating teasing us with a view of the free world beyond may as well have been prison bars reinforced with triple security locks. We discussed it no more. There was nothing to say. And there was no time to indulge in hopeful maybes.

In our pause beneath the grate, somewhere between scant hope and conceding defeat, I had listened. I couldn't hear that thing. It was coming for us, though. Of that, I had no doubt. My brother knew it, too.

Without my prompting, he turned the light in the direction from which we'd come. The water rippled from the rain, from the flow, from us. If it moved because of anything else, we couldn't tell. After a quick but thorough search, Jacob shinned the light ahead and we walked on, leaving the grating, its light, and its merciless tease of freedom behind. Fear and frustration came with us.

Soon there was another turn and it thrust us into solid blackness broken only by the too thin, too short, beam of Jacob's flashlight. Again, I bemoaned the loss of my own flashlight, even more than my belongings. The light we had wasn't near enough. The complaint running through my head must have jinxed us, for Jacob's light suddenly dimmed.

He shook the flashlight, the cheapest one we'd found in the store. It flickered bright a few times before shutting down completely, leaving us in rising water, surrounded by concrete, and in darkness so absolute I could believe I no longer had eyes.

"No," I said, the whispered word a plea.

Jacob shook the flashlight again, the rattling louder in the dark confines. It flickered, lit a dim beam for a few seconds, and then died out in a swift and steady fade.

"This happened to me before," he said, a voice in the dark. "I took out the batteries, switched them around, and then put them back in. It started working again."

"You knew the batteries were bad and you didn't change them!" I crossed my arms and clenched at my sides to keep from punching him.

"You're the one always nagging me to make everything last to the end!"

He took in a quick, deep breath and then released it. Whether it was to gain patience or gear up for a fight, I couldn't tell. I was hoping for a fight. When my brother spoke next, he didn't yell, but the attitude in his voice he learned from me.

"Do you want to argue or do you want to help me switch these batteries around? Or maybe you want to try and find our way out by feeling along the walls."

I wanted to argue. I wanted to yell and scream, and lose my mind so I would forget we were standing in a flooding concrete tunnel without sight while a creature born of evil was coming after us. That's what I wanted to do. But it's not what I *would* do.

"Hurry. Let's do this." I said, letting my anger pummel the wimp in me that wanted to toss away my sanity, and hoping I wouldn't regret it.

"Make a cup with your hands," he said.

By way of feel, he placed the back end of the flashlight over my hands so when he unscrewed the cap the batteries would go into my hands and not the water. He must have been holding the flashlight at a gentle angle because the two batteries slid out slow. He took the first one and I listened to the easy scrape as it slid back into the cylinder. After I felt him take the second battery, I dropped my hands. Jacob gasped.

The small splash made me gasp, too.

"You dropped it!" I shouted. "You clumsy idiot!"

"You took your hands away before I had it!" he shouted back at me. I opened my mouth to scream my rebuttal, but Jacob was already shoving the flashlight and cap in my hands, shoving them against my chest and squeezing his hands hard on top of mine for emphasis. "Here, don't drop these. And don't tip the flashlight. The other one will fall out. I'm going down for that battery."

Before I could tell him to be careful, before I could tell him I was sorry, my brother sucked in a deep breath and dropped under the water. I waited in that complete darkness for what seemed like far too long.

With his movement, the water swirled around my legs. I hoped it was *his* movement. After an eternity, Jacob popped up from the water. I almost leapt from my skin. At least I had sense enough to hold the flashlight and cap to my chest in a death grip.

"I got it!" he shouted in triumph.

Again, by way of feel he did his best to wipe dry the battery on my damp shirt before he put it back in and replaced the cap. Suddenly, we had light! The relief at being able to see again put our anger to rest.

Not long after, we found another tunnel branching off to the left. Following a brief conversation, we decided to stay the route we'd been going. Fifteen minutes later, I had doubts as to whether we'd made the right decision.

The floor sloped downward at a more drastic angle. Moments later, the water engulfed our hips. I didn't know if turning left back there would have been better. It was possible it could have been worse that way. But as the cold water crept up our stomachs, I found myself wishing we had gone that way instead of this.

I stopped, tugging on Jacob's hand so he would stop too. "Shine the light behind us for a second," I told my brother. I couldn't worry about frightening him now. Besides, he was smart enough to be scared already.

He spun around and shined the inadequate light into the darkness behind us. Something atop the water caught in the beam of light. Jacob and I both jumped and didn't bother to feel ridiculous at the sight of a filthy, yellow rubber ducky floating in the water. With a dopey grin on its face, it looked happy and carefree. Stupid duck.

I forced a chuckle, to lighten the mood. Jacob forced one too. We both failed. We were breathing hard, savoring the small break in our journey as I worried over its toll. The walk had become so very difficult in the rising water. My legs were cramping, and exhaustion dragged on me.

"It's just a rubber duck," Jacob said, putting some more effort into his chuckle before finding the child's toy with his beam of light so we could see it again. It bobbed up and down on the waves, smiling as though it was in a nice warm bubble bath.

And then in an instant the toy disappeared, as if sucked under the water by a sudden and violent undertow.

Then the water where the duck had been swelled upward, pulsing with the rhythm of a heartbeat, growing larger by the second.

It wasn't a wave.

The swell was a fat mound, black and shiny, like the skin of a wet seal, like a shadow born fresh into life.

The bulge in the water did not shift with the waves. The waves washed around it. I could see the knobs of a spine arcing in perfect intervals over the sleek center. The monster emerged further. It was rising up to stand. My heart pounded like a fist against my ribs and terror bit all the way to my bones.

My skin was utterly electric.

"Run!" I shouted.

Our legs plowed through as best we could while our arms shoved water behind us. With all our effort, our progress was at best sluggish, as we were laboring against a rising tide of water. We were living one of those nightmares, the kind where you're running from a monster and no matter the fear, no matter the effort, you can only run in slow motion.

I had an idea but before I could voice it, Jacob shouted my thoughts.

"We should swim, Liz! It'll be faster!"

We both knew how to swim, but, not having a great deal of experience, neither of us was very good. He was right, though. The water had risen up to my chest and walking had become only slightly better than standing still. We swam our best, hoping it was better than the monster behind us.

Jacob's flashlight shone in erratic swipes as we swam for our lives. And as that thin, slashing ray gave me flickers of sight, it gave snapshots of hope.

Graffiti splotched the wall. Some pictures, some words outlined in fat black and filled in with color, but in the brief glimpses, I couldn't tell what they said. With very few exceptions, the graffiti in the tunnels is near the exits where the artists don't have to haul their materials too far. Jacob knew this too.

We swam harder.

"Ah!" Jacob shouted, and I was mute with terror thinking that the monster had gotten him. But then my brother grabbed hold of me to save me the fate he had suffered.

"It's a wall," he said through his heavy breaths. "We have to turn left."

I looked up at Jacob. He was rubbing his head where he'd collided with the wall. He lowered his hand. A red mark patched his forehead. It stood out in a dim but encompassing light. Twisting my head to the left I could see another corner that turned right seven or eight feet away. It was the source of the light.

Around that corner could be another grating, or it could be our way out. Water rushed faster here which gave credence to the latter. Then I had to stand on my toes to keep my head above water. Jacob, being a little bit taller, had his arm around me to help. We were breathing hard and we were tiring. But no energy drink can hold a candle to the boost terror gives, and the very real possibility of escape.

From behind us, I couldn't tell how far, a gurgling sound echoed in the tunnel. Then there was an odd burst of breathy laughter. We didn't wait to hear more.

Jacob and I swam, swam faster than ever. We both knew we were swimming for our lives.

Around the corner, we found the exit. It was broad and beautiful, and gushing water down its slope toward us. We swam our best, but we were swimming against a determined tide and our progress was scant, at times in the negative. Keeping at it, we swam through the large square and out into the real world. We had to swim up the slope and then we'd be able to walk out.

Jacob and I were side by side. We put our all into it. Our lives depended on our ability to make it through this last leg. That knowledge, however, could not long sustain us physically. My aching limbs launched a rebellion. I could assume Jacob fared no better. We were down to our last drops of adrenaline. Our burst of energy waned and ebbed.

The toe of my shoe scraped the bottom, so I knew the floor was sloping upward. I put my feet down to run while my arms still swam. It helped. I yelled at Jacob to do the same.

With a quick twist of my head, I had a look back. All I could see was the tunnel opening and water flowing in. That thing was there, though. I could feel it. Even with water rushing over my skin, it tingled electric.

I didn't know whether it had developed enough to come out into the world. What I knew for sure was we could not let ourselves wash back into the tunnel. I forced my head, my attitude, and all my efforts forward.

On a wave, my head bobbed up high and I got a glimpse of the desert floor. Freedom was right there, *right there*. I glanced at my brother beside me. His face showed the strain of desperate determination, as well as mounting exhaustion.

We couldn't come this far just to let the water take

us back where that monster would devour us. We couldn't. But I could no longer ignore the heaviness of my arms and the vicious cramping in my legs. We were so close! I would have shouted at the unfairness of it had I an ounce of breath to spare.

While I battled the current, I squinted at the slope before us through the droplets assaulting my eyes. It was a waterfall in the desert, and it gushed at us like a gleeful foe.

We'd progress three feet only to have it wash us back two. My arms and legs fought with me, rejecting my commands at an increasing rate. My lungs burned and coughed as water made its way down my throat. Jacob coughed beside me. He was weakening, too.

We'd managed to swim about five feet out of the tunnel. Ahead there was a good twenty feet of river trying to force us back. Twenty feet until the cement wall surrounding us would be low enough to climb. From where we were, the distance looked great, too great. Still Jacob and I continued to make the effort.

Our arms and legs flopped in near rootlessness. It was all we had left. We were losing ground. Our burst of energy was depleted, our reserves, our resolve, sinking under the greater weight of reality. It became clear to me we were not going to make it.

I lurched toward my brother, to take hold of his hand instead of swim for my life. Jacob paddled without drive. He was going under. I was, too.

At least we would die together. My heart broke at the years we would not have, at the second chance we would not get, and I sobbed like a little girl in the face of my surrender. My only hope became one of a quick and painless death for my brother and me.

"Here!"

The shout called from somewhere above us. When I rotated my head, something caught my eye. Bobbing in the water, a gleaming white life preserver with a red rope tied around it. I couldn't see who was holding the other end. It didn't matter. I was sure I had very little time before my limbs would ignore even one small command.

"Jacob!" I called to my brother as I swam for the life preserver. It lifted out of the water and then landed again, closer to me so I was able to loop my arm through it.

I stretched my free hand out to Jacob. His eyes met mine, widened when they landed on what I was holding, and he stretched for me. Our fingertips clung to each other for a moment, but before he could grab on for a firm hold, a gushing wave pried us apart.

I hoped whoever had hold of the rope would not try to pull me out before I got hold of my brother. If they did, I would have to release the life preserver.

Jacob tried again. At the same time, whoever had hold of the rope was dragging me toward him. Our rescuer was trying to help me get to my brother. Once I was close enough, Jacob mustered up enough energy to grab my arm with one hand and the life preserver with the other.

Jacob's flashlight was gone. The thought was pure nonsense because it didn't matter now. Holding onto the life preserver and to each other was all that mattered. In the next few minutes, Jacob and I were going to either live or die.

While we held on for our lives, our rescuer hauled us up the concrete hill and into shallower water. When we were able to, Jacob and I used our legs to help. It frightened me how much effort it took, how weak I had become.

Then Jacob was shouldering me upward along the wall. Hands grabbed me. Big hands, strong hands attached to strong arms.

I let go of Jacob and the life preserver. Without even looking at who had saved me, I turned back on my hands and knees as soon as I touched the ground to make sure my brother made it out. No sooner had I looked, than Jacob was beside me.

Exhaustion, the likes of which I'd never known, fell upon me like a soaked blanket. In our weakened, sodden states, Jacob and I clung to each other as best we could with arms shaking in mismatched rhythm with the trembling of our bodies. I think we were both crying, but it's hard to say. Everything was too real to seem so.

After such a close surrender to what had been our imminent deaths, I needed time to accept we'd made it out alive. Displacement stupefied my mind and body. Reality tumbled into thoughts, and thoughts dissipated into a swirl of surrealism. It was hard to separate the world around us from the one inside my head. Both were muddled to me, slogging in a slow, tilted rotation.

Vague passages of time drifted over me, through me. Maybe we were crying, maybe we were just trying to catch a breath that wasn't supposed to be there.

I had a sensation of lacking solidity, as if I was half-melted. Still, Jacob and I leaned against each other, holding on as best we could with our feeble arms in the drizzle and the mud. We clung to one another with the knowledge we had escaped a death that still watched us with outstretched arms.

As my head cleared and my breath steadied, a man said, "Can you stand? I have a place to take you. If you can't make it to the car, I can carry you one at a time."

It was the voice of our savior, and it was familiar. With more effort than I cared to think about, I lifted my head. My gaze met a face I knew. He was kneeling beside us with his hands on his thighs. His beautiful suit was drenched and muddy. Concern hardened his handsome features. His voice matched his expression.

For the life of me, I could not understand why he was there. I was too stunned to speak. All I could do was stare up into Joe's handsome, wet face, and wonder how the casino worker ended up here, saving our lives.

Chapter 11

At a fleeting but painful twinge deep in the calf of my right leg, I blinked my eyes. Passing minutes dragged me from my sleep. I resisted, though. The dream I'd been having was heaven.

In it, I was comfortable and cozy, sleeping in a clean, air-conditioned room nestled in layers of bedding so fresh, and snug they could only exist in a dream. Yet when I opened my eyes, I found I was still dreaming.

The first thing I identified was a set of heavy, salmon pink curtains with soft pleats covering most of a large rectangle of a window. In the three or four open inches in the center of the drapes were translucent sheers such an immaculate shade of white, they made me think of angel wings.

There was enough light coming into the room for me to see, but not so much as to be over bright. That might have been luck, might have been chance, or it might have been someone's thoughtful consideration.

Against the wall, opposite the bed, was a dresser made of dark wood shining glossy in the morning light. Above it was a spotless mirror trimmed in the same kind of wood. To my right was an open door. It led to a bathroom almost as big as our whole camp in the storm drain.

I blinked a couple of times thinking maybe I was leaving one dream and entering another. And then in one swift and jarring instant the memories all popped into place.

Yesterday, Jacob and I had come so close to death I'm sure we bore its fingerprints.

We'd been soaked and filthy, and exhausted to a level not much above death, lying in a heap on the muddy desert floor. Joe, with an arm supporting us both, helped us to his car and drove us here, to the hotel section of the Desert Star.

I remembered him sliding a card through a keyless entry so we could come in through a back door. He showed us to a suite where we each had our own lovely rooms with our own elegant bathrooms. Jacob and I took long steamy showers and then slipped into thick, pristine white robes awaiting us on the backs of the bathroom doors. The robes were made of the softest, plushest fabric I'd ever felt in my life. I could live in the one I wore. I had in fact, slept in it.

Beside the sink had been a brand new toothbrush, still sealed in the long, thin package, and a new tube of toothpaste. Also on the creamy marble counter was a new hairbrush, a new bottle of lotion, and a cherry-flavored lip balm, and aspirin. And there was a tube of anti-bacterial ointment as well as a box of Band-Aids. I used it all.

After my shower, I'd left the bathroom, crossed the bedroom, and walked into the living room area separating the two bedrooms. I realized after living in the storm drains, even a cheap motel room would seem plush, but this suite was luxurious beyond anything I'd ever seen outside a movie.

Last night, through my bleary eyes, I could see how half a dozen of our camps could fit into the spacious living room decorated in mauves and white with pale green carpet and complementing accents. Jacob was already there, exhausted and happy, waiting for me.

Fresh from his shower, he sat at a table by the window wearing a robe that matched mine. He wore his like a king's mantle, and when my eyes shifted to the table, I felt his attitude.

Before him was a rich and colorful feast of vegetables, fruits, breads, and desserts, enough to please a fussy queen. Jacob's grin was broad, albeit tired, as he motioned for me to sit in one of the other chairs. I obliged and we proceeded to pig out.

Between mouthfuls of food, he told me Joe had left the room a few minutes before and that he'd said to eat and to get some sleep and he'd be back in the morning. Too tired to have an effective discussion about our situation at the time, we ate the largest meal we'd eaten since the buffet. I had a vague memory of putting a Band-Aid on my brother's shoulder before Jacob and I crash-landed in our beds.

I remember thinking, as I made my way to the layers of fresh sheets and soft blankets, that after sharing a bed with Jacob for so long I would have trouble sleeping all by myself. But exhaustion the likes of which I would never have believed possible overtook everything, including my many, many concerns.

My eyelids were weighted. My need to sleep was desperate. My arms and legs were already drifting off. For a moment, I'd been tempted to lie down on the thick carpeting and take a nap before having to walk all the way to the bed. The ridiculous notion made me chuckle. I was so tired I'd gotten silly.

There were things I needed to think about, plans to be made. All of it was urgent, but it would all have to wait. My body was going to claim sleep whether I granted permission or not.

I'd dragged back the covers and half crawled, half fell onto the bed, and was dead to the world before I could so much as tug the sheet over me. The sheet, the blanket and the comforter were over me when I awoke, snug, as if someone had tucked me into bed.

Shifting my head on the pillow a bit, I caught sight of a clock on the night table. It read 9:42 a.m. I needed to see my brother.

I sat up, or rather, tried. It was more of a slow, hurting grind to a seated position. If I had gone several rounds with whoever was the present heavyweight champ, I imagined that was how it would leave me feeling.

I don't think there was so much as four square inches of skin on my body that didn't show at least a minor scrape or mark of some kind. Some of the bruises made me look licked by a fair-sized paintbrush dipped in blue/black paint. It was the aches running beneath my skin, deep into my overtaxed muscles, that were going to harass me the most.

Every motion stirred up fresh pain. In some places, it was on the surface, but in others, aches stabbed deep into my bones. I appreciated every sting, twinge, and grimace, though, for it meant I was alive. The icing on the cake was I didn't think any of the damage was permanent.

Although I must have slept close to a dozen hours, I was still tired. A physical weariness had settled itself throughout my battered being. My body was trying to heal from yesterday's abuse.

I was tempted to fall back into the multitude of pillows and blankets fluffing that fabulous bed and stay there for at least a week. But I needed to check on Jacob. I needed to see again that he was all right. Besides, for all I knew we'd be tossed out of there at any moment. It was best I was awake and ready, no matter how much I didn't want to be.

A sudden dart of alarm shot up my spine. It shouldn't have taken this long. The fact that it did was a testament to my exhaustion. I sucked in a gasp while running a quick scan of the room and my stiff neck groaned in protest. As I was about to cry out my panic, there it was, my patchwork purse.

It was on a folded towel, I assumed because it was soaked, and sitting on the floor right in front of the nightstand. It was as if someone wanted me to see it as soon as I sat up on the bed.

I snatched it up and checked my long wallet. All our money was still there. Wet, like my purse and everything else inside of it, but every dollar was there. I let out my breath, and almost wept with relief. That money was more important to us than ever before.

Last night, I'd left my sodden clothes in the bathroom. After my shower, I'd rinsed them out in the bathtub and hung them over the shower rod so they would dry with as few wrinkles as possible. I'd seen more rips as well as a wider gap in the side seam of my shirt than I had expected. I was sure there were more, but I had been too tired to inspect my clothing further. A seamstress I was not, but this morning I found myself wishing hard for a needle and thread.

I wondered if my poor old clothes were dry yet. It

occurred to me then that my second bag had not been with me when Joe rescued us from the water. At the time I'd been so joyous with life and exhausted from fighting death I hadn't noticed everything I had was gone.

Both of Jacob's bags were gone, too, now that I thought about it. We had nothing but the clothes we'd come here with. And the condition of those had to be within spitting distance of worthless. The realization was disheartening. We were more destitute than we had ever been.

It was too big to take on at the moment. My sore shoulders couldn't bear the weight. I would think about that later. Not much later, though. I would fret about it right after I checked on Jacob. Once I saw he was fine I'd be better able to think. With the speed of a tired old woman, I leaned over and set my soggy purse back on the towel.

I slid my legs over the side of the bed and tested my weight on them. They would hold me, but with an aching, wobbling weakness that conveyed their grievances.

I lifted my arms hip high for balance. That took some effort, too. My limbs were weak, sore, and not entirely obedient to my commands. Painful knots punched like fists into the muscles of my thighs. My neck was stiff, reluctant, as if tightened to my body by the giant wrench of current events.

I hobbled into the bathroom. My clothes were gone.

Even my shoes were not where I'd left them. Maybe Joe had taken my things somewhere for washing. Or maybe, they were in such poor condition he threw them away like the trash they were. That would mean the only thing I had to wear was a robe that didn't even belong to me.

We were alive, I reminded myself. Jacob and I were alive.

Limping, I made my way into the living room, feeling old and beaten, worn thin, sore as hell, poor as hell and extremely lucky.

Pausing two steps into the living room so I could appreciate what I was too done in to appreciate last night, the luxury took me by surprise. The casino at the Desert Star was old and small, and I'd always assumed they had plenty of regular rooms, but I never figured they had a suite like this. It was as grand as any I would imagine at the big resorts.

The drapes were pale salmon, like in the bedroom, the carpet a calm hue of sea foam green. There was an almond-colored, sectional couch covered in a super soft fabric, and two cozy chairs of the same fabric positioned before a huge television. Beside the picture window with wide-open curtains was a smoky glass dining table without so much as a smudge or a speck of dust, and silver chairs with white seat cushions where Jacob and I had devoured our feast last night. There wasn't a trace of the feast now.

Everything was elegant and immaculate. The place looked like a vacation brochure for people with pockets deep enough to hold happily-ever-after security.

I remembered the window overlooked the swimming pool. Last night the light was on in the pool. It shone iridescent blue, rippling with what little the clouds had left to drop. Beyond that was a wonderful view of the Las Vegas Strip.

Crossing the room I stepped light, as the carpet, still fresh with vacuum lines, was so thick and new I didn't want to crush it.

Through the doorway to the bedroom on the other side of the suite, was Jacob's room, the same as mine. His form was obvious beneath the covers. Still, I limped to the head of the bed so I could look at his face. I had to see for myself he was all right. He was.

Jacob breathed a contented sigh, curled up on his side, snuggled deep into the blankets. He looked like a little boy. The sight made my chest tighten and at the same time made me smile.

Out of the corner of my eye, I caught sight of a comfortable looking dark green chair. I suppose there was one in my room too, I just hadn't noticed.

I headed for the chair, thinking to sit and rest, and enjoy watching my brother sleep in a real bed. Before I got to the chair, however, a lock clicked, and then the door to the suite opened. A moment later, I heard it close.

There was a rustling sound, like maybe shopping bags. I took quiet steps to the bedroom door and stopped. Joe, dressed in a fresh suit of ash gray, peeked into the room where I'd been sleeping.

He turned around and faced me as I stood in the doorway opposite him. Beneath the pale gray of his suit jacket was a shirt of deep burgundy, so crisp it had to be brand new. I could see a couple of small, pearl-like buttons peeking around a midnight blue tie. Like the room, he was too gorgeous to be real.

For a moment, we stared at each other. I didn't know what to say, and he appeared struck with the same affliction.

"Thank you," I finally said. I wrapped the robe closer around me; all too aware I was naked underneath. Joe gave me a small nod.

"How are you feeling?" he said in his smooth, deep voice as he stepped into the living room.

He moved with caution, as if he worried I might run away again. Like I would leave my brother, and walk out of here wearing nothing but a robe. Joe's eyes never left my face. I had the feeling he was studying me, maybe to see if I was all right, maybe something else, though I couldn't think of what.

I walked into the room trying not to let my limp show, doing my best to look as dignified as I could while wearing nothing but bruises, Band Aids and a big fluffy robe that didn't even belong to me. "I'm fine."

"Sit down. We should talk."

His tone was gentle, his words a kind invitation, not an order. We both settled in, he in one of the chairs that looked to me like it might recline, me near him on the end of the couch so clean I was hesitant to touch it.

"A doctor was in to see both of you last night."

I was sure he could tell by the look on my face I had no memory of that.

"Nothing appeared to be broken. You're badly bruised and scraped. But you don't need me to tell you that. You need time to rest and get back your strength."

"What about Jacob?"

"The same. He said you both did a good job of cleaning and dressing your wounds. He'll come back if you want to see him, talk to him. I would have asked you before calling him in, but neither you nor your brother were in any condition to consent and I was worried."

I nodded. The fact that a doctor examined me without my being aware of it was disconcerting. But Jacob had received medical attention too, and for that, I was glad.

"Are you hungry?" Joe asked.

"I'll wait for my brother."

"It's all right if you want to eat now. You can have more sent up later, as much as you want, as often as you want. There's a room service menu on the table over there next to the phone," he said, pointing to a small table at the other end of the couch.

"I'll wait," I answered, and then without preamble, I asked, "How did you know?"

He didn't feign ignorance, pretending he didn't know what I meant. I'll give him credit for that.

"It was raining, and I've known where you and your brother lived for a while now. It wasn't hard to figure out you could be in trouble if you were…home." Joe paused then. He ran his hands down his thighs and patted his knees twice. I believed he was deciding how to proceed.

After a short, thoughtful silence, he said, "Actually, that's not quite right. The fact is, sometimes I get strong feelings that let me know if something is truly bad or truly good. Just like you."

"Like me?"

"Sometimes you know things," Joe said.

The intensity of his aqua eyes was gripping and held an elevated degree of awareness I could not explain. It was as if Joe was looking right through my eyes and into my brain, peering into corners unlit by subconscious design.

"It's not so much actual knowledge as feeling," he

continued. "Really, it's more intuition than anything else. Some people, a few of us, anyway, are able to tune in to our intuition better than most. We never learned to ignore it. Like you. You knew you could trust Silvia with anything but money. You knew Benny wouldn't harm you. You knew these things within minutes of meeting them. You didn't need proof. You *knew*."

Joe tipped his head to the right, just a little. It made him appear more concentrated, as if the shift had strengthened his expression.

"I'll bet at times the feeling is so strong you practically know something for a fact. Like how you knew about that thing in the storm drains when it wasn't much more than a shadow."

I sat up straight. "How do you know about that?"

"We've known for a while."

"We?"

"There are others, like you and me. We can sense good because we're able to focus our attention in ways most people can't. We can sense evil the same way, especially when it's extreme like that. None of us can sense it as strongly as you, though."

"How many others are there?"

"A few hundred of us that I know are out there around the world. I'm sure many more exist. It's been less than a decade since we started learning about each other and getting organized. Even using the internet, that's not such an easy thing to do. There's so much nonsense out there. It's endless."

For a minute or two, I could find no words. There were others like me and Benny who knew that thing was real. Did these others, like me, know what caused it to develop and grow? Did they know how it started, and more important, did they know how to stop it?

My mind worked to sort through and organize all the thoughts and questions flooding my mind. Joe sat with unending patience. I had the feeling he would wait all day until I was ready for more.

"I still don't understand how you knew about me and Jacob yesterday. You felt we were in trouble, but how did you know where you would find us? We were all over down there. *We* didn't even know where we were going to come out."

"I feel very connected to you. It's never happened with anyone before, not to this extent. The first time I felt it was a couple of years ago, at the St. Patrick's Day parade downtown. I got no more than a glimpse of you, but I felt you. I followed the feeling, but I lost you in the crowd. After that, I searched the crowds at every event, trying to find you again. Then, a little over a year ago, I was at the hospital visiting an employee who'd been hurt on the job. Jacob was in the same hospital at the same time. I found out later it was because he'd been in a car accident. I felt your presence, but you left before I could find you. From Jacob's admission forms I learned where you lived."

Before I could ask Joe how he got access to those records, he said, "We have someone who works at the hospital. While I was trying to figure out the best way to approach you without sounding like a lunatic, you two were evicted from your apartment, and I lost you again."

His hands balled up into fists and tapped his thighs once before flattening out again.

"I felt it strong a couple of months ago when you and your brother walked through Caesar's Palace.

When you left, I followed you," Joe said, sounding and looking apologetic at the confession.

He was not ignorant of the intrusiveness of his actions and that made me like him more. It was nice to have someone acknowledge civil boundaries in regards to me, even if he had crossed them.

For a moment, Joe cast his beautiful eyes toward the thick carpet and I could give him a close look without him seeing. He was clean-shaven. I got a whiff of what must be his soap. It was kind of musky, but not strong enough to be cologne. Trying not to be obvious, I breathed in through my nose. He smelled so clean and so good. I found myself leaning in his direction. As soon as I recognized my embarrassing position, I sat back.

The movement aggravated the soreness in my back and nipped at my dignity. Still, I couldn't stop myself from looking. When my covert inspection stopped at Joe's lips and thoughts played in my mind where I could not afford a playground, I shifted my gaze upward.

A small scar about the size of a jellybean marred the skin just above his right temple. Even that attracted me, for somehow I knew he'd earned it through nobility. I glanced at his strong body and wondered if there were other scars. Yes, yes, there were, I knew suddenly. Or, maybe I'm crazy, and he is, too.

I thought of the first time I'd seen him, when he caught me credit hustling. I was leery, afraid of what might happen to me, but I'd never actually *feared* Joe. When I'd met him for the second time, the day he'd invited me for coffee, I *had* felt his presence before I'd seen him. I remembered how my head turned toward him, like a dial tuning into a radio station. My intuition wanted me to go to him, and I'd fought it. Well, I'd fought it with loose fists.

"That's how I knew you were living in the storm drains. I wanted to get you two out of there in the worst way, but you wouldn't have believed anything I said. You weren't ready. All I could do was watch and wait. The next day I transferred here, to the Desert Star. I figured since this place is so much closer, you'd come here more often. My boss thought I was nuts," he said with a half-smile that was adorable. "I told him I needed a change, but the truth was I wanted to be closer to you."

Joe's words left the girly part of me pleased. From there I turned ashamed at the joy over such a silly, superficial feeling. For a person living my life it was inappropriate and wasteful. With the mountain of troubles before me, I had no right to the frivolities of sweet talk. Still, I felt it. Worse yet, I liked it.

"I knew you were like us, but there's more to it than that," Joe said. "I haven't been able to stop thinking about you, and not just because of our abilities. You touch something inside of me, the likes of which I've never experienced. You're in me, Liz. I'm only saying so because, I think you feel it too."

He looked at me in a deep way and I could feel him voyage into my mind again. It frightened me, but at the same time, my mind grasped for his, like a hand that needed holding.

At my continued silence, Joe said, "You do feel it, don't you? You thought about me for a long time after we met."

That was true, but I was reluctant to admit it. And

as I'd already scolded myself for indulging in wasteful whimsy, I moved on to things that mattered.

"What is that thing down there?" I asked.

For a moment, disappointment flickered in his eyes, dimming the light I wanted to believe shined for me. I wondered if Joe regretted speaking his heart. I was a jerk for being so rude. Staying on track, though, I had to hold onto that, for my sake as well as Jacob's.

I couldn't drift into the lure of romance no matter the want. I had to take care of so many things before even thinking of such pleasures. Maybe someday. I gave an inward sigh. My 'maybe someday' container was the only thing in my life that was full.

Following my deliberate change of subjects, Joe gathered himself. After all, he too had matters of more importance that required his focus.

In answer to my question, Joe said, "You know what that thing is."

He was right. I did know, but I wanted him to tell me I was wrong. Since it soon became obvious he wouldn't, I said, "All the evils of mankind."

"It is the embodiment of all of the evils of mankind."

"That thing lives because we are flawed?"

"It's not our mistakes that live and breathe and carry on. We believe it is the intentional, the deliberate malice." Joe took a deep breath, then, and let it out. "There's some evidence that benevolence has a retarding effect. That's something."

I nodded. "…Do you think someday that thing will be able to leave the storm drains and come out into the real world?"

"Yes," Joe said without hesitation. "I think it's

getting close to that point. I'm sure you've felt it. Have you seen it developing into something more than a living shadow?"

I thought of its teeth, some of which looked like knife tips. I recalled what sounded like wet, bare feet slapping on the cement floor of the tunnel in awkward turns as it learned to walk. It was building itself into something more proficient, something that, if it progressed, would fill top secret, government files with its accomplishments. It didn't matter if I had not wanted to know any of this. I already did.

"Yes," I said. "It doesn't have to stay on the wall anymore. It can walk."

"It's walking?"

"Yes. I didn't see it walk, but I heard it. It can walk and it can swim. If it can't come out in the sun yet, it soon will." As he'd said, I knew this. "Joe, what happens when it can come out of the tunnels?"

Joe said nothing. He kept looking at me as if I was supposed to know.

And I did.

Evil would do what evil does; destroy everything that's good.

"Can it be stopped?"

I asked the question, but I already knew the answer to that, too. Maybe Joe was telling the truth, some things I know by way of feeling. Maybe it had always been that way for me and I assumed it was like that with everyone so I didn't pay it much attention. Silly me, thinking anything about my life could be normal.

"It's developed further than we thought," Joe said. "But I think it can be stopped, by you."

It was like listening to Benny again. The very idea

was ridiculous. I am nobody. Joe was making it sound like I had some sort of superpower, like a comic book hero. I don't. I had been face to face with it and could do nothing but stare before running away.

Joe spoke the truth. I don't know how I was so sure, but I *was* sure. That truth terrified me.

As my future unfurled, like a Venus fly trap sensing imminent death, I said, speaking fast, as if that would change the course of my destiny, "Why not you? Why not any of the others you told me about?"

"You're the strongest. Before you, your father was the strongest."

My words stumbled over my shock and made me doubt everything Joe had just said to me. My father's strengths were in drinking and womanizing.

"My father? My father was a drunk."

"The man you knew, Sam Linden, the man you grew up with, that man was a drunk. But he wasn't your father. You…I'm sorry. I…I assumed you knew, that you had a strong sense of…I'm sorry."

Anger flashed through me, resentment at Joe's highhanded knowledge of things I had never been brave enough to face, hadn't even the courage to acknowledge. "How would you know such a thing?"

His mouth opened to speak, but the words faltered and the sympathy on his face was as galling as the facts. It was true. He was right. I did know it.

I knew I was the result of my mother's infidelity. The truth had always been there, cowering behind all the clutter in my life. Always I had refused to look, to admit it. I'd never given the thought time to fester. Dad was a crappy father, but he was mine, my connection to the past, my lineage. Except he wasn't.

My vision blurred. Joe got up and walked into the bedroom where I had slept. He returned a moment later with a box of tissues. He set them on the table in front of me.

I slid a tissue from the box and held it against my running eyes with both hands, trying not to cry. I didn't want to break down like this, not in front of him, not over something so very personal.

The soft pad of Joe's footsteps on the thick carpeting registered on the fringe of my thoughts as he walked behind the couch. A moment later, his hands were on my shoulders, warm and caring, kneading, working at the mounds of stress coiled between my battered flesh and weary bones.

"I'm sorry," he said. "Since I'd felt it so strongly I assumed you did too."

On two occasions, in a state of sloppy drunkenness, my mother had told me straight out I was a mistake she'd made on a crazy night out with the girls. I ignored it, chalked it up to her cruel streak enhanced by alcohol. As was often the case when she drank, the truth had danced past her lips.

Whenever those words came around to gnaw at me I told myself it was my father who she took up with that night. He'd gotten her pregnant with me and then they got married. At some point I'd become convinced of it.

Voicing the direction of my thoughts, Joe said, "Jacob is still your brother, well, your half-brother. But you two are blood."

Like the hands kneading my shoulders, the words soothed me where I needed it most. Half or full, he was *my* brother. "I don't want Jacob to know," I said to Joe.

"Okay."

"Was Dad…Sam, Jacob's father?"

"No. Your mother discovered it on one of Jacob's hospital stays. I don't know who his biological father is."

I wondered if my mother knew who fathered her second child. I wondered if she'd ever made the same vicious confession to my brother she'd made to me.

Jacob had never said anything. Maybe, like me, he wove pretty themes into our mother's ugly stories, trying to forge a nicer life out of the mess she'd dealt us. Then I wondered if my mother's words were what paved the way to Jacob's drug and alcohol abuse.

I wish our mother were alive so I could rant at her for all the ways she screwed up our lives.

"I don't want my brother to know," I repeated. Such a burden could tip Jacob over the edge on which he was so often perched.

"I won't say anything. It should be a consolation that, if your real father knew about you, he would have taken responsibility for you. He was a good and decent man."

"He's a good and decent man who had a one night stand with my mother." Even if I'd wanted, I couldn't have strained the sarcasm from my words.

Joe's hands stopped moving, but remained on my shoulders. His fingers tightened. Not enough to be painful, but I got the message.

"No one is perfect. He was carrying a lot of weight on his shoulders. Because he believed he had the ability destroy that thing, he never stopped worrying he would fail in his efforts, and the world would suffer because of his failure."

Joe was passionate in his defense of the man who

had sired me. Maybe my father truly had been a good man. They must have been very close. Jealousy roughed up my pride with a harshness to which I should have long ago become immune. So often I've wished I could shun all my emotions and feel nothing.

"If he'd have known she was pregnant," Joe continued. "He never would have walked away."

"What makes you so sure he was my father?"

Obviously, Joe knew things, but he couldn't know everything and that was a stretch even for someone with extraordinary intuition.

Joe began his gentle massage again. Strong hands, aware, control of the pressure so he wouldn't hurt me. His thumbs worked on the tightness in my neck and my shoulders. It was heaven.

Wanting more physical from him played against what I *should* want. I was aware of that, even if I was ignoring it. The physical won out, though, with too much ease. I wasn't up to a fight, and for the moment, I didn't care. I leaned into Joe's hands, wanting more of the blissful relief, more of the human touch.

Joe spoke while he massaged. "When you were in Caesars Palace that day, I sensed your father's presence before I even saw you. It was strong. Because I was closer to you then, it was even stronger than at the parade. Except for the hair color you look so much like him it was undeniable. His eyes, his nose, even the way you look at me when you're aggravated."

I could hear a touch of humor in his voice when he said that last part. His gentle teasing would have amused me had I been in a state of mind to be amused.

"Also," Joe continued. "I knew because I feel his nobility in you, feel it strongly, like I always did with him."

"What's his name?" I asked.

"Dean Coulter."

Dean Coulter. I'd never heard the name. My curiosity grew, as did a hope I should know better than to indulge. Regardless of what some may think of people like me who live with less comfort o the average American pet, I was still in possession of basic human needs. If what Joe said was true, then maybe I had a father who would care about me.

"Where is he now?" I asked, twisting around so I could look up at Joe's face.

His hands stilled, keeping a steady grip on my shoulders as if to give comfort, or maybe take some. A painful memory spread from Joe's eyes to the rest of his face and the faint lines of aging barely creasing his skin grew deeper. It was as if a horrible past was dragging him back and he had to fight to stay in the moment.

For almost a full minute Joe would not look at me. Then he walked around the couch and sank back into the chair. Disappointment bashed me before he said the words I knew were coming.

"He's dead. He died two years ago, fighting one of those things."

"There are more of them?"

That statement struck me more than the loss of my father. The man was someone I never knew. Up until a few minutes before, I didn't even know *about* him, not really. Dean Coulter was little more than another dashed hope, and one I hadn't held long enough to treasure.

More of those things, though, more of those shadows that were becoming…becoming much more.

That was something I could relate to, and fear.

"None of them have ever developed as much as this one." He turned his head then, and muttered in awesome fear, "It's walking."

"How many are there?" I asked, even though I wasn't sure I wanted to know.

"We don't know, exactly. But their numbers are growing. Every few months now, we get a new report. They exist in storm drains all over the country, probably all over the world. With the exception of this one, they're all still shadows as far as we know."

More of them. A chill crawled up my arms at the thought. "I still don't know what you expect me to do about it."

Joe stood, but he did not turn to leave. I had to tilt my head far back to look him in the eye. Again, I was taken aback of his size, and the fact that I had no fear of him.

"You have enough to think about right now. We'll talk about that later."

"I want to talk about it now."

Staring up at Joe was akin to staring up at a mighty oak and put me at a disadvantage, so I stood too. I did my best to ignore the protests of my many aches and pains.

"You need to rest…"

"What am I supposed to do about that thing? What is it you think I *can* do?"

"I don't know," he said, the words rushing out. With a more halted flow, he said, "I know that's a lousy answer, but it's all I have. Your father believed he could figure it out. He believed when faced with it, he would know."

"But he didn't figure it out. He died!" Could Joe not see the idiocy?

"Yes," he said in a muted tone. "He died."

I took a breath before speaking again. "Did he even have a clue?"

"He told me once he felt there had to be some sort of sacrifice, though he didn't know what, and his own fear was its weapon. He was certain about those two things." Joe shook his head. "I don't know how anybody could go down into those tunnels to fight that thing and not be afraid."

"It would be impossible."

"Right."

"But my father still went after it."

"He did," Joe said, nodding, yet saying nothing more.

My biological father was either heroic or foolish. I had to lean toward foolish. "Was it here in Las Vegas, where my father died?"

"Yes. I was with him." Without realizing it, I think, Joe touched the scar at his temple.

The torment constricting Joe's voice was unmistakable and I understood then that while my father had died an honorable death, it was also a terrible one.

"What was he like?" I asked, sitting down. I wanted to continue to stand, but my aching legs bore a weakness that had already granted as much standing as I was going to get.

Joe sat back down, his gaze directed at me when he spoke.

"He was a good man, strong and brave. Doing the right thing was his nature. Before accepting his lot in life, he'd been a police officer. But even then, Dean knew. Since he was a child, growing up near the storm drains, he'd sensed it, knew it was dangerous. That's what he told me. As a teen, he wanted to do something about it. Like you, though, he didn't know what he *could* do.

"That day, like the others when we'd gone down there, he walked into the storm drain with a flashlight, a gun, a knife, and a mission. You should know neither of the weapons did him any good. I don't know if they would now, since that thing has changed. Maybe it's become more vulnerable to guns and knives, but maybe not. We don't know. Your father died a mile or two from where you and Jacob set up camp."

"But how…" I began, and then stopped. I turned my head. Jacob was standing in the doorway of his room. How much had he heard? I looked at his face, surrounded by mussed hair that was too long. Beneath the blond whiskers on his face was the solemn mask I always wore, the one that gave nothing away.

Jacob had always been an open book, at least to me. Even when he was sneaking around I knew when he was up to something. I think that's because a little bit of the child in him never grew up, the portion of unpolluted innocence we're all born with that he'd somehow managed to maintain through all our troubles, until now.

This new level of maturity in my brother inflicted a profound sadness on my heart.

Jacob walked into the room and sat down on the couch next to me. His hand closed over mine. I hope he hadn't heard our conversation.

"I'm sorry I didn't believe you about the monster,"

Jacob said.

He'd heard. He knew everything. I squeezed his hand, my brother, my family. "It's okay, Jacob. Who wants to believe such a thing, especially when we live down there?"

"Lived," said Joe, emphasizing the past tense. "You don't live there anymore." His tone had changed, became as big and hard as his stature, and he didn't sound open to debate.

"We'll find another place to live," I said. I could never repay Joe for what he'd done for us, but I wouldn't be indebted for more.

"This suite is for you to stay. People who support us have already paid for it, and they'll continue to do so. Some of them have a lot of money and know where it's best used. They understand what will happen to the world if we don't find a way to stop this."

"I still don't understand what it is you expect me to do." My voice rose a degree with frustration.

Joe looked away from me. I think because he didn't want me to know yet.

"Tell me," I said. "Tell me now, or we're leaving."

He cast a meaningful gaze on me. He understood I meant what I said. I didn't doubt Joe intended to be honest. He didn't want to frighten me.

"It'll take a few days for the tunnels to dry out. When they do, we'll go in."

"You want us to go back?" Jacob said.

His outrage was understandable after what we'd been through down there. He lifted an inch or two off the couch. Jacob flinched, grabbing a muscle in his thigh before sitting back down. Joe saw it, but did not insult him by remarking.

I wanted to laugh it off, like Joe was crazy and his story of monsters in the storm drains the product of a wild imagination. Joe turned back to me and our gazes locked. Denying his stories would mean I'd have to deny mine.

I knew I would go then, that I had to, and it made me want to stomp my feet and cry.

I was not the man who fathered me. I wasn't brave; I wasn't even adventurous. All I wanted to do was make a normal life for me and my brother. Those very words sat parked on the tip of my tongue, engines revving wild before becoming quiet and succumbing to fate.

Maybe I did carry some of my biological father in me, because I knew with such utter clarity I could not walk away. In my mind, I saw it, dozens, then hundreds, then thousands of those dark, slimy monsters. They would invade cities and towns, devouring everything good that crossed their paths until all the world was nothing but a cauldron of fat, slithering evil.

"I have to go back down there." I said it to Joe, but I said it for Jacob. I was stunned at my own words and glad I was already sitting down.

"Liz, no, you can't be serious!"

"Jacob…"

"No, Liz. We almost died in those tunnels. That thing isn't afraid of you. It was coming after us!"

"What happens if I don't go? Jacob, think. It'll get stronger. It'll come out into the world. Once that happens we won't be safe anywhere anyway."

This gave Jacob pause. In his usual style he hadn't thought that far ahead, had not bothered to connect the dots from now to the future. At my words, he did so.

The progression was clear on his face. My little brother had not become such a closed book after all.

Jacob turned to Joe. "It's all true, isn't it?"

"Yes, it's true," said Joe. He leaned back in the chair then, giving Jacob time to think.

Eventually, those things would take over the world. We wouldn't be safe anywhere. No one would. Jacob must have been picturing it. His face sagged as anger and fear gave way to despair.

"It'll come after us. We'll die anyway," Jacob said. Acceptance drained his voice of defiance.

"Yes," Joe said.

For a moment, I worried Jacob would break down and cry. He didn't. With a fair amount of dignity, he managed to stand. His stiff legs carried him to the window. He stared outside, his back was to me and I couldn't read his face.

I said to Joe, "What about the others that are developing? How can we get them all if they're all over the world?"

"Your father believed this one is the leader, and they are all somehow connected to the one here in Vegas. That this one is so far developed gives credence to his belief. Dean thought if we killed the one here before it's full-fledged, the others would die."

"You don't know that for sure," I said.

"We don't know for sure," Joe conceded. "It's just a theory. That thing wasn't as developed then. Maybe Dean would feel different now. We don't know what capabilities the future generations hold. What we do know, thanks to you, is this one is getting close to ready to leave the tunnels. We have to stop it."

Jacob turned from the window to face us. His

features firmed. I swear my brother was growing into a man right before my eyes.

"Then that's what we have to do," Jacob said.

"Not you, Jacob," I told him.

"If you go, I go."

"Jacob, no…"

"If you go, I go," he repeated. He limped over to the couch and sat beside me, took my hand, and squeezed. "We take care of each other, always."

The passion with which he spoke made me want to cry. We were family. There was only the two of us, but we were as much a family as any other, more so than many. We would never set out to harm each other, and either of us would die to protect the other. *Family*.

Joe stood up. "We'll wait a few days. It'll give you two a chance to rest and to heal, and to get back your strength. In the meantime, the tunnels will dry out. You both need to put on some weight. There's a menu on the table over there, Jacob. I already told your sister, order whatever you want from room service. Everything is covered, even the tips. So don't worry about the cost."

"Oh," Joe added, nodding toward the door where sat several shopping bags.

"I bought some clothes for you. I used the tags in your old clothes to figure out what sizes to buy. In a couple of days, I'll arrange for you to go to the mall and you can pick out things for yourself. You'll need more than what I got for you. I'll be back at six. We can eat dinner here, or go out if you two feel up to it. We'll talk more then."

He stood up, slipped a hand into his pocket, and took out several business cards, which he set on the table. They were simple, plain white, flat black lettering with his name and a phone number.

"You can call me at this number anytime for any reason."

With that, Joe left. Jacob and I sat quiet for a while. Thoughts ran through our heads for a long time before they were organized enough to put into words.

And then my brother and I talked.

Chapter 12

The shopping shouldn't have been fun, not with what lie ahead of us. But it was the most fun we'd had in an awful long time. We had plenty of cash as well as a credit card with a limit far exceeding our needs, and I would not take advantage. I was proud Jacob felt the same. Lately, he was maturing by the minute.

Buying new clothes did make us both feel wonderful. Dressed in the new clothes Joe bought, showered and with fresh haircuts, the people in the stores treated us like normal people. Store clerks did not stare at us, semi-covertly as they so often did, as if we were about to steal something. We could browse, and we could try things on, laugh and joke around with each other, like everybody else in the mall.

We stuck to simple shirts and shorts, a couple pairs of jeans, pajamas and another pair of shoes. Even with the card, I shopped for discounted items. Buying things on sale was a good habit, one I intended to keep.

It had been three days since we'd escaped death at the mouth of the tunnel. Our bodies healed faster than I had expected. I suppose an endless supply of healthy food and ample rest is to credit. Being able to sleep in safety didn't hurt either. I hadn't realized how often I awoke in our concrete camp to scan the darkness for something darker.

The last couple of days, Jacob and I did nothing but

lay around the suite, eating, napping, and watching movies. They were, without a doubt, the most wonderful, self-indulgent days of my entire life.

Joe stopped by often, checking on us, making sure we had everything we needed, and more. His kindness was sincere, and remarkable in its abundance. With each visit, I found myself growing more and more fond of him. I could no longer deny he had become my first real crush. It's silly, I knew, but I couldn't help it.

When I knew Joe was coming, I made sure I combed my hair and brushed my teeth.. That was less embarrassing than it was exciting. I was finally getting a taste of what other girls took for granted.

Joe made me feel like a normal woman, even in such abnormal circumstances. When he was near, my heart was exhilarated, and desirous. Sometimes when he looked at me, I could swear he felt the same.

Once when he stopped by to see us, Jacob was napping in his room. For a while, Joe and I talked about things hollow of any real relevance. I enjoyed that. It had been a long time since I'd had a normal conversation with anyone but my brother, and I'd forgotten how nurturing it was to my mind and to my spirit. I also realized how necessary it was in order to feel connected to the big, wide world that existed outside the confines of my fight for survival.

Or maybe I hadn't forgotten. Maybe, no, there was no maybe about it. What I loved, what I craved more of, was this life I'd never known beyond daydreams, planted in my head by television shows that were pure fantasy to me.

During the first stages of our talk, I'd kept the details of my family to myself. Joe was already aware of Jacob's problems, but by virtue of his youth, my brother deserved some forgiveness. My parents were heartless screw-ups and my relation to even one of them embarrassed me. What Joe already knew was more than enough.

Then he told me about growing up in foster homes since the age of twelve after his father had murdered his mother. His father got himself killed that same day in a shootout with the police. Joe had witnessed it all.

He told me what a brute his father had been to both of them and how for a long time afterward he would get angry with his dead mother for not having been strong enough to take her son and leave. Then he would get mad at himself for getting angry with her. Sometimes he still grappled with his feelings, and often felt shame for it.

After he told me all that, I was as open with Joe as he was with me. It was so good to talk without fear he would judge me by my roots.

That night, I walked Joe to the door of the suite and we said goodbye. He didn't leave though, not right then.

We stood there looking at each other, less than two feet of empty space between us. He leaned toward me, just a little. His eyes drifted toward my lips. For a moment, I was sure he would kiss me. I believe he was thinking about it. He paused, and then I felt his uncertainty claim my moment.

Maybe he thought it would scare me off, or I would be offended if he kissed me. His intuition should have told him he couldn't have been more wrong.

I closed the door behind him, both thrilled and disappointed. That night I fell asleep dreaming Joe *had* kissed me. In the morning, I was still happy because even though I hadn't gotten my first kiss from my first crush, I'd almost forgotten what it was like to have a good dream.

Yes, even with all that lay ahead of us those had been the most wonderful days Jacob and I ever had. For in that moment nothing was an issue. Food and shelter were a given. We'd had more extras than we had ever known, even before we became homeless.

At first, when the young man from room service wheeled our food in on a silver cart, I felt strange about it, like I was a fraud, an impostor sneaking around with somebody else's identity. I half expected him to call me on it and toss us out. He was so nice, though, so happy to be doing for us.

It was the same when the maids rolled their carts in to clean our room, which was very strange to me. Everybody was working so hard to make us comfortable. After spending a lifetime in poverty, and the last year living in the storm drains, it was a little bewildering. I knew better than to get used to it.

Sitting in the food court at the mall, looking and feeling like everybody else who had eaten whatever they wanted, was wonderful. We didn't even play 'next time I'm getting that' when a tray with something tasty passed by us, for we could have it right then if we wanted. We had that option.

No millionaire ever felt as rich as Jacob and I did that day at the mall, with all choices of food at our will, and shopping bags full of our new belongings at our feet.

Jacob stuffed the last bite of mega-sandwich into his mouth. He used a napkin to give a thorough wiping to his hands before digging into his pocket. He slipped out the smart phone Joe had given us, and was so patient in teaching us to use.

"Should I call for the car now?" he asked.

He was so near to giddy with anticipation, it inspired a bright spark of bliss for me. As much as we'd enjoyed shopping for all of our brand new things, I think Jacob had been looking forward to that moment all day.

Several times, I'd seen him dip into his pocket to touch the cell phone. Neither of us ever had one before. It had always been a luxury far beyond consideration. Sitting there holding it, wearing new clothes and a fresh haircut, my brother looked happy, normal, and healthy. My heart ached with joy.

I glanced down at the bags surrounding us. We had plenty. We even had extra shoes, which Joe insisted on even after I told him one new pair each was enough. After checking off the things we'd gotten, including plenty of new socks and underwear, I nodded at Jacob. He tapped and slid his finger on the screen with a reverence bordering on comical.

I wasn't any better. Earlier I'd made a stop at the bathroom when I didn't even have to go. I just wanted to see my hair again. Joe had made appointments for us both at the salon right there at the hotel. They'd treated us like movie stars. By the time we left, with a bag full of products and lessons in using them, I felt like one.

There was a blow dryer in the bathroom at the hotel, but still, I allowed myself the splurge of buying a curling iron and a few cosmetics. With my new haircut and some make-up on, I couldn't help but enjoy flipping my waves, indulging in a bit of vanity. Beach curls, the lady at the salon called them. They bounced clean and soft with fresh cut ends.

Jacob's extra treat was a hand-held video game he found in a clearance bin. My first instinct was to tell him no. Eventually the batteries would die and that would get expensive. I didn't have the heart. Nor, after my own silly splurges, did I have the right.

Sitting here steeped in newness and normalcy, I was glad I had allowed us each those indulgences. Tomorrow we were going back into the tunnels. As much as I'd have liked to deny it, to lean on ignorance I did not possess, I understood there was a fair chance we might not be coming back out.

Chapter 13

My eyes were open long before the sun could light a glow around the pretty drapes in my room. I stared into the darkness where I could see nothing beyond my wayward imagination. In my mind, against my wants, I was in the tunnels again facing that damp, black mass as it continued to evolve right before my eyes.

A shadow darker than Hell's basement, the dampness of the shadow as it shimmered and slithered along the walls of the tunnels. The demon glow of its eyes, the sharp points of its teeth, and its grin boasting smugness and ill intent.

Maybe seeing it in replay mode was my mind's way of desensitizing me to the terror that gripped me every time I thought about going back down there. It was a logical plan. However, it wasn't working.

Again, last night I did my best to talk Jacob out of going with us. He wouldn't budge on the issue. I was both proud and sick. My brother was not going to leave my side. While his chivalry gave me a great deal of comfort, I was still tempted to tie him to his bed while he slept. I smiled into the darkness and wondered if he had the same thoughts about me.

Joe told us two others would be joining us on the mission. Jacob and I hadn't met them yet, but Joe was confident in their abilities and assured me they would be an asset, as if I'd turn down help. While he was trying to convince me to accept them, all I kept thinking was 'thank goodness', and wishing there would be even more of us to go down there. An army would be good.

Over the last few days, thinking about my life, about my *intuition,* at some point I accepted my belief in what Joe had said. I had to.

At school, at work, in the tunnels, my intuition was always there guiding me with a strong yet gentle hand, even if I didn't realize it. In fact, the times in my life when I'd made my own trouble were the times I had not listened to my intuition. As I said before, I assumed it was like that for everyone. The knowledge that I was different made me feel as special as it did cursed.

I still had powerful doubts in regards to my being able to do anything about that monster. It's one thing to have a bad feeling about a guy I'd meet and not allow myself to be alone with him, but to destroy a monster no one even understood was all together something else.

I truly didn't know what I would do when face-to-face with it. Joe, however, had a tremendous amount of confidence in me. I tried, and to a point was successful in letting his beliefs bolster what little confidence I had in myself. Just when I felt as if I was gaining ground, another thought kicked me back; maybe we are all fools.

When the sun nudged me with a gentle glow, I sat up and stretched. My plan had been to sleep in this day, get as much rest as possible before the mission. That wasn't going to happen. It was better to get up and sort my thoughts, to make peace with my destiny before my fears distracted me.

While my legs carried me to the shower, my mind

took on that hearty task. I suppose I was as successful as I could hope to be.

After dressing in my new clothes, I put on a touch of makeup and styled my hair in a simple fashion. I didn't want to appear as if I was trying to look nice, even though I was. Then I walked over to Jacob's room to check on him. He was still asleep. Joe wouldn't be here for another hour and a half, so I left Jacob alone and hoped he was having a pleasant dream.

I spent the next twenty minutes standing at the window and gazing out at the Las Vegas Strip. The sight was mesmerizing. Morning lay a golden, storybook blanket over the long line of exotic resorts, creating a vision more suited to a city in a fairy tale than Sin City.

I considered the oddness, as I stared down at the town from this beautiful hotel suite. Apparently, there was no middle ground for me. I'd lived beneath the city, now I live above it. I've hustled credits for money to eat, and now people delivered food to me on silver trays, free of charge.

A few days before, I wanted nothing more than to have a job and a halfway decent apartment for my brother and me, such a simple goal. Now, what I wanted most is for my brother and me to live through the day.

"Hey, earth to Liz."

I turned at the sound of Jacob's voice. Mussed hair topped his head and he was bundled in his big white fluffy robe. There was a sheet crease across his cheek. He yawned and grinned at me.

"You were really off in another world."

"Sorry."

"I'd ask what you were thinking about," Jacob said as he took a seat at the smoked glass table. "But I'm pretty sure I can guess."

I left the window to take the chair across from him. "You don't have to go, Jacob. No one will think any less of you. In fact, you could be a distraction to me."

Leaning forward on his elbows he said, "Like I distracted you when that gush of water knocked you off your feet?"

He didn't say it in the cutting, sarcastic tone of the boy I had always known. In fact, there was a touch of humor in his voice. He sounded more like a parent making a point to their developing child than a little brother getting the better of his big sister.

My mind turned back to our last day in the tunnel, how Jacob had taken charge when my raging panic caused me to be unreasonable. My brother had an emotional growth spurt that day. Maybe it had begun earlier and I hadn't noticed his gradual change, as my focus had been on survival.

I laughed. I couldn't help it. He was right. Had Jacob not been there with me, without a doubt I would have died. He saved my life and there was no rational reason to think he couldn't do it again.

"Why don't you go jump in the shower," I told him. "I'll order up some breakfast. What do you want?" I wasn't hungry, but I had to eat. I would make sure Jacob ate too. Maturing or not, he is still my little brother.

On a big yawning stretch he said, "I'm feeling oatmeal today."

"Oatmeal it is; and fruit."

He laughed on his way back to his room and

glanced at me over his shoulder. "Yes, Mom, and fruit."

About ten minutes after we finished our breakfast, there was a knock on the door. It was Joe. I knew it. I knew it sounded funny to say I recognized his knock, but I did. Or maybe, as he'd said about me, as I had that day in the casino, I sensed his presence.

Jacob opened the door and Joe entered, saying hello to both of us. He was dressed in jeans, a dark blue T-shirt and blue Nike's. I'd never seen him in casual dress before. Somehow, he managed to look even better than he did in his fancy suit, or maybe it's that dressed more like me, he didn't look quite so unattainable.

He had an army-green backpack slung over one shoulder and he had two smaller versions of the same backpack in his hands, which he set on the carpet near the door.

Following him into the suite were two other men, also wearing backpacks. One looked to be in his early twenties, but he had such a baby face he could be older and not show it. At about five foot eight, he carried at least an extra twenty or so pounds. He had full, ruddy cheeks and dark blond hair he wore in a bowl cut. With a Star Wars T-shirt stretched across his soft body and a meek uncertainty about him, he looked more like the target of a bully than a tunnel warrior. But then again, who was I to talk?

The other man looked exactly like what I had expected. Late thirties with the air and manner of a man long steeped in soldier training. Before he had even come all the way into the suite his ice-blue eyes made a complete scan of the room, and of us, I'm sure looking for possible dangers. I didn't take it personally. I got the impression if he walked into a nursery school he'd do the same thing.

He was tall, well over six feet, broad across the shoulders. He wore his salt and pepper hair in a neat buzz cut. His features were rugged and sun-stamped, his body solid. I doubt there was a smidgeon of fat on him.

With the sleeves torn off, his faded black T-shirt displayed arms boasting of muscled power and dark with tattoos. I didn't want to stare at his ink, so I just glanced long enough to see a skull or two. There was a white bandage wrapped around about four inches of his left forearm and I could see a couple of pinkish spots where blood was starting to seep through.

"Liz, Jacob" Joe said. He nodded to the younger of our teammates. "This is Augie." Nodding to the tough-looking guy Joe said, "And this is Cake. Cake is an expert in weapons and tactics. Augie's talents lie in his knowledge of the supernatural and other such things. They're both like us, Liz, in that their intuition is superb.

"Thank you for coming with us," I said to them both.

"Actually," Augie said. "*Thank you.* We've been planning this mission for a while. I feel a lot better about it now."

I was humbled, and at the same time, I wanted to apologize. I didn't know if I would be any help to them. I may in fact, become a hindrance. I don't have their knowledge or talents. If it weren't for the brave actions of my little brother, and then Joe, I wouldn't even be here now to doubt myself. I worried my ineptitude might get them all killed.

"We all have our doubts about our abilities," Augie

said, looking at me with kindness and understanding.

His hazel eyes appeared rather small in the plump surface of his face, but they were warm and without guile. Augie was going to be easy to like. He smiled then and raised one eyebrow. His bottom teeth were a little crooked and the tops ones were perfectly straight.

"Well," Augie amended. Except for Cake, that is. He has enough confidence for all of us."

Cake didn't agree or disagree. The only sign he gave of even hearing the statement was a very slight lift to the right corner of his lips.

Jacob stared at the dangerous-looking guy and said, "You don't look like a Cake."

A slow grin split Cake's face. The brackets around his mouth multiplied, as did the creases around his eyes until they met in the middle of his sunbaked cheeks. "It's not the name I was born with. I gave it to myself back in high school. It was a good way to get guys to pick a fight with me."

Joe, Jacob, and I laughed. Augie shook his head at Cake's confession, but he was smiling too. Like he'd heard this before and it still amused him.

Jacob asked, "How many times did some joker call you Cupcake?"

Cake raised his eyebrows and glanced at his fists with a rascal's gleam that took the chill off his eyes. "I'm surprised the skin on my knuckles could grow back so many times."

Everybody laughed. For a man whose initial impression was of a person who couldn't have a sliver of a funny side, Cake sure had a good sense of humor. However, when his smile faded his face formed back to the hard look of a man who, should he deem it necessary, could kill you with little effort and less conscience. Under any other circumstance, I would avoid a guy like this. Today I was happy to see him, happy he was on our side.

"Have you guys gone down there before? Have you felt or seen it?" Jacob asked.

"Yes," Cake said. "Augie and I have both felt the thing, but we haven't seen it since it was a shadow. But I may have found a way to track it."

"How?" I asked.

"That feeling it gives off, you know, that electric kind of tingling on your skin? I used a sander to scrape a couple layers of skin off my forearm this morning," Cake said, raising his left arm, the one with the stained white bandage. "I'll take this wrapping off when we get down there. I'm thinking my skin will be more sensitive to its presence."

Jacob and I stared at the bandage and I'm sure he was thinking the same thing I was. That is one tough guy, to scrape two layers of skin off his arm to turn his body into a tracking device. I was impressed, and a little sickened.

"Does anybody have even a clue as to what we can do when we find it?" I asked. I didn't know what Joe had told them, but it was best they knew I didn't.

The men all glanced at each other before turning to look at me. They didn't have to say it. They all thought I would have some ideas on what to do. I don't. I don't. I wanted to scream that at them. I wanted to chicken out, grab my brother, and run. I did none of those things.

They were risking their lives as much as we were and we all understood why. While that thing *might* kill us today in the tunnels, it or one of its brethren eventually *would,* no matter where we were. As far as how we would kill the thing, well, we'd have to figure it out later. Maybe something would come to me. Maybe it worked that way.

Of course, it didn't work out that way for Dean Coulter, my biological father.

"Let's go," Cake said, opening the door. Augie followed him. I walked out behind Augie, Jacob behind me and Joe at the end.

Joe parked in a gully in the desert. Cake retrieved some things from the trunk. When I heard it slam shut, I glanced over at him. Over one shoulder laid a fat, green strap holding a long firearm. I know very little about guns, but I suppose it was an assault weapon of some sort. A handgun was in a holster at his side. A fierce looking knife balanced out the other. I'd bet Cake wore another weapon or two out of sight.

The rest of us shrugged into our backpacks, and we walked. A few minutes later, the five of us stood at the north entrance of the storm drains, the one Jacob and I had used a million times. I guess that day would make a million and one. I hoped the total of our exits would be equal.

Chapter 14

We'd been walking through the tunnels for a little over an hour when Cake suggested we take a break. I think he could have walked ten times more without so much as a pause. He did it for us and I was glad.

While I had regained much of my strength over the last few days, apparently I was not back to normal. The ache in my legs was more a reminder than a hindrance. The weakness, however, was something to which I was not accustomed and it concerned me.

I worried over Jacob. He seemed fine. But then again, to look at me I probably seemed fine too, as pride kept me from letting on. Augie was keeping up, though I think he was also glad for the break. In the quiet of the concrete tunnel, I could hear him breathing.

We sat along the wall, legs stretched out, and everybody had a drink of water from the bottles in our backpacks. Joe said there was food in there too, but nobody was hungry.

I thanked him for seeing to it we were so well equipped. My fears and worries had muted all thoughts of food, water, even flashlights. It shook me how I would have come down here so unprepared. Again, I felt utterly inept. If anything, my ineptitude kept deepening. That I would come down here without first thinking to bring even a flashlight was proof.

After we sat down, Jacob and I set our flashlights

on the floor beside our legs. Augie set his in his lap, never letting his hand lose touch. He clutched it like a security blanket. I got the feeling even at the best of times he was afraid of the dark.

While all our gazes made regular sweeps of the area, Augie's eyes darted about with no particular pattern. Often, his visual pouncing did not even stay within the beam of his flashlight. He wasn't accustomed to such lightless surroundings like Jacob and me. My heart went out to him. I thought Augie was the bravest of us all.

Cake adjusted well, moving about as if he did this sort of thing every day, with a methodical eye and great awareness. Joe looked far more the capable warrior than the casino suit. He kept his eyes on the tunnel the same way he did in the casino; keeping a casual yet disciplined watch for anything that wasn't normal.

"Do you sense anything?" Joe asked Cake, nodding toward his scraped arm, now exposed without the bandage.

Cake had removed the wrapping in the car right before we entered the tunnel and I had a good look. The self-inflicted injury was so raw it glowed. My skin ached at the sight of it. If Cake had pain, he didn't show it. In fact, it was as if the only thing that reminded him of his terrible abrasion was Joe's question.

Cake glanced at his arm, and then up and down the tunnel. "No, nothing," he said.

After a few minutes, I said, "Whenever you guys are ready." I had the feeling they were waiting on me.

We all got up and followed in what had become our pattern, Cake in front, then Augie, me, Jacob and Joe. We never walked side by side and I was exactly in the middle. That may have been coincidence, but I didn't think so. Whether by deliberate design or unspoken agreement, I think they were all trying to protect me.

The tunnels were mostly dry, but it smelled dank with plenty of signs of the flood that had been. Dirt that days before had rested on the desert floor made a sandpaper sound beneath our feet. Debris of all sorts was scattered here and there; beer and soda cans, boards washed away from some construction sight, plastic grocery bags lay about like deflated ghosts.

Occasionally we passed a clumped-up article of clothing and I wondered if it belonged to one of the subterranean residents, maybe someone we knew. It made me think about the other people who lived down here before the storm. Suddenly I was afraid of not only the monster, but of finding one of my neighbors who did not make it out.

At my request, when we first entered the storm drains we made a stop at our camp. I wanted to see if anything was salvageable. Nothing was. The place looked awful enough to make me regret our coming.

Our hard-won mattress was askew and had been so thoroughly soaked it still dripped water. The drops landed on the desert-encrusted floor and formed a muddy mess.

Our chest of drawers had tipped over and was five feet from where we'd left it. Strewn along with the rest of our belongings was one of our plastic crates, at least I thought it was ours, as well as some things I'd never seen before.

A child's yellow dump truck lay next to a large red tennis shoe and the sweatshirt I'd gotten for fifty cents at a yard sale. Several short boards and a thick cluster of desert scrub had washed against the wall and landed in a pyramid form, looking like a campfire waiting for a match. The top of the pile was dry, but the bottom was still dark with floodwater. A muddied white sock dangled from a branch. Our little home reeked of fouled water and loss.

Precious slices of our bread had come out of the torn bag and lay on the floor, buttered with filth. A tin can of something, maybe from our drawer, lay nearby. I didn't know what was inside. The label was gone so it was just silver, and dirty, like everything else in our retched little home.

Scanning the floor with my flashlight, I found my copy of Paper Moon lodged between a broken wine bottle and one of the buckets we'd used as a toilet. A clump of its own soggy pages lay beside it. My precious book looked gutted.

"Let's go," I said. "There's nothing here for us." And there never would be. Even if all ended well today, Jacob and I would never live here again. I sucked in a shaky breath. We would find a place. We always do.

No one minded if we stopped by Silvia's camp. We were on a search mission anyway. I didn't expect to find her there, but I had to make sure. Jacob seconded my request as soon as it was out of my mouth.

Silvia's home didn't look quite as bad as ours did simply because she had fewer things. There were small piles of clothing and a blanket lying around. They were still damp and they stunk of wet mess. A couple of beer bottles lay on the floor, along with a tube of lipstick. The cap was missing.

"I hope she's all right," Jacob murmured. I took his

hand and squeezed. He squeezed back.

"Is there anyone else you'd like to check on?" Joe asked.

Benny had left before the storm. I was sure Chester had made it out. Chester was always sober and alert. There were others we had a passing acquaintance with, but I didn't know where their camps were. Maybe we'd pass someone who had word of our friends. I didn't know what else we could do.

"No," I said.

The next hour passed in silence. We took another break. Cake insisted everyone eat something, hungry or not. From our backpacks, Jacob and I, like everyone else, ate half of a peanut butter and jelly sandwich. We saved the rest for later. Though nobody said it, making our food last was the second reason we ate only half. The first was because no one wanted to be too full to run at top speed.

We also found some apples and crackers in our packs. After another moment of exploration, I found a few granola bars, a small package of ginger snaps, and some dark chocolate squares individually wrapped. Jacob had some too. I looked up to see Joe smiling at us.

Joe said, "I know how you two like sweets."

"Thanks," I said, and nudged Jacob to do the same.

Beside me, Augie plowed into his pack. His hand flew out with some chocolates and the same little bag of cookies.

"Ha!" he said, waving it in the air and smiling bright like a child who'd found the prize in his box of cereal.

We all laughed. Augie and Jacob ate their cookies.

I had one dark chocolate square, but saved my cookies for a better stomach. When they were finished, Cake reminded everyone to drink more water and everyone did. Soon we were back to walking.

Moving through the tunnel after a little food and water, I got a second wind to energize me. Almost immediately, I worried about the source of that energy.

Maybe the buzz was due to the chocolate I'd just eaten. Or maybe it wasn't anything human-related at all. Maybe the buzz playing with my senses was something electrical, and alive.

I kept the worry to myself because I wasn't sure and I didn't want to look like a paranoid fool, be the girl who cried monster.

The fact was I didn't feel the same electrical current I did when I was near the shadow monster. This was more of a tingle I could maybe attribute to the caffeine in the chocolate, or fear, or even a chill from the leftover dampness in the tunnels. Likely, it was a combination. The feeling was so faint I couldn't even swear it was there.

It could be I wanted to get this over with and that meant the monster had to show itself, sort of wishful thinking, or rather, feeling. I told these things to myself as I tried with all my might to find some bravery within and elevate it above my dread.

Maybe my imagination was trying to liven up the monotony. Step after step after step took us through an all-encompassing night that was figurative, and the terrifying confines of a concrete tunnel that was not.

It may well have been these extreme circumstances were playing with my judgment. It wasn't a far-fetched scenario. After all, we were essentially waiting for a creature to attack, one that wanted to kill us. While I focused on identifying what I was feeling, I still kept my watch. The tension of waiting dragged on and the tingle that was too slight to mention continued to trouble me.

I'd never walked through these storm drains with so many others before. That alone made the feel in here different. We were moving, which meant the flashlights we all carried were also moving. Every once in a while, I wasn't sure if one of the shadows I saw traveling along the walls was from us.

Images of fluctuating darkness shifted at the corner of one eye and then the other. I swung my head back and forth, sometimes up, shining my light, trying to catch something that traveled just outside the beam. All this action of five people with lights was throwing me off. This shadow was Jacob's, that one, Cake's. A snake-like shadow slithered off to my right and I sucked in my breath. Was that Augie scratching his nose?

It didn't look like anyone else noticed anything. If Cake's scraped skin told him something was amiss, he did not pass on that information to the rest of us.

I made a few more passes with my flashlight across the ceiling when no one else did. I supposed I didn't see anything that didn't belong. For a moment, I felt better. Then a slight tingling rolled across my skin again, but I couldn't tell if it was electric monster or electric fear.

I was afraid, very much so, and maybe over-sensitive. I worried for Cake and Augie, with whom I already felt connected. I worried for Joe, who had taken up residence in my heart and in my life where I thought I had no room. I was worried sick for Jacob and I worried for myself. If the worst happened to me, what would become of my brother? The mingling of all this extended worry blended with the existing pack and confused the tactile aspect of my intuition.

I focused on my skin, on my physical feelings. But the crowd of shadows moving in my peripheral distracted my concentration, knowing one of them may not be a simple obstruction of light. Maybe I really am getting paranoid.

I shivered and hoped nobody saw. I had a chill. Yes, I was sure that was all it was…almost sure.

Cake and Augie forged the way in front of me, Jacob and Joe had my back. I was not alone. I would not fight this thing alone.

Odd as it sounds, for some reason the full impact of that, until that very moment, hadn't sunk into my way of thinking. After a lifetime of having virtually no one to depend on but myself, I supposed it should not have been surprising. Before this, to put in the hands of anybody else even a small portion of our well-being would have been foolish. Things weren't like that for us anymore. The realization settled me.

Crazy, but down here in the storm drains and in mortal danger, my chest tightened with wonderful, newborn emotions.

These men were not merely my allies in this mission; we were like a family. No, not *like* a family, I corrected, thinking of my cruel, selfish mother, and the drunkard she had me call dad. We *were* a family because we were what a family was supposed to be, partners in life, willing to sacrifice for each other, to do right by each other, having each other's backs.

Even Cake and Augie, who I'd only known for a

few hours, would risk their lives to protect Jacob and me. I felt that truth running through my cynical veins. *I knew it.* And I knew we would both do the same for them.

I was not alone. I was not alone. Those four words repeated in my head like a time-proven magic spell, and worked like one too.

We stopped at a crossroad. Everyone shined lights both ways, looking, listening, and trying to feel. The tunnels were identical in that they were both full of darkness too thick for our beams of light to penetrate very far. The flashlights we carried were far superior to the ones Jacob and I used to have. Still, even the upgrade had a limit as to how far it would shine through the dense darkness.

Cake held his scraped arm out in front of him, shifting it one way and then the other, much like a divining rod.

After a moment, Joe asked, "Does anybody have a take on which way we should go?"

"Left," Cake and I both said at the same time.

Everyone turned to look at me. I was as surprised as they were.

"I don't know why." I said with a lame shrug.

And I really didn't know why. It was as if the word had come from someone else, but as soon as I said it, I knew Cake and I were correct. Still, I was uncomfortable with everybody's eyes searching mine. They looked at me with too much confidence, waiting for answers I could not provide.

"Do you feel it?" Augie asked.

I shook my head and said, "No, I don't feel it, not for sure. I just think we should go left."

"Then left it is," said Joe without hesitation.

His belief in me was disconcerting. For one thing, no one had ever given me that kind of credit before and I didn't know how to handle it. Mostly, though, it was because I didn't want to be wrong. If I made a mistake, it would cost us all much more than my credit. I reminded myself Cake said left too. So why weren't they looking to him for answers?

As we all turned left at the crossway and started down the tunnel, Jacob said, "Hey, before we go on, I, um, need to take a leak."

Then Augie said, "Yeah, I could use a bathroom break too."

Pointing in the opposite direction in which we were heading, Joe said, "Jacob, Augie, you two go first. We'll stay here with Liz. When you come back, Cake and I will go." As the boys walked away, Joe looked at me with concern.

"It's okay, Joe," I said. "I'll go back a way. I'll be fine by myself for few minutes."

Joe paused a beat or two before he said, "I'm going with you. I'll turn my back,"

The very idea mortified me. Whether by intuition or likely the expression on my face, Joe read my feelings.

"Take Jacob, then."

"I'm not taking anyone with me, not for *that*." I was glad for the lesser illumination of three flashlights instead of five. I had to be blushing all the way to my toes.

Joe was displeased with my firm decision to go off all alone. Even in the dimness, I could see the frown lines deepen between his brows.

"Liz, this is no time to be concerned with modesty."

In the firm voice I'd often used on my little brother when he aggravated me with something outrageous, I said to Joe, "I'm going alone."

Joe looked as though he would argue with me. Instead, he turned his head, and then his body and walked away angry.

Cake stood a few feet away so I knew he heard. I thought he would argue with me, and try to force me to take someone. He didn't. Maybe he knew it was pointless. He was staring, though. The angles of his sharp features didn't budge. They thought I was being foolish. Maybe I was, but I only cared a little. I was going by myself. I refused even to think of doing otherwise.

A few minutes later Jacob and Augie returned. Jacob shot Joe a juvenile grin and said, "We used the left wall so stick to the right."

Joe chuckled through his aggravation. "Thanks for the tip."

Cake grinned at my little brother, too. Again, I was taken with how much his smile softened the life-roughened features imprinted on his face, exposing a tender side I'm sure not seen by many who had crossed his path.

Cake looked over at me and winked. The warmth in his expression touched my heart. He still thought I was being foolish, but he forgave me. Maybe it was because he'd acted foolish too, and he knew sometimes that's what you do. If I could have handpicked an older brother to keep for my own, Cake would be my choice.

After Joe and Cake left, I said to Jacob, "I can go

now, save time."

"No," Jacob said. "We should all be here, in case you need us."

"He's right," Augie said.

"I don't need you guys for that," I answered, with a fair amount of attitude.

They said nothing, but I waited anyway. From their point of view, they wanted backup in case I called out, or screamed.

When Joe and Cake returned, Joe took me aside and before I could repeat my refusal, he whispered in my ear. I was grateful he did not say aloud that in the pocket of my backpack I would find tissues and hand sanitizer. He might have been mad at me, but it didn't stop him from caring. *Family*. I nodded my thanks and left, blushing again.

A few minutes later, in my moment alone, I was battling a shy bladder, and then cursing it. No matter my insistence on wanting to be alone, I was afraid.

The anxiety of needing to hurry wasn't helping. If I took too long, the guys would come looking for me. While listening for their footsteps, I made a great effort not to think about that humiliating possibility. Instead, my mind turned to their motivation.

They would come looking for me because they cared for me. Still, I didn't want to be embarrassed. I closed my eyes, took a breath, and pretended I was in the bathroom back in our suite. I pictured the shiny white tile, imagined the pine-scent of the clean bathroom. It worked, thank goodness.

On my walk back, in an effort to keep my thoughts from dwelling on my vulnerability, my mind latched onto Joe and the kiss I knew he thought about but didn't pursue. In a sudden, mind-jolting burst with which stupidity so often gives way to the obvious, it occurred to me I could have been the aggressor.

As my steps faltered, I huffed out a breath and shook my head. Why didn't I think of that at the time? I could have kicked myself for acting like an inexperienced dunce. The fact that I was an inexperienced dunce was no excuse. I'd seen enough movies, read more than a few books. I could initiate a simple kiss.

Next time, I thought. If there was a next time, I definitely would. If I didn't chicken out, that is.

For a moment, I imagined it. I considered how I would do it, how it would feel to put my lips against his, the physical and romantic entanglements to which such a kiss could lead.

Yeah, right. I shook my head again, but without aggravated frustration, just pure exasperation. What it would lead to is more ineptitude on my part. Yes, I probably *would* chicken out. With any luck, before I made a complete fool of myself. For one minute, though, I coddled the fantasy. That much I could do.

In the dreamy freedom of my imagination where I could choreograph private indulgences, the kiss was perfect. I was as smooth and confident and as capable as any woman I'd ever seen on television or read about in a book. My sensuous moves and his eager responses were right out of a romance novel. It was beautiful.

I savored the moment before sweeping it into the bin with all my other wasteful dreams. In real life, things never go as well as they do in my imagination. Of course, I knew this. I'd survived by it. And I should have known better than to even consider slim possibilities. A good, fat *probability* was as lenient a luxury my normally good senses permited. I'd do well to stand by that guide.

Wiping the silliness from my head, I forced my thoughts back to the present. That's when alarm jolted me, sudden, as consuming as it was cold, freezing me in my tracks.

It was possible that while I was busy embellishing my romantic competence I lost track of time and it only *seemed* like I had walked much farther to get back than I had to get there. But it seemed it nonetheless. Had I disoriented myself and not turned back? Was I walking the wrong way, taking myself farther from the guys and deeper into the storm drains, all by myself?

I stopped to listen for their voices. There wasn't a single sound. And then, every inch of my skin became prickly.

My head spun around, following the slash of my light. There was nothing to see in my beam of light, nothing to hear in the concrete tunnel. It might have only been fear tightening my scalp. What to do?

My sense of direction was good, always had been. But underground, infused with fright, surrounded by nothing but thick darkness, solid concrete on all sides, and shadows that might or might not be alive, it was no wonder I would doubt myself.

Worst of all is that it was my mistake, my fault. I'd let myself get distracted. By indulging in a pointless fantasy, I had been more stupid than I'd ever been in my life. And my life might be the cost of that stupidity.

How far should I go before realizing I'd gone the wrong way and turning around? Maybe I hadn't gone far enough yet and turning around would take me farther away. In an effort to ease my panic, I concentrated on the intuition Joe so believed in. It was useless. No answer poked its head through the muddle of my uncertainty. I wasn't sure which way to go, and as my anxiety grew, so did my panic.

I shined my light down one black corridor and then pivoted to look the other way. There was nothing but darkness. For a moment, I could swear the tunnel was shrinking, becoming the width and depth of the trench of a grave.

My intuition, if I even had such a thing, was beyond my command. I was lost.

I considered calling out to my companions. However, foolish as it sounds, my pride was not yet ready to surrender. They wouldn't condemn or belittle me. They wouldn't have to. I'd do a good job of that myself.

Those thoughts ran through my head a few times, carrying meaning on which I could not at present focus. For, as I stretched to grasp it, my peripheral caught movement.

My entire body spun around and I slashed my flashlight as I would if it had it been a sturdy sword.

There was nothing, not in the beam of light, or in its edges. In that same instant, a breeze blew on my back and I spun around again.

There was nothing to see. Maybe the rush of air was from my quick turn. I was making myself crazy. For a minute or so, I stood there. Darkness surrounded me on all sides, and nothing but cement walls encasing the unyielding night.

Did I hear breathing? Was it mine? Maybe. I held my breath. After a couple of seconds, I let it out. Was that the release of another breath? Maybe it was an echo. Had there always been an echo in these tunnels? I couldn't remember. How could I not remember? I had to move. I had to move.

Facing the direction in which I'd been going, for no other reason than a random guess, I walked. More out of desperation than faith in Joe's belief, I tried again to summon my intuition as my feet took me where they would.

Suddenly it felt right, so I walked faster. At the sound of my brother's laughter, I slowed and took a deep breath, trying to pull myself together before I faced them. I didn't want anyone to know how bad I had scared myself.

When I walked into their view, they all gave me a glance before gathering up their backpacks. Only Joe paused, running his eyes over me as a parent would over an injured child. For a moment, worry crossed his face, so fleeting I could almost doubt my eyes. I was certain Joe sensed the fear still clinging to my semblance of calm.

Joe said nothing, though. He would not make a point of it in front of everyone, for which I was grateful.

Within minutes, we were on our way. I felt better, stronger, surrounded by the others. That wasn't being independent and tough, the way I was trying to be, but it was the truth. And if living in the tunnels taught me anything, it was no matter how I felt about the truth, I was better off acknowledging it than denying it.

Strutting behind a façade of grit and guts would be to disregard what assets I had, assets I needed, and render them useless. I could keep the depths of my uncertainties to myself. That shame was mine. But the fact that they were a part of me was irrelevant to my companions.

It didn't matter to them I was more than a short journey from perfect. They saw me better than I saw myself. Since they were smarter, braver, and more experienced in life than I was, self-belief had started to feel less a delicate thread of a daydream and more a rope to salvation.

I thought about that. It calmed me, much like being with this family. Even in regards to the two newest members, I was sure they would always accept me. I felt it from both Cake and Augie. I'd felt it from Joe right from the start, though I hadn't let myself believe it until the day he saved our lives. I had to accept myself the way they did. It had already begun.

Back there while I was alone in the tunnel I had admitted to myself that while indulging in daydreams I let myself get lost. Not paying attention when I needed to, it had been a foolish mistake. I'd been an idiot. I'd been human. I'd been human.

The acceptance, well, at least the acknowledgement of the possibility of my intuition, helped me to find my way. It was when I dismissed it I had my trouble. By not engaging in warfare against my nature, I am better able to direct my skills, whatever they may be. That's how I knew to turn left back at the crossroad. That's how, when the time came to face the monster, I thought I would know what to do.

From these revelations, I garnered a sense of peace. It lasted almost one full hour.

Chapter 15

We stopped for a short rest and a long drink of water. To my left sitting against the wall was Joe, long legs stretched out, crossed at the ankles, his backpack was beside him.

On my right was Jacob sitting like Joe. Augie and Cake were across from us. Cake rested his scraped and muscled arm on one bent knee as his eyes roved over the walls and the ceiling, ever vigilant. Augie sat in a loose cross-legged pose while he rummaged through his backpack. In such a way, he looked even younger than my brother did.

"Any more cookies in here?" Augie asked.

"Sorry," Joe said.

Cake dipped into his backpack and, after a brief scavenge, took out his little bag of cookies. He handed it over to Augie, saying, "Happy early birthday, kiddo."

Augie's entire face blossomed into joy, bunching the fair skin around his eyes until they looked like glistening raisins pressed into rising bread dough. His happiness over a little bag of treats made me smile. In a way, he reminded me of Jacob, a man on a mission who was still just a boy.

"Thanks, dude!" Augie all but shouted. After positioning his finger and thumb at the edge of the little bag he slid a glance back to Cake. "You sure you don't want these?" he asked. The way the question perched on the edge of the treat, it was obvious he hoped the answer was no.

"All yours, kid. Better eat them before I change my mind."

Augie tore open the bag and feasted. Cake glanced over at his young friend and chuckled. There was warmth in that chuckle, the softer side of him showing again.

Cake would be a formidable enemy, of that I had no doubt. The man was hard and tough and I had a feeling he'd done things he would never discuss, likely because not all of it was for the good. I thought there was a great darkness in his past. I felt it. Maybe the mission was his way of making amends.

To us, to our little family, he would be our defender. I had a strong feeling Augie wished Cake had been around when he was in school, I'm guessing harassed by bullies.

For a while Jacob and Augie discussed, and then debated, their favorite candy. They both had wondered why commercials always say 'care-a-mel', but regular people pronounced it 'carmel'. They differed in opinion about candy with nuts versus the purity of solid chocolate. Jacob liked about any little treats added to his candy while Augie claimed nothing could beat a plain bar of dark chocolate.

"Augie," I said, when their conversation waned. "You know a lot about the supernatural, myths, legends and things like that?" He puffed up a bit. I'd touched on his specialty, his point of pride.

"I've been fascinated with all that kind of stuff my whole life. There's a lot of bull, most of it, in fact. But some of it's real. If you take the time to use science and common sense, it's not hard to tell which is which. Most people don't make the effort. It suits them to believe what they want to believe, period," he said, with a swipe of his hand.

Augie scratched his head before continuing. "I think it makes them feel smart, or wise, or something, like they have this supernatural answer for everything. And if you ask, they can always come up with some vague reference as proof. You know, like, "Hey, this really happened to a 'friend of a friend.'"

Augie chuckled. "I love that; it's always a friend of a friend. What an easy out."

"So, what's not real and what is?" I asked. "Give me some examples."

"Well, like the full moon for instance. People have this theory—more crazy things happen during a full moon than any other time. Statistics show that's not true, but people still believe it even though there's proof saying otherwise." Augie shook his head. His thick swag of bangs swished over his brows.

"Another example," Augie said. "There's this ridiculous belief celebrities die in threes. It's absurd, of course. Those people count them in threes. You could count dead celebrities or anybody else in threes, or twos or fives and say that's how they die. I think a lot of people want to attach some kind of magic or mysticism to everything. I think it makes them feel more powerful, like they can make predictions, or have a say in things."

"I can see that," Jacob said. "So, do you think people who pray are trying to perform magic?"

I was surprised Jacob's mind went there. We'd never discussed religion. But he'd seen the mural of Jesus in the tunnel, so maybe he wondered about it too.

"More like they have an inside line to *The Magician*," Augie answered. He glanced upward, wary, his shoulders bunched in a very slight cringe, as if lightning might split the concrete to strike him, thrown by a God peeved at Augie for referring to Him as a nightclub act.

I kept my smile to myself. Cake repressed his amusement, too. He looked over at me and when our eyes met, we shared a burst of silent laughter.

Once assured God spared him of retribution, Augie continued. "Other things though, like certain ancient beliefs, some of which align exactly with various other cultures with which they have no connection, geographic or otherwise, and existed long before. Like the one I connected to the shadow monster."

We hadn't discussed the monster. I knew that was strange, considering it was our sole purpose for being in the storm drains. Maybe it was something we had to ease in to, like hot bath water, or, more aptly, acceptance of a terminal disease.

"What beliefs?" Jacob asked.

"I studied several things," Augie said. "But the one that sticks to me because it makes the most sense is 'moral causation'. The Buddhists call it Kamma. We say karma. It's simple, really; cause and effect. One explains the other."

"When you produce evil, you cause further evil," I said. "It spreads, it grows."

Augie nodded. "Yes, that's exactly it."

Joe said, "The Reverend Merriweather, for example, who was just here spewing his rhetoric of hate under the guise of piety."

Looking at Joe I said, "When I heard he was

coming to town, this jittery sickness came over me. I knew he would make that thing worse."

"Ah," Cake said, and then twisted his lips in disgust as he shook his head. "He is one pompous, self-righteous little shit. Yeah, I think we all felt it when he strolled into town. Guys like that give religion a bad name."

"They feed the thing, make it stronger," I said.

"Yes," Joe confirmed. "Thugs like that nourish it."

Nodding, Augie said, "I believe that, too. I don't know when it started developing, but I think, like a lot of toxins, evil has a cumulative effect. I think that maybe it takes a series of things, maybe even over many, many years, snowballing over time as the great evils make their contributions. Look at history. Look at Hitler, Stalin, Ho Chi Minh, and so many others. They emitted evil like fertilizer, and I think that's kind of how it worked. The compilation of all their evil deeds, well, I think they created that thing. If you think about it, it's actually very logical. Karma: cause and effect. And the good things people do, well those things give it a setback. We've seen that, too. Even small acts of kindness matter."

"Amen to that," Cake said.

"Do you believe in God?" I asked Cake. It was a very personal question. Oddly, though, I was comfortable asking him.

"Well, they say there are no atheists in fox holes and in my vast experience, that's the truth. I'm not ashamed to admit sometimes I talk to the Big Guy," Cake said, jerking a thumb upward.

One yes. "Augie?" I said, sending him the question.

"I was raised Catholic. It's kind of woven in to who I am."

Cake tipped his head toward his young friend and said, "Yeah, at one time our little Augie here wanted to be a priest."

Augie nodded. "That's true. I was an altar boy and everything."

Cake grinned, raising his eyebrows twice after saying, "I think the no sex thing was a deal breaker."

Augie blushed and I wondered if, like me, sex was an experience he'd yet to have.

After a moment's thought, I said to Augie, "So, being Catholic, do you think this thing was caused by the evil deeds of others, or fed by them after being created by Satan?"

"I think it's all the same. Karma can figure into Catholicism, sort of. I mean, you're supposed to do your best to live a righteous life so you can get into Heaven and if you're bad, well, it's straight into the fiery pit. That's good coming from good and bad coming from bad. Both paths of action lead to more of the same. When you do good things, more good things come of it. Like when someone does a good deed and it inspires others to do the same. There's a phrase for it."

"Paying it forward," I said.

"Yes," said Augie. "That's right. Even little things count. Like when someone is in the drive-through and that person pays for the car behind them. Then that person is inspired to go and do something nice for someone else. The good spreads. It works the same way when, for example, somebody gets bullied. Sometimes that person fights back in a big, excessive, and unfair way and innocent people get hurt, or worse. That's bad, sometimes *really* bad, coming from bad. This monster, this embodiment, I think it's kind of the same thing only on a much larger scale, a more, extensive scale."

For a minute or so, we all sat in quiet contemplation. Then I looked at Joe. "What about you, Joe? Do you believe in God?"

I thought Joe repressed a look of absolute disbelief, maybe even to the point of condescension that would have offended Cake and Augie. For the briefest of moments, the expression formed before he ironed it out. If Cake and Augie noticed, they let it go.

Joe said, "I believe there is good and there is evil. If some people want to name them God and Satan, it's their right."

"But you don't believe in the actual entities." I was pushing, maybe too far, but I wanted to know. It was important to me. I needed to know if his beliefs were the same as mine.

"No, I don't," Joe said in an even tone that held neither insult nor apology. "I believe good and evil are both manmade." Looking at Jacob and me, Joe asked, "How about the two of you?"

Jacob shrugged his shoulders. "I don't know. I never really thought about it. It'd be nice if there were such a thing as God. But I don't know."

All eyes turned to me. I thought of the mural of Jesus. I wanted to believe. I'd tried to believe. I wanted to be one of those people who could put her troubles in God's hands and rest easy, believe an entity, a kind, and loving Father reigning with supreme power over mere humans would take care of me. But using logic and science, as suggested by the Catholic in our group, I thought with no small amount of irony, I accepted I do not believe. My troubles are my own to handle, as they always had been.

"No," I said to the group, though when I spoke the last of my sentence my eyes were on Joe. "I don't believe there is such a thing as God."

Everyone got quiet after that. I don't know if Cake and Augie were disappointed in me or pitying me. With God in their hearts, I supposed they were praying for me. Even though I didn't believe, I thought that was nice of them.

"Out of curiosity, what other theories did you consider?" Joe said to Augie, changing the subject I'm sure, because he sensed my discomfort. I was grateful to him yet again, grateful for his intuition coming to my rescue.

Augie readjusted his position and, shifting left and then right, re-crossed his legs before saying, "The theory of spontaneous generation was one I found interesting."

"What's that?" Jacob asked. He was leaning forward, looking like an interested student.

"Spontaneous generation was the belief that life could come from non-life. Early philosophers, like Aristotle, believed life could come from non-living matter. You know, without seeds or eggs or parents or anything."

"That life just sprouted from nothing?" Jacob asked.

"Well, you have to remember the science they had to work with. This was like, 300-something BC. They didn't know about microorganisms and such. Without microscopes, all they knew was what they could see with their bare eyes. At the time it must have seemed logical."

"Spontaneous generation," Jacob said with thoughtful consideration. "That'd be nice, life coming from non-life."

"How so?" asked Joe.

My brother grinned and said, "You could just buy a couch, and then it would give birth to a couple of matching chairs."

Everybody burst out laughing. The sound was loud in the tunnel. It felt good, like laughing around a dinner table. All that was missing was dinner, and the table. I could see it, though. Maybe when this was all over we could have a nice dinner together, like a regular family. For a moment, I imagined us all living together in a house, sharing in the chores, and the joys and the laughter. We would have occasional disagreements, even arguments, but they'd never tear us apart. No one would be tossed out because they had a different opinion. Picturing it was effortless.

One heartbeat after that image gave me joy, the electric prickle blazed across my skin in a sudden, undeniable, and vicious rush.

My eyes zoomed in on Cake. He was staring at his scraped arm. His smile was gone. His expression hardened and his sharp gaze shot up to meet mine. We both knew one of those things was right there with us.

In that same second-tick of time, before either of us could speak or jump into action, the shadow bulged from the wall right behind Cake. There wasn't even time to scream before it was too late.

Half a dozen black tentacles as thick as logs and tapered to nubs shot out and wrapped around Cake in solid layers like stacked tires. Then, as if using Cake for leverage, its entire being heaved from the wall and fell on him in a dense heap.

The thing appeared to be a solid entity, yet it was liquid enough to meld its separated parts back together, thick, and slimy, as if infused with all the dirty, dark, and oily deeds of mankind. It smelled sour, like rotted garbage. It slithered and pulsed, and buried Cake.

We all jumped to our feet. Augie scurried away, nearly falling in his panic before grabbing his backpack and shoving his hand inside. The shadow monster molded itself to and around Cake's body. We could see Cake struggling inside.

Together we shouted and kicked at the thing. It was like kicking watery clay. My foot stuck, but not bad. I was able to wrench it free to kick it again, not that it did any good. Jacob was kicking too. Profanities blasted from his mouth like cannon fire.

I kept screaming, "Let him go! Let him go!"

I grabbed the thing from the bottom and lifted. Its weight was substantial and what I was able to lift crept through and around my hands in a thick goop.

In the scattered beams of our flashlights that lay on the floor, we all fought to save our friend. Joe had a large knife and was on his knees trying to cut around Cake. It was like trying to carve thick sludge. Every slice closed almost as soon as he made it.

Joe tried prying it apart after making the cuts, but he had the same trouble I did. The damned thing closed around his hands and then oozed through his fingers. But he kept trying. We all did.

Augie yanked a thermos from his backpack. In an instant, he was tossing clear liquid on the beast and shouting in a language I didn't understand. Holy water, words in Latin. I borrowed profanities from Jacob to hurl at the monster along with my feet and my fists.

The thing might well have been laughing at us for all the damage we were doing.

All the while Cake continued his valiant fight. One of his fists punched outward, and then both boots kicked. For a moment, the contour of his face stretched against the thing from the inside, mouth open in a scream we couldn't hear.

While we continued to fight it with all we had, Cake's form diminished. It appeared as if he was shrinking. No. The horror of it sickened me. Cake wasn't shrinking. He was being absorbed.

From the inside, Cake's fight weakened to little more than pulses, if that was even him at all. We didn't quit. We didn't slow. Cake was ours, and this thing couldn't have him.

Suddenly, the monster withdrew, though I'm sure it had nothing to do with our fight to save our friend. It was finished. The thing suctioned itself to the wall and flattened into a wet shadow, and as fast as a flashlight beam could glide against the wall, it was gone. And so was Cake.

It was less than two minutes from the last time I saw Cake until the moment that thing slithered away.

I pounded on the wall, screaming, "No! No!" Crying, and losing my mind to rage and to grief. I didn't know when Joe wrapped his arms around me. I didn't know when he dragged me away from the wall, or when emotion reduced my screams of grief and fury to sobs. All I knew is the harder I trembled, the tighter Joe held me.

I dropped my head against his chest. One of his big

hands cupped the side of my face while his other arm held my body tight against his, as if to keep me from falling apart. My legs gave out and we sat, wrapped in each other as much as we could.

When I looked up, we were in the center of the tunnel, not touching any of the walls. That wouldn't make any difference, though, if that thing wanted us. Shadows can travel on the floor as easy as they can on the walls.

The weight of my shock subdued my weeping into broken breaths. In the quiet wake, there was still crying. I didn't need to look to know it was Augie. He was closer to Cake than any of us were.

I turned my head. Jacob was sitting, staring in muted shock at the place against the wall where we lost Cake. Augie sat between me and Joe and my brother, his arms wrapped around his thick legs, his forehead wobbled on his knees with each violent sob. I crawled to Augie and hugged him and for a while, we cried together.

"I don't understand," Jacob said. His words sounded swollen, confused, as if it was all more than his brain could hold. "According to Liz, it was already developing. It had feet. It could walk. It wasn't on the walls anymore. What did it do, go back to being a shadow? Can it do that?"

"No," Joe said. "I don't think so. The one Liz saw was too far along to go back to being a shadow. It would be like an adult trying to become an infant. That was a different one."

"There are more? How many more?" Jacob asked in disbelief as his head rotated to face Joe. I'd forgotten he didn't know. He hadn't heard when Joe told me and

I'd never passed on that information.

"Nobody knows for sure," I said to my brother. "A lot."

Jacob stood and paced. His breathing hastened. "I thought we were coming after one. Now you're telling me there's a whole nest of those things down here?"

"They're all over the country, probably all over the world," Joe told him.

"I thought I would know how to stop it," I said. "I thought when it happened, I would know, that the answer was inside of me. I didn't have a clue."

"I thought I would too," Augie said. Every few words hitched on emotion. He wiped his wet face with his hands. "Even when I was reading all that material, I felt it, like, like I didn't feel worried I couldn't find anything in writing because when the time came, I would know."

Sitting shoulder to shoulder with Augie, I said to all of them, "You all believed I had some sort of special ability, something more than you. Well I don't. I don't! And now Cake is dead!"

"We just haven't figured it out yet, Liz." This from Joe.

I turned on him. "When do we figure it out, Joe? When that thing comes back for you, for Augie, for my brother, for me?"

"I don't think it can absorb you," Augie said to me, and then he sniffed and wiped his face again.

"Why not?" I shouted. "Why the hell not!"

"You're too good," Augie answered.

"That's ridiculous, I shot back."

Joe said, "We all have a certain quality that keeps it at bay. Yours is the strongest."

"Oh?" I said with complete sarcasm. "And what about Cake? He sensed it, too. It didn't keep that thing away."

Joe said, "Cake made some big changes in his life. Impressive changes. He had a very dark past, though. It made him more vulnerable."

I didn't ask about Cake's past. I didn't care. It didn't matter. He was good. I felt it. I knew it without a sliver of doubt.

"It's not fair!" I shouted, coming to my feet. My legs were wobbling and Joe got up to help me to stand. I shook off his grip. My anger was indiscriminate. I swung around, facing the darkness where that thing had taken Cake. "It's not fair! Bring him back!" I screamed down the tunnel. "He's ours! Bring him back!"

Five seconds later an answer floated back to me out of the darkness. A loud whisper, a voice within a hiss.

"*Mine*."

Chapter 16

We all scrambled for our flashlights. Standing shoulder to shoulder with Joe on my left, Augie on my right, and Jacob beside him, we shined our lights down the tunnel.

The four moving beams showed nothing. All was silent. We suppressed our breathing to listen with the greatest possible intensity. A mild tingle rolled over my skin. Nothing like the electric prickling it had been before. Had I not been so on edge, not been so presently sensitive to the thing, I might not have even noticed.

Keeping my light pointed in the direction from which we'd heard the voice, I shifted my eyes toward the walls, the ceiling, and the floor. There was nothing in the dim peripherals of our beams. But, as we'd just seen, that could change at any second.

Together the four of us waited for the confrontation. I think we all understood the time had come.

"Show yourself!" Joe shouted.

There was movement, but it was far enough beyond the light so we couldn't make out any kind of definition. All we could tell for sure was it was moving toward us.

Augie's light trembled, but he did not cower, did not run away. I shifted my beam of light so it touched his and made a bigger, brighter light, and from Augie I drew courage. Joe and Jacob followed my lead, shining their beams of light together with ours so the edges all touched and we had one bright circle of light.

As the thing came closer, tension tightened its grip on all of us. We could hear its approach, like soft shoes on cement. And then, as if walking into a spotlight on a stage, the thing stepped into the bright cluster of our joined beams.

We all stared, frozen, taking it in, needing time to adjust our preconceived images because the monster was so far from what any of us had expected it left us stunned. I was prepared to see something hideous, something slimy, and fanged. My partners must have been too, because I felt their shock at what stood before us.

It looked, quite simply, like a man, a very normal, very average, man. But I, and I'm sure my partners would say the same, felt the evil seeping from its every pore, could even catch a hint of sour rot it couldn't help but emit.

With its good posture, the thing stood about five feet ten inches tall. It carried an average weight on an average build, much-used sneakers covered its average-sized feet. It had on a pair of dirty and wrinkled jeans. Its short-sleeved cotton T-shirt at one time had been dark blue. The aged shirt bore an air of dustiness that eventually affects all dark-colored shirts.

In the center of the T-shirt was a yellow happy face. Part of the chin area of the decal had peeled off and what was left of the iconic image had cracked with age and wear. I'd seen the shirt before, that exact shirt. I'd seen it down here in the storm drains. It struck me then. Everything the monster was wearing had come from someone living down here in our underground community, from a person it had absorbed.

Beyond my control, certainly beyond my want, my gaze zeroed in on the baseball cap it was wearing. It bore the Detroit Tiger's logo. The thing tipped its head for a moment, letting me see. Near the edge of the bill was an old mustard stain in the shape of an upside down teardrop. Benny's baseball cap, the one he had been wearing the last time I saw him.

Benny never made it out. He'd never gotten his fresh start. He'd never gone to rehab or moved in with his brother. He was dead, taken by this thing. My rage boiled anew. Poor Benny, who tried to leave the tunnels while worried about us, striving for a better life. I forced myself to keep my feelings hidden. Later I would mourn Benny, our friend. Right now, I needed to keep my head, keep focused on the lethal monster before us.

The thing appeared to be a man in his early thirties. Its clean-shaven face was pale, but not *very* pale. Eyes, nose, mouth, all nondescript and average in that they were not particularly big, or particularly small.

The man/monster standing before us wasn't what I'd call handsome, but no one would say he was unattractive. Its stance was nonthreatening as it grinned through average lips. If it could even semi-master charm, the thing would not have a difficult time attracting a woman, or befriending a man.

Its sandy brown hair lay down neat and grew a little bit below the bottom of the baseball cap. Matching eyebrows rose a little. Its head lifted and tipped once in a nod just for me. It wanted me to understand. And I did.

Its looks would not cause others to rest their eyes upon him for any specific reason. With its faux normalcy it was clean cut enough so it could blend into the business crowd, but it wasn't so neat as to exclude him from the edgier sect. It would all depend on how he dressed and held himself. The disguise was perfect. It looked, for all intents and purposes, like an average human man.

The normalcy of the monster made it more terrifying. I looked into its eyes that were a subdued green, glittering with the sparkle of life. It grinned at me showing straight teeth, white, but not glaringly so.

Its face, bearing no remarkable features, sharpened to make a point. Yes, I understood. Looking as it did, the thing could go almost anywhere. Its inconspicuousness allowed it easy assimilation. It could creep into street gangs or corporations, politics, Main Street, Wall Street, city streets, or country roads. The thing would not draw suspicion, not raise fear, until it was too late.

Its grin tightened to a smirk, brimming with the smugness of victory. The thing knew it was what the world had wrought upon itself.

The monster, the thing that looked like a man but was in truth, the destruction of mankind, turned to Augie. "Care to toss some holy water on me?" it asked, and then laughed.

Its voice was also indistinct, not high-pitched or too deep, not a smoker's voice, not commanding, nor was it meek, an average man's voice. Although it exuded a fair amount of arrogance, I think it was only to suit its present purpose. In public, it would conceal its ego. And it would do so with ease. For, working beneath its ordinary appearance were the combined minds of all who had created it. The monster would be proficient in deception. I knew all of this. My mind touched its virulent intentions, and I knew.

The thing was still laughing when it turned its sharp green eyes to Joe. "So we meet again, Joseph. My, how I've grown!" it said, holding out its arms, presenting its developed self with a proud smile. "Not much thanks to your friend, Mr. Coulter. He wasn't, how did you put it, oh, yes, nourishing."

Dean Coulter, my actual father. Joe tensed beside me. Dean Coulter was his friend. Now he'd lost two to this monster and its brethren. And if we did not win this day, it was just the beginning. I glanced at Joe. He appeared calm. He wasn't. Restrained tension held his body taut. I wondered if the monster could tell.

And then Joe's expression flattened to reflective. It took him a moment to voice his thoughts.

"You didn't absorb Dean," Joe said to the monster, though he sounded as if he was speaking to himself. I thought about that, too. I said to Joe, "You told me that thing killed my father."

"It did," he said, glancing at me before turning back to the monster. "When it wasn't much more than a damp shadow, Dean and I trapped it. We cornered it in an area still under construction."

"You didn't trap me!" the thing yelled. Its eyes grew large, its skin reddened with anger. Joe's statement had insulted it. Then it collected itself and said in a self-satisfied tone, "I lured you."

After a moment Joe said, "Yes, I think you did. I think you had to lure us there because that was the only way you could kill us. But you didn't get me."

"How did he die?" I asked Joe.

"Dean and I had hunted this thing down to a dead end and then lost sight of it. Where we'd stopped we were standing beside a huge stack of discarded materials; pipes, cut metals, big chunks of concrete piled all the way to the ceiling. I stepped away only a bare second before this thing bulged out from the wall and shoved much of it on top of Dean. Dumb luck was the only thing that saved me. Dean was half-crushed beneath it all. He lived for about twenty minutes while I worked to free him."

Joe looked so pained. They must have been the worst twenty minutes of his life. I can't even imagine. But like my mourning for Benny, and us mourning Cake, Joe put it aside. He cast a thoughtful glare at the monster standing before us and said again, "You killed Dean, but you didn't consume him. In fact, you didn't even touch him."

"I didn't want to consume him," the monster shot back. "I found him…too bland to waste my time."

I didn't believe that for a second. There was a reason he didn't absorb my father. I don't think it could absorb Joe either, or it would have that day. From beside me I sensed Joe didn't believe that thing either.

I slanted a glance his way, and hoped the monster could not read me. My mind worked to make connections I might be able to use, if I could figure out how. I think Joe was doing the same.

Joe's free arm hung straight along his body, though he kept his hand hidden behind his thigh. He held the knife in a firm grip. The blade hadn't done us any good against the less developed monster, but maybe now that this thing had developed into a humanlike figure, he was also more susceptible to injuries. I was certain it had vulnerabilities, though what they might be eluded me.

The thing turned its human eyes toward Jacob. "Now you, young man," it said.

Evil twisted its widening grin. As it gazed at my brother, I was sure it was thinking not so much about Jacob's drug and alcohol abuse of the past, but of the unscrupulous things it led him to do.

"*Yum,*" the monster said, its brows rising again before settling over green eyes now rounded with a terrifying expression of anticipation.

I stiffened and the thing pivoted to look at me. It wasn't quite as smug as it had been a moment before. But it also didn't appear to be afraid. I could swear, though, I caught a trace of, of something akin to trepidation. I got the impression the thing's well-crafted façade was putting more effort into its camouflage.

Hoping to keep its focus on me and away from my brother, I said, with as much boldness as I could muster, "We're here to stop you."

It laughed again, but this time its display of humor sounded a little bit forced. Maybe it was my imagination. Maybe not.

"After all the great many who came before you to create me, you think the four of you can stop me, can stop us?" At the word 'us' the thing raised both hands over its head and swirled them forward several times. In an instant, my skin prickled so bad it hurt. Joe and Augie cringed too.

Shadows emerged from the darkness, dozens, no, hundreds. Some were in a vague circular shape and were as dull as ordinary shadows. Others had a damp sheen to them, as they were further along in their development. We turned our flashlights on them. They didn't scurry away and hide. They wanted us to see them.

Many of the shadows continued to change their shapes, stretching out to become oblong, and then contracting, as if playing with their progressing abilities. All of them were in constant movement.

They traveled in varying directions along the walls, slow, and I could swear, methodical. Glancing up, I could see them moving around on the concrete ceiling. I then looked down. Shadows passed near our feet. They had us surrounded on every side.

Augie, after looking from the man/monster to the shadows encircling us, and then back again, said to it, "We figured out how you were created, and what makes you grow."

Augie was terrified. He was also angry and hurting and from that, he was able to gather courage. How I admired him.

Swiveling its head toward Augie, the thing said, "Well, I have to give you some credit there; but just some."

The thing held its human hands out in front of its body and curled its fingers upward into closed fists. It drew its hands in, then, holding them close to its chest.

All the while, the shadows continued to circle us, unhurried, in a loose but definite pattern. They reminded me a little of the innards of a lava lamp. One caught my eye when it bulged half a foot or so from the wall before sinking back to join the others. I couldn't help but wonder if that was the one who took Cake.

"It wasn't so much the big names who directly

gave me what I needed," the monster continued. "The Hitlers, the Pol Pots, the Amins, and all their kind, they were the tastiest morsels, sure. They were not, however, the ones who developed me to this point. There simply haven't been enough of them."

The thing paused, scanning us, as if to make sure we were still paying attention. We were.

It lifted a finger, a teacher making a point. "You see, it is their *followers*. It is the countless minions marching blindly, obediently, doing their bidding. It's all of them in their great masses. The followers aren't the one who taste the best, but *they* are the ones who feed me most."

Flashing through my mind, an image of Nazi soldiers, watching with a complete lack of humanity, of compassion, as their fellow human beings suffered, tearing frightened children from the arms of their hysterical parents, herding them all to their deaths.

I thought of the street gangs, hurting, and killing because it's what a leader wanted them to do, terrorists, blowing themselves up, murdering innocents, for the same reason. Then I thought of the evil lurking in religious and political subterfuge, a malevolence that was in the news daily as we stood before the offspring of cruelty, greed, and bigotry.

Genocide, slavery, brutal and mass annihilations, human history is a cascade of endless horrors breeding more, breeding *this*. The followers. Yes.

The thing looked at me, and then its gaze roved over the others who stood at my side. The shadows continued to swim around us as if we were in a walk-through tube of an aquarium.

"Ah, I see you understand," it said. "So smart, you

are, you do-gooders. It's too bad you haven't organized better, haven't mastered leadership like your counterparts. Too many of your persons in charge are so busy with the pettiness of besting the opposition and bickering for their own interests, they've forgotten their place. They've lost sight of the greater good and who they are paid to serve. And now it's too late."

That last sentence, though, sounded more like an argument than a statement. It was trying to convince us it had the right to claim victory. It didn't. But we all knew its future was promising.

"Serial killers," the thing continued. "Are lovely, but there are so damn few of them. It's the great abundance of smaller contributions. Thieves, for example, hold a special place in my heart. It's because there are so very many, and such variety! The purse snatchers, shoplifters, car thieves, techno thieves, the cheaters, the swindlers, the embezzlers, all that conning and defrauding and the insatiable greed that leads them to only want more, no matter what it takes."

It paused for a dreamy smile before continuing. "They all contribute to us. Some have a more special place in my heart than others do. For example, I especially like the villains who break into homes, into a place people consider sacred, safe, their *sanctuary*. They take what doesn't rightfully belong to them because they can, because they see opportunity and due to a wonderful absence of ethics, of conscience, they steal.

"I *love* racists," it said, slapping a hand against its chest. "They raise their children to be just like them, ignorant, hateful, and cruel. And the bullies! Ooh, I *love* them," it said, eyes hooding, as a look of utter ecstasy lifted its face. "They come in all ages, all styles; the mean girls with tongues sharper than their brains, the tyrant males who use their muscles to intimidate, to beat their girlfriends, their wives, their children."

It paused long enough to give a quick tuck of its bottom lip under its top teeth. "The rapists, the pedophiles, oh, and the animal abusers, let's not forget them. Your factory farms are cauldrons of savage abuse. Give me my bacon and burgers, give me my bird sandwiches, and I'll pretend those sentient animals didn't live lives of horrific suffering. You abduct and imprison tigers, orcas, and any other free creature you please, for your entertainment. Mankind's brutality is boundless. And I love you for it."

It smacked its average lips together several times. "Those who abuse animals and children," it said. "They're *especially* tasty."

After a pause, it resumed its speech. "I like the bad neighbors, the bad bosses, the nasty co-workers, rude clerks, and rude customers. All of them strutting around, stirring up small, steaming pots of misery. With the internet, they can all pour out their nasty thoughts by the bucket load and send them all over the world in seconds. And they're good at getting others to join up with them, to follow their lead. Oh yes, I do love the bullies! They're *delicious*," it hissed.

Following that statement, the thing licked its human lips. Its tongue was a deep plumb color, as if engorged with the darkness contained beneath its fake human skin.

We gaped in utter horror as its tongue extended from its mouth another five or six inches before splitting down the middle and becoming forked. The two separate tips moved independent of each other in a snake dance meant to shock us. The tips curled out in opposite directions, each one licking the corner of its lips before straightening again to waggle.

And then, a jagged, white arc of electricity the width of a pinky finger jumped from one tip to the other and then back again. It sparked and sizzled, illuminating the monster's open grin and the wild delight in its eyes. The thing then made a circle of its lips and drew its tongue back in for a moment before letting it slide out again to show us how it now appeared normal.

At our horrified expressions, laughter bubbled from its chest and rolled from its mouth. Before its glee faded, Joe threw the knife he'd been holding with an expert speed and precision I would expect to see at a talent show.

The knife sliced through the air so fast it wasn't more than a blur until with a solid thud, it implanted deep into the heart of the monster. The thing stumbled backward and, arms outward, looked down at the handle protruding from its chest. It made a sound, pain, maybe a whimper.

I waited to see if it would fall to its knees, or maybe drop dead. It did neither. Instead, it lifted its head to look back at us, straight faced, before breaking into another bout of laughter.

"Again with the knife, Joe?" it said, before shaking its head as if amused with a child's antics. "Didn't you try that last time? Well, I suppose you thought since now I look like everybody else, you could kill me like anybody else, right? So cute."

It was still chuckling when it wrapped its fingers

around the knife handle and slid the blade out of its chest. No blood poured from the wound. In fact, there wasn't even blood on the knife. Holding it in front of its face, the thing gazed at one clean side of the blade and then the other. In an instant, it lost all its humor.

The thing tipped its head down and glared at Joe. It meant to punish him. Since I felt it, knew it was going to throw the knife straight into Joe's heart, I had time to act.

I don't know what I was thinking. I don't know that I was thinking at all. I just reacted. An instant before the knife would have embedded itself in the center of Joe's chest I leapt in front of him.

Instead of the sharp blade slicing into Joe's heart, it lodged deep into my left shoulder. I cried out in pain and at the sight of the knife protruding from my shoulder, lost my balance to dizziness, and fell back against Joe.

Jacob cried my name. At the same time, I heard Joe shout, "No!" The cold blade burned and in seconds, the shirt I wore was soaked with my blood. Suddenly I was on the floor, leaning back against Joe who cradled me in a gentle hold. Jacob and Augie were on either side of me.

"Don't move," Joe said to me.

And I wouldn't have considered moving had I not seen the direction of the monster's gaze. It had turned to my brother. I shouted, "Jacob, get behind Joe!"

"You think that will help?" the thing asked me in a loud, scornful voice.

The shadows around us accelerated, jerking, as if they'd become agitated, nervous too, maybe. I feared at any moment they would pounce.

"He couldn't stop me with a knife. What will he do with his bare hands?" The thing took a deep breath and then yelled at me, "I get what I want!"

Augie jumped to his feet and stood between us, shouting at the monster in Latin, holding a cross out in front of him. A terrified, crazy part of me nearly laughed at Augie treating the monster like a vampire.

The thing lunged toward Augie, but did not get close enough to touch him. Its tongue flicked out several times, forked once again. From the split-tips shot jagged spears of lightning. Short bolts of electricity hit Augie, piercing him before disintegrating. The pain of the electric shards crumpled him over.

With each strike, Augie cried out. He flinched and turned, but the strikes kept coming, snapping horribly each time one hit. Though Augie didn't bleed, thin tendrils of smoke appeared from dime-sized burns left on his clothing.

Jacob leapt to his feet and shouted at the monster to stop. It shot off two more bolts, and then watched with enjoyment. Augie trembled and the trembles intensified into convulsions so severe he lost control of his muscles. His flashlight fell from his hand but did not break when it hit the concrete. It rolled a few feet, swirling a beam of light that emphasized the sensation of surrealism.

Augie's legs gave out and he dropped to the floor. He curled up on his side facing us, his limbs twitching, eyes unfocused but blinking, albeit erratic. He was alive. Breathing hard, nevertheless he was breathing.

I still didn't see any blood but I couldn't tell how bad he was hurt. There must have been a dozen smoldering holes in his clothes. Augie's compressed lips muted his cries of pain, and my heart broke.

And that thing wasn't finished with him.

The monster closed in, the two tips of its tongue rubbing together for a moment like a fly with its legs. Revving up more current, the two sides split and serrated bolts jumped from one tip to the other, brightening, as if infused with fresh power, and the sharp and dangerous sound of electric crackle grew more intense.

It was ready to finish off Augie for good.

Jacob rushed to Augie, laying an arm over him while positioning his body between Augie and certain death. When I looked up at the monster, rage and terror flooded the whole of me. The thing had turned its focus on my brother.

It grinned at Jacob, letting the two sides of its forked tongue waggle, electricity snapping loud, small bolts of lightning jumping from tip to tip. It was showing off for us, while tasting victory.

"Don't let it hurt my brother!" I cried out to Joe as I leaned away from him.

The command was unnecessary, as Joe was already rushing toward them. At my movement, pain surged through my shoulder and more blood gushed from the wound. Blood ran warm down my body, soaking through my shirt. My attention didn't waver.

As the monster stepped toward Jacob, Joe attacked. He threw punches and landed kicks with the vicious proficiency of a man well trained to fight. A couple of times the monster stumbled, but it didn't appear to be hurt. In fact, I'd say it enjoyed the challenge, grinning after Joe delivered a full-face punch and then beckoning with the fingers of both hands for more.

All the while the monster spit out small bolts of lightning from the tips of its tongue. Though Joe was able to dodge many, he couldn't evade them all. The strikes soon took a toll. Joe's arms quaked with spasms, and then his legs did the same. He had to fight for balance.

The monster flicked both tips of its dark tongue several times in quick succession. Crackling bolts of electricity struck Joe, and again, and then again. He lost the ability to get out of the way. Joe's body tightened up on him, and after the series of strikes, he jerked backward before falling, landing hard. His head slammed on the concrete floor.

The monster then knelt beside a semi-conscious Joe. It leaned over, bending to his ear. I think it wanted to say something to Joe before killing him. I think it wanted to gloat.

Before it had a chance, Jacob grabbed the thing around its middle to yank it away from Joe. It spun around, twisted out of Jacob's grip, and spit two quick bolts at him. My brother cried out and stepped back. With a grin, the thing rubbed the split tips together again, working up more power.

Holding my left arm against my stomach, I crawled in their direction, moving like a lame tortoise. To do what, I didn't know. Something, though. There *had* to be something. The knife in my shoulder crippled all my efforts, the slightest of which dug the blade around. Cracks of pain shot through me and I bled even more, but I couldn't stop. That thing had my brother.

Around me, the shadows whirled in rapid motion, as if whipped into a frenzy of excitement, or panic. They broke their pattern and parted for me, creating a clear path as I crawled toward Jacob. Why would they do that?

The ones near to me darted back and forth, always keeping a certain distance, like vicious dogs fenced from attacking. There had to be a reason for this strangeness, but I didn't have time to analyze. My head swiveled at the sizzle and snap of electricity. I looked up to see Jacob flinching with pain as more of those little bolts of lightning struck him. I had to get to my brother.

Pain, no less sharp than the blade lodged in my flesh, shot through my arm. The wave of dizziness that followed almost rolled me over. Closing my eyes for a moment, I did my best to will it away.

I opened my eyes to see fat drops of blood falling from my drenched shirt. When they hit the floor, the shadows near me darted away, as if running from explosions. They returned cautious, only to flee again when more blood fell.

I hadn't understood that odd behavior. Then I thought I did. If I was right, this was something I could use. I touched my right hand to my bloodied shirt and then flicked droplets from my fingertips. The shadows scurried away. They were afraid of my blood.

I looked up. The monster kneeled over my brother. It had him pinned on the floor. Thin tendrils of smoke rose from burn marks in Jacob's shirt. He was squirming, trying to get away from the thing.

Maniacal laughter rolled over the monster's forked tongue, wagging over my brother's face. Long, jagged sparks arced from one tip to the other and it laughed harder at Jacob's struggles, enjoying my brother's fear.

With my right hand, I tugged on the knife. The skin

around the blade protruded outward big enough so it was obvious even through my blood-soaked shirt, but the knife didn't budge from my flesh. My stomach roiled with nausea. I nearly passed out from the pain and had to let go.

For a moment, I gasped for air. I forced my lungs to take a deep breath. I couldn't wimp-out. From my partners, my family, I drew the will, the courage, and the strength I needed.

I took a firm grip on the handle, and yanked as hard as I could. The knife slid from my flesh, painful and grotesque, feeling like a fresh slice. I pinched my lips together to hold back the scream.

Wet warmth gushed from my body, further saturating my shirt. Tears poured from my eyes and I had to wipe them away so I could see. I had to concentrate to maintain focus. With the bloody knife in my hand, I crawled closer to the monster.

Using what had to be the last of my strength, I managed to get to my feet, the blood-covered knife clutched in my right hand. Dizziness washed over me again and for a moment, I feared I would lose my balance, maybe even land on the blade I was counting on to save us.

I took a quick, deep breath, once again forcing focus, and then raised the dripping knife as high as I could.

The thing must have sensed me, because its body stiffened, its head lifted, and it spun around to stare up at me. Its eyes landed on the knife I was holding, narrowed on the blade coated in my blood. And then, for the first time, fear showed on its face.

Before it could react, I plunged the knife deep into

its chest.

The monster's scream was horrible, high pitched, more of a tortured screech, like metal twisting on metal in a violent car crash. The awful sound echoed off the walls.

Jacob scrambled away as the thing surged to its feet. It stepped away from me, as if it could escape the knife by moving backward. Its hands shot outward, and then wavered around the grip of the knife. All the while, its screams continued. The thing grew wild with rage and horror at what I had done.

This time its wound bled, oily black blood, gushes of it. Its pale skin became gray, and then it darkened in broadening patches like hasty bruises. It was as if the darkness at its core cropped up, seeking escape, expanding in blotches over the surface of its skin.

The monster grabbed the knife and was able to yank it out, but it was too late. My blood had already infected it.

As the knife clattered to the floor, the thing leaned forward, and then curled, yielding to its fate with helpless fury. It twisted its head and glared at me with such boiling hatred I shrunk back.

Unable to control the wash of dizziness, I sank to the floor. Jacob, Joe, and Augie all made their way to me. We huddled together on the floor and watched.

Violent convulsions took over its faux human body, twisting it at unnatural angles until the man/monster was grotesquely misshapen.

It looked as if the bones of the thing were dissolving, for its arms bent where there were no elbows, its legs where there were no knees.

Its eyes protruded until they looked like they would

pop from their sockets. Sparks poured from its slack mouth in sporadic flows. This time it was not deliberate. The sparks were without dynamics or propulsion and the monster was choking on them, its chest heaving, wheezing instead of screeching.

The thing staggered to the wall where it leaned back for support, its head jerking and wobbling on its thickening neck. Its bugged-out eyes stared at the shadows, now spinning in chaotic races along the tunnel walls, ceiling, and floor.

"You won't win!" the thing shouted at us.

Dying sparks clung to its lips, crackled on the surface of its oily chin. It then repeated the words, but was unable to elevate them into a shout. Said them again, I think, though I couldn't be sure. The words garbled in the vomit of dying sparks and they were difficult to make out for sure.

It twisted, leaning its shoulder against the wall. Raising its arm, moving in rubbery, abnormal directions, it swiped one flopping hand across the black ooze pouring from its chest.

As the thing smeared its oily blood on the wall, it said through the slowing stream of sparks, "Go my children. The world is yours."

Its skin darkened further, began crumpling inward in some places, bulging outward in others, and taking on a bright sheen of dampness. It was regressing, losing form, dissolving. Its clothes slid from its liquefying body. Its arms shriveled to malformed flaps.

It continued to wipe its black blood on the wall. Its face folded in on itself. Its fluxing jaw jutted outward right before its forehead folded over on its face. As it slid down the wall, it left traces of itself, wet and sludgy. And then it was nothing but a thick puddle of black, lumpy muck. The bill of Benny's cap poked out near the center.

We waited. Maybe the others worried about the same thing I did. That it would become a shadow once more, and travel the wall. It didn't. For a few seconds it shimmied and pulsed, and then it was still.

The shadows all swirled around us for a moment, none of them coming too close. Then, as if in a mob rush, they swarmed to touch the wall where the thing had left its oily blood, to skim where its body had devolved into a lifeless mass of sludge.

Once they made contact with its remains, the shadows all rushed off in the same direction, the way we had come. They were going to the exit. I knew this. With its death, the thing had given freedom to the less developed, freedom it hadn't gotten the chance to enjoy for itself.

They would leave the tunnels.

They would go out into the sunlight, out into the world.

Chapter 17

Wrapped in the hotel's fluffy white robe, my own soft pajamas beneath it, I sat in one of the dining chairs in our suite. A sling supported my left arm. The robe protruded a little at my shoulder from the bandage. Staring out the window, I gazed at a good stretch of the Las Vegas Strip.

Even in the light of day, it was still a beautiful town. The distinctive designs, the grand scale of creativity, all the great diversity that works so well together in imaginative splendor never failed to impress me.

Now, however, other matters captured my attention. And would have it for a very long time.

It had been three days since we left the tunnels. Three days since we witnessed the beginning of the end. Augie was always quick to correct me in that line of thought, as he was far more optimistic than I was. He still thought it was not too late.

It could be Augie was right and my outlook was overly grim. After the twenty-two years I have lived, it *had* become my habit to view a situation for the worst-case scenario. So often had been the way of things for me that I couldn't help it.

Readjusting my position in the chair, I tested the mobility of my arm and the next instant, regretted it. A sharp pain darted through the flesh of my shoulder and well into my bone. After forcing a few deep breaths, I glanced at the glass of water and the little orange prescription bottle of pain pills awaiting me on the table.

The guys were sure to leave them close to me. I'll take one in a little while and then lay down for a nap, as I promised them I would. Not yet, though.

At my request that was almost an order, Jacob, Joe, and Augie went down to the arcade to play some video games. I wanted to take advantage of the time I had to myself to think. At least one of them had been with me since we left the tunnels, and I finally had to demand a little bit of solitude.

I explained to them that since none of us was part of the corruption that created the shadow monsters, I was reasonably safe. I remind them those things can't absorb us. Our blood would destroy them.

They could kill us, though, as the first one killed my father, shoving a stack of construction materials on top of him, crushing him. There are plenty of ways to kill a person without touching them. The further they developed, the more able they would become to cause our death. They are very motivated to do so.

My cell phone was on the table next to the pain pills and I made a solemn promise to call if even the slightest tingling touched my skin. They were still hesitant to leave me, especially Joe. He's more or less lived here since we returned. I swear he must have timed my showers so he would know how long it takes me, so he would know if something was wrong.

Jacob was no better. He hovered about me like a personal security guard. Augie was less intrusive, but his eyes watched the walls wherever I went. While I did value and cherish their concern, it had begun to feel a bit smothering. I needed a break.

It took me coming close to a real mood, but the guys finally agreed to give me some space. They wouldn't be far, though, and they wouldn't be gone too long.

That was okay with me. It was. In truth, I wouldn't have it any other way. It felt good to have loved ones from which I needed a break. It made me feel normal. For a little while, however, I wanted to explore my own thoughts without their input.

We knew how to kill those things, but it didn't do us much good. We couldn't go around splashing our blood on every shadow we saw.

Still, the guys held hope for the future of the world. Without them here to shove it down my throat, I felt a little more open toward their optimism. What other choice was there? Besides, I liked the hope they felt, and exuded. Even though I hadn't admitted it to them, I liked it quite a lot.

I had always cherished the *idea* of possibilities, and the guys made it seem real. I couldn't say why I hadn't been able to admit that to them. Maybe keeping enthusiasm under wraps had always been a way for me to minimize the disenchantment that had followed me since I learned to walk.

I needed to work on that problem, and there had never been a better time.

I glanced at the pills on the table again. My shoulder was aching and getting worse by the minute, the stitches pulled and stung. The skin around the wound hurt in a wide radius. A few more minutes of clear thoughts first, and then I'll take one.

Everyone would have to start doing the right thing, Augie had said in one of our many discussions over the last few days. Then there would be nothing to feed those things, nothing to help them grow, to let them develop. And with enough good deeds, we could dry them to dust.

Yeah, right, I thought. All we had to do is get the word out without sounding like a bunch of kooks. We'd just call all the news stations and tell them to report that if everyone didn't start behaving themselves, they'd feed the shadow monsters. Yeah, that would work. I also kept that pessimistic, albeit realistic, thought to myself. But Augie got the vibe from me.

I had to smile at Jacob. "The answer is simple. It's just not easy," he'd said. So much truth condensed to so few words. Still did us no good, but I liked the philosophical sound of my little brother's statement. It was good to hear him thinking.

Joe was more pragmatic. He talked about starting a new society. In his description were tones of the communes of the 1960s except we would not pollute our brains with drugs and we would not welcome everyone. Those people with darkness in their hearts, in their deeds, would not get in. And as time presented evidence to what we already knew, everyone would want to get in.

For all who wanted to gain entrance into our new world there would be a panel from which they would have to gain approval, Joe explained.

The idea had been circulating throughout the country amongst people like us for a while. Those of us with the best intuition would make up the panel. People who were not deserving of our new world would not get in, no matter how they pleaded, no matter how they promised to change their ways and be good.

I couldn't help but wonder if such an unforgiving act of forbiddance would taint us.

The strategy was, we would breed the good with the good, raise the children to be so, and wind up with a population the shadow monsters could not absorb. We would, in effect, starve them. After all, Joe had said, there are a great many good people in this world. Though most of them didn't have our intuition, and certainly, no one was perfect, they were good at heart and would be an asset to the new human race.

Joe told us about a huge mass of land in Colorado where we would start, eventually branching out. Plans were already in the works. Such communities would spring up all over the world. In the meantime, the shadows would take the others. We would be starting a new world while the old one paid its tab.

Jacob sided with Joe in his beliefs for a new world. Augie's views, of course, are the most optimistic of all of us. It was impossible not to love that guy. He thought that once the world saw what it had created, the people would come around. But they'd have to notice first. And they'd have to notice and believe before it was too late for them to right their wrongs.

While I still didn't know what bad things Cake did in his past, I knew it was a recent past. The good he'd become had needed more time to flush it out. There are many for whom it was already too late, for their wrongs ran deep, and time was running short. These thoughts too, I kept to myself.

Augie was either living in a fantasy world or holding on to the last bit of promise this one had to offer. I couldn't decide, and the skepticism dragging from my past didn't help. Maybe Augie was right. Maybe people would see the way of things and do better while they still could.

I glanced at the pain pills again. It was time. My shoulder was begging. I lifted the cap. Joe had made sure it sat on top of the bottle, unsecured and easy. I tipped one out and swallowed it with the water. After a few minutes, I stood up to go to my bedroom.

Before I turned away, though, I paused to look outside the window again. It was something we'd all done a lot since we got back.

It was late afternoon. If I touched the glass, it would still be warm, but not hot like earlier when the sun shone directly into our rooms. The world on the other side of the glass shone golden and bright. Tourist from all over the world wandered along Las Vegas Boulevard. They didn't know it, but they all had shadow monsters in their storm drains back home too, wherever in the world back home was.

Ours were now traveling above ground, discreet in their consumptions. How many of those people I was looking at were good at heart? I wondered. How many would be with us in the new world?

Raising my line of sight, I took in the varied skyline of tall resorts running the length of the Las Vegas Strip, colorful even without the night to showcase their extravagant lighting. Roundish shadows passed from building to building as if crossing an invisible bridge.

No one realized the shadows far outnumbered the few clouds floating between the sun and the ground.

There weren't as many shadows as there had been

yesterday. Tomorrow there would be less. They were moving on to other towns. The guys and I had been wondering if they would be able to free the shadow monsters living in other tunnels, if their leader gave them that power. If they could, that would accelerate the end of the world, as we knew it.

I stood there for a long time, until my eyes grew heavy and my body, eased with less pain and ready for sleep, craved the comfort of my bed. The sight out the window didn't change. Neither did my pessimism, no matter the effort.

Still, I had to overcome that. I didn't want to carry it with me to the new world. Maybe when I was feeling better that wouldn't seem as difficult.

I wished I had the optimism I felt from our enemy.

They swept through the world a giant step closer to their goal. They journeyed far with their freedom, gifted from the dying remains of their leader, and roamed with growing confidence.

The shadow monsters played with their shapes, mocking our animate and inanimate lives, posing, moving; taking advantage of our many distractions.

Tourists walked up and down the sidewalk, the late day sun casting their innocuous shadows against the glossy sides of the resorts. Nobody noticed there were more people-shaped shadows than there were people. Nobody noticed that sometimes a person-shaped shadow paused when not a single person had.

The shadows never stopped. They never needed sleep, or even to rest. They mingled with other shadows on the walls. They twirled in a merry dance across the tall buildings of the city, of many cities, as unnoticed as a breeze across a cemetery.

A word from the author…

I lived most of my life in the wondrous city of Las Vegas, Nevada. For ten years my husband and I traveled several months of the year in an R.V. and I was fortunate to see every state in this amazing country. Now I live in beautiful Michigan, where I've learned about layering clothes and that boats don't have brakes.

Thank you for purchasing
this publication of The Wild Rose Press, Inc.

If you enjoyed the story, we would appreciate your
letting others know by leaving a review.

For other wonderful stories,
please visit our on-line bookstore at
www.thewildrosepress.com.

For questions or more information
contact us at
info@thewildrosepress.com.

The Wild Rose Press, Inc.
www.thewildrosepress.com

Stay current with The Wild Rose Press, Inc.

Like us on Facebook

https://www.facebook.com/TheWildRosePress

And Follow us on Twitter
https://twitter.com/WildRosePress